UNTIL
Then

The Organization-Book One
M.K. MANSON

One Night Publishing

UNTIL THEN
Copyright © 2024 M.K. Manson

Edited by: Editing4Indies
Proofread by: Karen at Barren Acres Editing
Formatted by: Bravia Books
Cover photo by: Ellen Christy Intimate Portraits
Cover model: Anonymous
Cover Design by: Frank Manson and Ellen Christy Intimate Portraits

Printed in the United States of America

Trigger Warnings

Murder
Kidnapping
Explicit language
Sexual Abuse
Sexual Assault

To my husband.
I knew you were the one for me the night we met.
Thank you for this life we have shared for 34 years and counting.
You believed in me, even when I didn't believe in myself.
Your support throughout this process has never wavered.
No matter what you say, I will always love you most.

Prologue

I just want to be normal. I don't want to look over my shoulder anymore. I'm always waiting for someone to take me out. Or even worse, worrying that someone I love will be taken or killed because of me. I want a life without murder and betrayal. Why won't my father just let me go? I want to fall in love and marry the woman of my dreams. Start a family and be... happy.

A chance meeting at a restaurant threw us together. We had a whirlwind romance, and then she was gone from my life as fast as she came into it. No reason was given. Just gone. I hated the world and everything in it. I wanted to burn it all to hell. I needed to forget her. Meaningless fucks with women who can't handle my rough ways weren't working. All the boxing, running, and weightlifting I did weren't enough to release the pressure.

When my father forced me to do the unthinkable, I knew it was too late for Lola and me. She can never be mine now.

Chapter 1
Lola

How could this day get any worse? It's only eight o'clock, but I'm ready to go back to bed. It poured all night, and the basement of my Cape Cod flooded. I had to spend the first hour of my day setting up an appointment with the water restoration people to come and dry it out.

On the way to work, my shitty car broke down. I've needed a new car for a long time. Taking the time to look at them has been impossible with my work schedule lately. Why couldn't this piece of shit make it a little farther before leaving me stranded?

"I hope someone hits you, you, you, piece of shit!" I scream as I leave it parked on the side of the road. My black pencil skirt and Manolo patent leather pumps are drenched by the time I walk the remaining mile to my office. The giant golf umbrella I had in my trunk did no good to shield them from the pouring rain.

I make a squishing sound with every step I take as I pass by my assistant Amelia's desk. She lifts her gaze to look at me. When she opens her mouth to speak, I lift my hand to cut her off. "*Don't* say a word."

After dropping my things on the chair in the corner of my office, I kick off my shoes, then set them on the vent to dry and pull out my walking shoes from under my desk. I head straight to the bathroom and remove my skirt. Standing in my white shirt and panties, I do my best to dry it under the hand dryer.

Returning to my office, I ring out, "Amelia, can you please find a tow truck company and get them on the line for me?"

"Yes, ma'am." Only a few seconds go by before Amelia chimes out over the intercom.

"Tow truck company holding on line one, Ms. Patterson."

I arrange for a tow truck to pick up my stupid car, then I get to work finalizing the details for the biggest presentation of my life. I've been busting my ass for three years working for Kingsley and Masters. Six months ago, I was promoted to head of advertising. Finally, all my hard work is paying off. I got an assistant, a big office with a window, and a nice pay raise.

I'm the lead on the presentation for Mahdavia Corporation. If we can land this account, it will be the largest Kingsley and Masters has acquired in five years. I've put together a great team of people who are all at the top of their game. They've been working feverishly to get me all the numbers I need to complete the project, and I know we can do this.

I work straight through lunch and think maybe my day is turning around when the electricity goes out a little after two. *What else is going to happen today?* I take a deep breath. Light comes in through my window, but the staff in the cubicles down the hallway are plunged into darkness.

As I walk through the cubicles, I notice a lot of chatter as everyone tries to find their phones and turn on their flashlights. The procedure is to make your way to the vestibule for further instructions. I pride myself on being a put-together person. I don't get upset often, but this day is really testing my limits.

"Everyone, settle down," I say, trying to calm employees walking around like ants who have lost their way. "We'll figure this out. Amelia, can you please call the electric company and find out what the hell is going on?"

"Yes, ma'am," she chirps.

"Joe, can you check with maintenance and make sure it's not internal?"

"Will do, Boss."

"Everyone. Check your socials and see if you can find any cause for what's happening." There's some grumbling, but everyone starts scrolling. It doesn't take long for people to speak up.

"There was an accident on Lowe Street," Marta says.

"Yeah, someone hit a pole and split it in half. Oh man, I hope they're all right," Karen says.

Amelia returns from her desk and puts out her arms.

"A semi-truck hit a telephone pole on Lowe Street and broke it in half."

"That doesn't sound too bad," I say.

She continues, "And then that pole broke four more poles in half. We will be out of power for several hours while they extricate the driver and fix the poles."

"Shit," I say a little too loudly. "Okay, people, I know we had planned on completing the Mahdavia proposal today, but we're going to have to complete it on Monday. Thank you all for your hard work, but you might as well go home. Everyone be safe. See you on Monday." Some are happy, and some groan, but regardless, they all clean off their desks and start the twenty-floor trek down to the street.

I head back to my office, put on my now drier high heels, and get my things together to go back to my flooded basement. *Shit.* I forgot; I don't have my car. I need to order an Uber to get home. Checking the app, I see they are backed up for the next couple of hours. After throwing my purse over my shoulder, I make my way down to the ground floor. At least the rain has stopped.

I've walked a couple of blocks and noticed the streetlights are working. Anthony's, a quaint Italian restaurant on Rogers Street, is just up ahead. I guess I'll go there for a late, late lunch before heading home. Entering the lobby, I realize I'm not the only one with the same idea. The place is packed. I have nothing better to do, so I stand in line to put my name on the list for a table.

The hostess behind the podium informs me that because of the rush, they are only seating tables of two or more. I turn around to leave and walk straight into a brick wall of muscle. The woodsy smell of his cologne fills my nostrils. Inhaling deeply, I slowly raise my head to look up into the most delicious brown eyes I've ever seen. He's at least six feet tall, with dark brown hair that's handsomely styled in waves on the top. He's impeccably dressed in a dark gray Tom Ford suit, white shirt, and cobalt-blue tie. His suit shows every muscle of his body.

"I am *so* sorry," whooshes out of my mouth.

"I'm sorry. I was standing too close," he says in a deep voice.

"Are you alone? I-I mean, they are only seating tables of two or more," I stutter like an idiot.

"Yes, it's just me. The power went out, so I thought I would come eat and see if it comes back on."

Snapping out of my haze, I ask, "Do you want to share a table with me?"

"Sure, that would be great, thanks," he says.

I turn back around, and the hostess is one step ahead of us. Menus in hand, she leads us to a small table in the back by the bathroom.

"The best seat in the house. I guess beggars can't be choosers in situations like this," I say, holding my arms out wide. *Could I sound any more stupid?*

"It doesn't matter to me. I have the best view in the house anyway," he says, making me blush. He pulls out the chair for me, and I sit, burying my face in the menu.

"I'm Ethan, by the way." He reaches his hand across the table.

"Lola." I smile, shaking his hand.

The servers are overwhelmed. After fifteen minutes, a young lady brings us a basket of bread and two glasses of water, and asks to take our order. She looks impatient as bits of hair hang in her face from her disheveled ponytail. We place our orders quickly. Spaghetti with marinara sauce for me and lasagna for Ethan.

"Where do you work?" I ask, ripping pieces of the Italian bread and putting it in my mouth.

"In the Atlas Building. Do you work close by?" he asks, taking a sip of his water.

"I work a couple of blocks up in the Santino Building. How old are you?" I ask.

"Twenty-six. Do you have any brothers and sisters?" he asks.

"No, I'm an only child. Do you?"

"I have three older sisters."

"Ouch. You're the baby." I snicker.

"Yeah, don't remind me of the torture I endured growing up. Next question." The server brings our food, and the game of twenty questions continues.

"Did you grow up in the city?" I ask.

"No, I grew up outside of the city. Did you go to college?"

"Yes. I graduated from Syracuse with a degree in advertising." We spend a few minutes stuffing our faces. "The electric company told us we would be out of power for hours," I explain.

"Oh well, then I guess I *won't* be going back to work."

"Probably not. I get to go back to a soggy house," I say, with a *lucky me* expression on my face.

"A soggy house, why?"

"With all the rain we had last night, my basement flooded. The restoration people are working to dry it out. Luckily, I don't keep a lot of stuff down there."

"Well, that sucks. How far away do you live?"

"About fifteen minutes. But my car broke down on the way to work this morning."

"Boy, you really are having the day from hell, aren't you?

"Yeah, I guess I am." Twirling the spaghetti around my fork and shoveling it into my mouth.

"You're calm. If all those things would've gone wrong for me in one day, I would be losing my shit," he says, cutting into his lasagna.

"There's not much I can do about any of it. I don't control the weather. I knew I needed a new car, but I've been putting it off, and I sure as heck didn't have anything to do with the poor truck driver taking out all those utility poles."

"That's true. But how are you going to get home?" he asks.

"I tried to order an Uber earlier, but they were booked. I started out walking until my stomach pulled me in here. I guess I'll try a cab or start walking again."

"In those shoes! Are you crazy? I'll drive you."

My feet *are* hurting after twenty flights of stairs and walking three blocks. *What am I thinking?* This guy could be a serial killer or something, with melty chocolate eyes.

"Oh, you don't have to do that. I'll figure out a way home," I say, waving him off.

"You shared your table with me. The least I can do is make sure you get home safely." He bows his head and puts a hand on his chest as if he is a knight or something. I'm not sure why I trust this guy, but I do. He makes me laugh. I won't let him come inside. I'll just let him drop me off.

"If you're sure you don't mind? But let me buy your lunch"

"I guess that's a compromise, but next time, I buy," he declares. Next time? Is there going to be a next time? A little twinge of excitement flutters in my stomach. I *hope* there's a next time.

We leave the restaurant and walk down the street to the parking garage. He ushers me to a candy-apple red Tesla Model S. After he opens the door for me, I slide into the passenger seat. He walks around the back of the car and removes his suit jacket and tie. He opens the driver's side back door, then lays them on the seat and slides behind the wheel. He unbuttons the top two buttons of his shirt and lets out a sigh of relief like he's wanted to do that all day.

"I've never ridden in a Tesla before. How do you like it?" I ask.

"It's a good car. It's comfortable and has a long battery life," he says, giving me a cheesy smile with his generic answer. He puts my address into the car's display, and we exit the parking garage. I watch as we go by the area where I left my car. Sure enough, the tow truck has picked it up. A few minutes later, we pull into the driveway of my little home. It's white with black shutters and just the perfect size for me.

"Thank you for driving me home. I really appreciate it, and so do my feet," I say with a giggle as I dig into my bag for my keys.

"It was no problem. Thank you for sharing your table with me today," he says sweetly.

"It was nice to meet you." I feel awkward, like I should shake his hand or kiss him goodbye or something.

Before I can get out of the car, he takes my hand. "Maybe we could hang out sometime? If you would like, I could take you to look at cars tomorrow."

"Um … sure, I guess that would be okay," I say.

"It's a date. See you tomorrow at noon."

"Can you pass me your phone?" I ask, and his eyebrows scrunch up. "So I can put my number in it."

"Oh yeah, sure." He hands me his phone open to the text screen, and I text myself a *hello*. Hearing my phone chime, I give it back to him. "Perfect, see you then."

Ethan waits until I unlock my front door before he backs out of my driveway. I give him a little wave and lock the door behind me. Leaning my head against it, I close my eyes and imagine his lips kissing me goodbye. I guess today wasn't so bad after all.

Chapter 2
Ethan

I'm sitting at my desk, working on a report for the Mahdavia proposal, when the lights suddenly go out. *Dammit!* The backup battery for my computer screams, so I save and shut down everything before I lose my report. After grabbing my phone and jacket, I lock up my office, then fall into step with the employees heading to the break room for further instructions.

After about fifteen minutes, John, the office manager, advises me of a truck accident. Several utility poles were downed, and the driver was trapped.

"There's been an accident up the street. We will be without power for a few hours. So I guess that's a wrap, people. I'll see you on Monday," I advise the staff. I walk down the twenty-five flights of stairs to street level and start walking to Anthony's, getting in line for a table.

I'm standing behind a woman who smells like a beach. Is it coconut? Or jasmine? Whatever it is, she smells amazing. I'm six foot three, so she must be around five seven because if I lean forward, she's right under my nose. I inhale deeply. While I'm in my own little world soaking up her scent, she's talking to the woman behind the podium. Before I know what's happening, she turns abruptly and slams right into my chest. I look down into the most beautiful blue eyes I've ever seen.

"I am *so* sorry," she says quietly.

She's gorgeous, and I momentarily forget how to breathe. Her dark brown hair is pulled up in a tight bun on the back of her head. My eyes scan her body, taking in every inch of her. She's wearing a white button-up shirt tucked into a tight black skirt with high heels that makes my cock twitch in my pants. I love a woman in high heels.

Snapping out of it, I say, "I'm sorry. I was standing too close." Before I know it, we've followed the hostess to a small table in the back by the bathrooms. She looks disgusted to be seated there, but I would follow this woman out by the trash cans for a table.

We make small talk. Her name is Lola; she's twenty-five and works in advertising. She tells me about her day from hell, and I cannot believe how upbeat and unfazed she is after the flooded basement and broken-down car. And now she *thinks* she's going to walk home. The fuck she is! I can't let her walk all those miles home alone in those shoes that make her legs look so sexy. Besides, it will be dark before she makes it home. I'll make whatever deal I need to drive her home.

Sitting in her driveway, I stare into those ocean-blue eyes. Should I kiss her goodbye? I feel a pull to her, but no, she'll think I'm a creeper. But I *need* to see her again. I take her hand and offer to take her car shopping tomorrow.

"It's a date. See you tomorrow at noon." Driving back to my apartment, I imagine what it would be like to kiss her soft pink lips.

Chapter 3
Lola

E than rings my doorbell promptly at noon. I'm ready to go in my low-rise jeans and pink sweater, with my hair pulled back in a high pony. He's dressed in dark blue jeans and a black Henley that's pulled tight across his muscular chest. I wish I could reach out and outline every single one, but I can't. We just met. Are we friends? Acquaintances? I don't know what we are, but I do know it's too soon for touching.

We drive around the city looking at cars. I have no idea what kind of car I want. That's one reason I put this off for so long. I'm a point A to point B kinda girl. I don't need anything fancy. Ethan seems to know all the questions to ask, so I'm thankful he came with me today.

"What's your price range?" he asks.

"Not as much as you spent on your Tesla." I chuckle.

"An electric car would be a great option for you."

"I know, but I don't really want to mess with installing a charging station. How about a reliable car that gets great gas mileage instead? One I don't have to think about for a while." He nods in understanding. I rarely have time to drive far from the city, anyway. My career takes up most of my time.

I like having everything I need close by. That's why I chose to buy a home in this neighborhood. I'm just a few minutes from the grocery store, gas station, and, of course, the mall. I have everything I need right here. Why would I drive somewhere else to find it?

The day is coming to an end. After wandering around five dealerships, we make our last stop at a Toyota showroom. My eyes are drawn to a reservoir-blue Toyota Prius Limited. The car gets great gas mileage and is small and sleek with a gray interior. It has all the bells and whistles. I think I'm in love. And it cost half of what Ethan's car did. I negotiated my payment with the salesperson and hit the road.

Ethan follows me back to the house, and I park my new baby in the garage. "Would you like to stay for dinner?" I ask, putting down the garage door.

"That would be great. What will the chef be preparing?" he asks with a laugh.

"Do you know how to use a grill?"

"I AM MAN," he grunts out, pounding his chest like a caveman.

"You're a goofball. If you grill the steaks, I'll make the sides."

"That sounds like a great plan to me." We've spent the whole day together, looking at cars, talking about cars, and driving cars. I want to learn more about *him* now. There's just something about him I like.

"I love your house. It's so quaint," he says awkwardly.

"I don't need much. It's just me, and honestly, I'm not here very often. My job keeps me busy." I gesture to the patio doors. "The grill is out there. I'll get the steaks ready." He pulls on the sliding door, and it's not locked. He doesn't comment, but he gives me the side-eye as he goes outside. He uncovers the grill and gets it started, scraping it clean with the brush. I put the steaks on a plate, season them, and place them on the island. He comes to the sliding door.

"I'm ready for the steaks."

"Here you go," I say, presenting them to him, and he goes back outside. I wash and season the potatoes and start them baking in the oven. Then I wash the asparagus, snap it, and set it aside to fry.

"I'm going to go change," I yell out the door.

"Okay," he says, waving his hand at me.

I pull out my ponytail on the way down the hall, and once I get to my room, I change into my soft sleep shorts with bunnies on them and a baby-blue baggy sweatshirt that says NEEDS COFFEE on the front. Returning to the kitchen, I fry the asparagus in garlic and butter and set it on the table. Removing the potatoes from the oven, they go on a platter. Just as I place the platter on the table, the patio door slides open, and Ethan joins me with the steaks.

"Which one do you want?" he asks, pointing at the two medium rare steaks.

"The smallest one, please." I hold out my hand like Vanna White showing a puzzle on *Wheel of Fortune* and say, "For your dining pleasure this evening, I have prepared oven-roasted potatoes and garlic asparagus."

"It looks delicious. Thank you for letting me tag along with you today. I had a great time, and I think you got a great deal on the car. Who knew you were such a hard-ass negotiator? That guy didn't see you coming. Looking all sweet and innocent and then BAM!" He claps his hands together. "You let him have it right between the eyes."

"You're so funny," I say, getting up and going to the refrigerator for the steak sauce and setting it on the table. "What do you want to drink? I have water, water, or water."

"If you have any, water would be great, thanks."

"I'm serious," he says, taking the sauce and pouring some on his steak. "Telling him what you wanted your payment to be instead of the price you wanted to pay really confused him. He was sweating while he was putting together all the figures. But then when he couldn't make the price you wanted, and you stood to leave. Oh man, it was so good!" he says, rubbing his hands together.

"I'm sorry, my limit is $500 a month."

"We cannot possibly make that monthly payment. How about $560?"

"No, I really don't want to go over five. Thank you for your time."

"Okay, okay, okay. Let me go talk to my manager again for you."

"He must have needed a sale for the month. Because you made his day when he came in and said he could only go as low as $509, and you accepted."

"I would've paid $560, but it can't hurt to ask, right? I think $509 was fair," I say, taking a bite of my steak.

"It was great! I bet you're a beast in the bedroom, I mean *board-room*." What the hell kinda slip of the tongue was that?

"I can hold my own," I say with a smile. I haven't told him I'm the boss. Some men can't handle a strong woman, and I'm not sure where he falls on that spectrum yet.

"I know you said you work in the Santino Building, but who do you work for?"

"I work for Kingsley and Masters."

"What do you do there?" he asks, cutting into his steak.

"I head up the advertising department. My department prepares media kits and ad contracts, and creates campaigns for our clients related to advertising. We make presentations regarding the services we can provide." I nervously talk to him like he has no idea what an advertising department does.

"That's great," he says with a crooked smile.

"Do you live downtown?" I ask.

"Just outside the city limits, in a condo. I hate to mow grass, so it seemed like the best option. You bought a house, so you must like mowing the lawn?"

"No, I have lawn service." There's an awkward silence. Why are we talking about grass?

"What I do like is having something that's *mine.*" He quirks a brow at me. "When I was a kid, we had to move a lot," I say, scooping out some potatoes. "It was hard changing schools in the middle of the year and making new friends. All the packing and unpacking. I didn't like any of it. I swore when I got a good job, I would buy my own house and never move again. I've been here four years now."

"Why did you move so much?" he asks.

"My dad died when I was twelve."

"I'm sorry."

"Thank you. He had been very sick... pancreatic cancer. My mom was a nurse, so she worked twelve-hour shifts at the hospital, then took care of him. He died in his sleep while I was at school, and she was at work."

"That's awful," he says, his eyes soaking in my every word.

"Mom became our only source of income, so she took whatever

nursing jobs there were to keep the lights on. Sometimes that meant moving to a different hospital or a whole new city. She could make more money as a travel nurse. But she could only take those jobs during the summer months, when I was out of school."

"Wow."

"We made it work, and we had each other." I try to smile.

"Does your mom live close by?"

"No, she passed away last year. She was struck by a truck while crossing the street after her shift at the hospital."

"Oh my God!" he blurts out. "You've been through so much. How do you stay so positive, especially on a day like yesterday?"

"I guess yesterday was nothing compared to some of the stuff I had to go through as a kid. So days like that don't bother me. 'It is what it is,' Mom always used to say."

"You have a great attitude. I hope it rubs off on me." His eyes lock on mine a little too long.

"Let's clean up and go out on the patio," I say, trying to lighten the mood. "We can watch the sunset. It's my favorite time of the day." I start to clear the table. Ethan loads the dishes into the dishwasher. I put the leftovers away, and he covers the grill. "Have a seat, and I'll get us a drink."

Walking onto the patio a few moments later, I hand him a glass and say, "I hope you like whiskey. It's Woodford Double Oak." I sit down next to him.

"That hits the spot. I thought you only had water?" He chuckles as he sets his glass on the table. Sitting back, he motions to put his arm around me, and I let him. I lay my head back on his arm, breathing in his manly scent. We watch in silence until the sun is gone and the stars appear in the night sky.

"Lola?" he whispers.

"Hmm?"

"Would it be okay if I kissed you?"

"I'd like that very much."

He takes the drink from my hand and places it on the table beside his. He turns in his seat to look at me. After taking my face in his hands, he places a gentle kiss on my lips, then pulls back and leans his forehead to mine.

"Mmm, that was nice," I coo. I open my eyes, and his eyes are on me.

"I'm so glad we shared that table yesterday," he says, brushing my hair over my shoulder and running his fingers lightly across my skin.

"Me too." He comes back for another kiss. This one is more intense than the last. Before I know it, we are licking, sucking, and exploring each other's mouths. My hands grasp his shirt, pulling his chest closer to mine. He takes in a deep breath and pulls away.

"Thank you for today, but I think I should go."

"Oh… right… sure… of course," I blabber out, not sure what just happened. Ethan takes my hand and leads me to the door. Turning when he reaches it, he pulls me into him for a hug. He holds my neck with one hand while he presses another soft kiss to my lips.

"I'll text you and make plans for next week."

"Until then," I say.

He smiles sweetly. "Until then."

Chapter 4
Ethan

Driving home from Lola's, I feel like I'm on a cloud. I replay our day together, remembering every detail about her—her eyes, her hair, and her soft lips when I kissed her. Then it hits me like a ton of bricks. We work for rival advertising agencies. Why didn't I catch this before now? I can't date a rival. *Shit. Shit. Shit.* This is awful, just awful.

Inhaling a settling breath, I decide maybe it won't be a big deal. I mean, I've never seen her at any meetings, so she can't be that high on the totem pole, right? I'll talk to her about this later. There's no need to mess things up before we even get started.

When we kissed on the patio, all time ceased to exist. I never wanted it to end. That little *hmm* sound she made sent me over the edge. I had to leave. I didn't want it to go too far on our first date. And if I kept kissing and touching her, I would've kept wanting more.

She's so different from the other women I've been with. She's smart and confident. And just… herself. She doesn't put on a show or try to be something she's not to impress me. I want to learn everything there is to know about her. I want to hear *all* the sounds she makes, like when she comes on my hand, my mouth, my cock. There's still so much to learn about her before we get to that point, but it needs to come soon, or I might explode.

I can't sleep. Every time I close my eyes, I see Lola. When she came out of the bedroom after changing into those bunny shorts and sweatshirt, her wavy dark hair hung over her shoulders, and she had removed her makeup. I'm sure my mouth was hanging wide open. I felt like I was seeing the *real* Lola.

She was so vulnerable telling me about her parents. She has been through so much in her twenty-five years. I need to know more about her.

Sleep needs to come before the need to relieve the pressure building inside my cock takes over for a second time tonight.

Chapter 5
Lola

It's Monday morning. The water restoration people are here to check the basement and pick up their equipment.

"The basement looks good to go," the tech says. "It dried up well since there wasn't much stuff down there. I would have a foundation specialist come out and check to see if they can tell where the water is coming in, but other than that, I think you're all set."

"Thank you so much for taking care of it for me. Have a good day," I say, closing the door.

I pull my brand-new car out of my garage and head to work. I think of Ethan as I pass the Atlas Building. I continue to our garage a few blocks down and park in my designated spot.

Approaching our morning huddle, I say, "Okay, people, I know we are a few hours behind preparing the Mahdavia proposal, but we can do this. Joe, we need the final numbers for the commercial."

"On it!" he shouts.

"Marta, do you have the final numbers for the print materials?"

"Yes, ma'am," she says as she hands them to Amelia.

"Kaitlynn, do you have the storyboards for the commercial in order and ready to go?"

"They are already set up on the easels in the conference room.

Marta and I are going to run through them again."

"Perfect, thank you."

I continue down the checklist of components we need for our presentation. We work like a well-oiled machine throughout the day and gather back in the conference room for an end-of-the-day huddle.

"Great job today, everybody. Let's be sure we are all set before we leave tonight, and tomorrow will be a breeze. We got this!" Everyone exits the meeting room to get ready to pitch the Mahdavia account tomorrow.

I rolled into my garage around eight o'clock. I was *not* leaving until every piece of the puzzle had fallen into place. I want to walk into the meeting tomorrow with no sense of urgency. I *am* nervous, but I think my team and I are prepared to bring this account home. I'm determined to relax and try to get a little bit of sleep. I eat the last two pieces of leftover pizza and take a long, hot bath.

Finally settling into my soft bed, I stop when I see I have a few texts from Ethan. I was so busy today, I hadn't checked my phone since lunchtime. He's been texting me since a little after six o'clock.

ETHAN

How was your day today?

Are you still at work?

Are you okay?

Please text me when you get this.

Ethan, I am so sorry. I had a long day at work. I came home and got straight in the tub.

I'm glad you're all right. I was getting worried.

I'm fine. How was your day?

I had a busy day too. I think it will all work out when we finish up tomorrow.

I was wondering if you would like to go
out on Friday night?

I'm not sure what I'm doing on Friday
night. How about Saturday instead?

That works for me

Dinner?

Sure, where?

Do you want to go back to Anthony's
for old times' sake?

That's fine. Can we try to sit somewhere
other than by the bathrooms? Lol.

Definitely

Until then

Until then

Chapter 6
Lola

The representatives from the Mahdavia Corporation arrive right on time. My staff and I have run through this presentation a hundred times and are ready to go. Our game faces are on, and we kill it. They seemed to love the concept for the television commercial and left smiling.

"We can't celebrate yet. Now we wait," I tell my staff, and we wait and wait.

Five o'clock on *Friday* rolls around, and we still haven't heard from them. I invited my team to Don's Pub on Main for drinks—for team building, of course. I think we all just need to blow off some steam and decompress. The anticipation of the results is killing us all.

The Pub is loud, but not too crowded yet. We find a table in the back corner, and I order some tequila shots to get the party started.

"I am so proud of you *all*," I say as we raise our shots for a toast. "You are the best team I could've ever asked for. Thank you for all your hard work. Now let's drink!" Everyone takes their shot, and the evening commences. We order snacks and more drinks. My phone chimes in my pocket.

"It's them!" I yell, running out the front door to take the call where it's quieter. I take a deep breath and answer in my calm, businesslike tone.

"This is Lola."

"Good evening, Lola. This is Alex Mahdavia."

"Good evening, sir. How are you this evening?"

"I'm well, thank you. I'm sorry to call so late, but I wanted to inform you that your presentation made a strong impact on the committee."

"Thank you, sir."

"We will be awarding the contract to Kingsley and Masters. Congratulations."

"Thank you for letting me know, sir. My team will be very excited."

"Have your assistant contact my assistant, Stephanie, first thing Monday morning for the details."

"Yes, sir. I will have Amelia speak to Stephanie. Thank you for this opportunity. Kingsley and Masters will not let you down."

"I'm sure you won't. Enjoy the rest of your evening," he says.

"You as well, sir. Goodnight."

I hang up the phone and scream, "YES! We got it! Fuck yeah, we got it!" I run back into the building and crash head-on into Ethan's chest again.

Chapter 7
Ethan

I came to Don's Pub on Main with my team to lick our wounds. Mahdavia passed on our proposal. I got the rejection call from Mr. Mahdavia's assistant about an hour ago. She said they decided to go in a *different direction* with the campaign. Sitting at the bar, nursing my beer, I catch a glimpse of who I think is Lola rushing out of the front door to the bar. She just about gave me whiplash. *What the hell?* I didn't know she was even here. I excuse myself and am heading out the door to find her when she comes flying in and bounces off my chest for a second time.

"Oh my gosh! What are you doing here?" she asks, giving me a big hug. Her body is vibrating with excitement.

"I'm here with my team. What are you doing here?"

"I'm here with my coworkers. We did it! We landed the biggest account in five years!" she says, jumping up and down.

"What account is that?"

"The Mahdavia Corporation!" Her face beams with pride, but I know theirs was the team who beat us out for the contract. I can't believe it. I don't want to ruin the night for her by telling her. She's so kind and considerate that she would've spent her evening comforting me for my loss. I couldn't let her do that. There will be time later to tell her who I am, but not now. Throwing a fake smile on my face, I congratulate her.

"That's amazing. I'm *so* happy for you," I say, hugging her again.

"Thank you so much." She plants a quick kiss on my lips. "Are you okay?" It's like she can see what I'm thinking.

"Yeah, yeah. I'm fine. Go. Celebrate with your coworkers. You deserve it."

"Thanks. I'll still see you tomorrow for Anthony's, right?" Her hand rests on my forearm, sending a thrill of heat through my body.

"Of course, but let's go to Lowell's Steakhouse to celebrate instead."

"That would be great. Especially since it's your turn to buy." She chuckles and elbows me.

"I got you. Go. Have fun. We can talk tomorrow."

After one more quick peck on the cheek, she's off to the bar. I see her with a tray of shots in her hands as she heads back to her table.

"WE GOT IT!" she screams, and they all fly to their feet, high-fiving, hugging, and yelling. I'm happy for her. I really am. But I needed that contract badly.

Lola and her team are partying up a storm on the dance floor. My team has long since gone home, and I sit at the bar, watching her. She let her hair down out of that tight bun she wears and untucked her red shirt from her skirt. She has *those* shoes on. Those damn high-heeled shoes. They make her legs look so incredible. I want to start at those shoes and lick my way up her legs, straight to her pussy.

I've lost count of the shots they've shared, and I'm starting to get concerned. I don't want her to drive home. When the lights go down low, it only takes me four strides to reach her. Stopping her before she can leave the dance floor, I wrap my arms around her from behind.

"Dance with me," I say as I breathe into her ear.

"Hey! You're still here!" she says, throwing up her arms and yelling as if we were the only two people in the room.

"I thought I would stay and drive you home. Is that okay?"

"Okay. But can we dance first?" she whines.

"Of course." I take her in my arms, and we begin to sway with the music.

As soon as I have her near me, I'm inhaling the coconut scent of her hair. Slowly, she relaxes into me, and she lays her head on my chest. Holding her with one arm around the waist, I rub my other hand up and down her back. We stay in each other's arms until the music cranks back up.

Everyone around us is pumping their fists and jumping up and down, but we stand here looking at one another. She stares at me with those deep-blue eyes, and I place a soft kiss on her lips. She threads her hands into my hair and pulls me in for a heated kiss. I can say I was a little surprised by how hot her kiss was, but I didn't pull away. Our tongues tangle around one another, and the need to fuck her is becoming too much.

"Let's get out of here," I whisper in her ear.

"Yes, please. Take me home, Ethan."

She says good night to her crew, and I take her by the hand, leading her out of the bar. I open my car door for her. She slides into the passenger seat, and I reach over her to connect her seat belt, then close the door. She kicks off her shoes, and I can't help but stare at her toned legs. I want to be between them with my mouth on her pussy until she screams my name.

She's quiet on the ride to her house. Her head leans back on the headrest, and she faces the window. When I take her hand, it's limp. She's passed out. Tequila will do that to you. I let her sleep until we arrive. I park and nudge her on the shoulder gently.

"We're home, baby." She says nothing. *Damn, she's out cold.* I get out of the car, walk around to her side, and open the door. The moon shines on her pale skin. She looks so peaceful. She's holding the keys to her house in her open palm. I take them from her and open her front door. When I return to the car, I carefully lift her into my arms. When we reach the front door, she mumbles something.

"What did you say?"

"Oh no. Oh no. Oh no," she repeats as we walk in the front door.

"It's all right, baby. I got you," I say as I close the front door behind us with my foot.

I start across the living room, and then I hear it…that unforgettable sound of vomit trying to escape her stomach. I walk a little faster, trying to get her to the bathroom before it happens, but … it's too late. She throws up all down the front of my shirt. I try to stay calm, but yuck! A gag chokes in my throat, but I continue my brisk walk to the bathroom. I want to get there before she does it again because I might hurl right along with her this time.

"Hang on, Lola, we're almost there." We make it to the toilet just in time for her to throw up a second time. I hold her hair back the best I can while rubbing circles on her back. She empties the contents of her stomach.

"Shit," she hisses as she turns her head and sees me standing above her.

I chuckle and then smell myself. *Blech.* "If you'll be all right for a second, I'm going to take off my shirt, okay?"

"Yeah." She waves me off while her head lies on the side of the toilet seat.

I strip off my shirt and find some towels, laying them on the counter by the shower. I let her sit there for about twenty minutes, and when nothing else comes up, I say, "Let's get you into the shower."

"I don't know if I can stand."

"I'll help you." I lift her off the floor and steady her against the wall.

"Why is the room so crooked?" she asks innocently.

"Well, that's because you drank all the tequila at the bar tonight." I chuckle as if I'm speaking to a child. "It'll stop soon."

She leans her head back against the wall, and I start to unbutton her shirt. I'm trying to be a gentleman and not stare at her chest, but it's so damn hard. I'm hard. *She's in distress. Don't be a jerk.* I lower the shirt from her shoulders. It slips from her arms to the floor. I unzip her skirt and slide it down over her hips. She's wearing beige lace panties that match her bra, and my breath hitches. Taking in a gulp of air, I talk to myself under my breath.

"You can do this. Be professional." But it's taking everything in me to keep myself under control.

Continuing my mission, I unhooked her beige lace bra. She leans her head forward onto my chest. I lower the bra down her arms and toss it onto the pile of puke clothes. Last piece. *You can do this.* I lower her panties down her legs, watching them travel over her soft, pale skin until they fall to the floor. I tap her feet one at a time, then retrieve the panties and toss them aside.

"Come on, baby, I need you to try to wake up, just for a little while." The hot water steams up from the shower as I carefully maneuver her back into the water. I lean her head into the spray and rake my fingers through her hair to get it all wet. She sputters and seems to wake up now. She looks up at me with hooded eyes as I pour shampoo into my hand. Bringing it to a lather, I use both hands to wash her hair. When I'm satisfied I have scrubbed all the puke away, I walk her backward into the shower spray again.

I'm careful to keep it from her eyes as I rinse the bubbles from her dark brown locks. I pour her coconut shower gel onto the puffball that hangs on a hook, gently caressing her back and arms, and come around to do her chest, neck, and stomach. She says nothing. She just stares at me with her pouty lips spread apart. I'm trying to keep my thoughts on the job at hand and not on my hardening dick in my now drenched pants. I rinse her and hold her to the side so I can quickly wash my chest and stomach where she got me. Turning off the spray, I reach for the towels. We exit the shower, and I stand her in front of the mirror.

"Put your hands on the counter and try to hold on while I dry you off," I say, and she nods. Never taking her eyes off herself in the mirror, she looks like she doesn't know who she's looking at. I towel dry her hair and then start wiping the beads of water from her body. I stand and see her eyes becoming droopy, and she's no longer holding on. *I'm losing her.* I wrap the towel around her loosely and sweep her into my arms. I'm sorry now that I left my jeans on because I'm leaving little puddles on her floor.

As I carry her to the bed, she says softly, "Thank you," and taps my cheek with her hand.

"You're welcome."

I pull the covers back from the bed and set her on the edge. After removing the wet towel from her body, I lay her down and cover her with the duvet. Returning to the bathroom, I remove my soaked jeans and dry myself off. I wrap a dry towel around my waist and head out to find the washing machine. After throwing our clothes inside, I turn it on and return to the bedroom.

I'm not leaving her. She might need me. She might get sick again and need me to help her to the bathroom. I won't leave her here alone until I know she's okay. *Keep telling yourself that's why you're staying.*

I switch off the light on the nightstand, pull back the covers, and climb into bed beside her. I gather her into my arms, her back to my front, and hold her, listening to her little sighs and slow, steady breaths. She's so peaceful when she sleeps. I brush her hair from her face and nuzzle my face in her neck. She lets out a soft hum, and I feel my cock harden. *Down, boy, you need to stay in control. Just for tonight. We can do this.*

Lying on my back, I consider how I'll tell her we're competitors. Will it make a difference? How do I tell her about my father? I like this girl a lot. I don't want to screw it up. Lola stirs around 4:00 a.m.

She rolls over to face me. "Hey."

"Hey."

"I'm sorry I threw up on your shirt," she mumbles.

"It's all good. How do you feel?" I whisper.

"Like my head is going to explode," she says, wincing.

"Let me get you some pain reliever and water, and then you can go back to sleep." Throwing back the covers, I'm headed for the bathroom.

"Thank you, Ethan."

"You're welcome. I didn't want to leave until I knew you were okay," I say, rummaging through her medicine cabinet. Returning to the bedroom, I can see her silhouette from the light in the bathroom, and she looks like an angel.

"Can you stay with me, please?" she asks.

"I would like that, plus I don't have any clothes to wear because they're in the washer."

"Speaking of clothes," she says, gesturing to her lack thereof.

"Yeah, you threw up all over yourself. I didn't want to rummage through your drawers. Point me, and I'll bring you something to wear."

"In the top drawer of my dresser is a nightshirt."

I pull open the top drawer, and before my brain can process the bright pink vibrator sitting on top of her clothes in the drawer, she blurts out, "No!" Too late. I already saw it. Where do I go from here? I turn and look at Lola. Her face is bright red, her eyes clamped shut, and her hands to her mouth. "Is there something pink on top of my clothes?"

"Yup."

"Oh my God. I'm so embarrassed." Her head is buried in her hands. "What else is going to go wrong tonight?"

"Well, technically, it's tomorrow. But it's okay, don't worry. It's not like I haven't seen one before. I have three sisters, remember?" I pull the nightshirt out of the drawer, and the vibrator falls onto a blue shirt below, and I close the drawer. She sits up and pulls the nightshirt over her head and down her delicious body.

"I'm not sure why I feel so bashful. You already saw everything."

"I didn't see... I mean... I tried not to look," I blabber out, handing her the medicine and water. She swallows them and takes a drink.

"Thank you for being a gentleman."

"You're welcome, milady," I say as she lies back down on the pillow. I cover her up, and she nuzzles into the bed. She seems to fall back to sleep. I move the laundry from the washer to the dryer and lie back down beside her.

"Ethan," she says.

"Yes," I say, drawing out the word slowly.

"I really like you."

"I really like you too, Lola."

"Ethan," she says again.

"Yes."

"Can we still go on our date tonight?"

"If you feel like going, of course."

"I hope I do because I want to spend more time with you."

"Me too, Lola. Me too. Now try to go back to sleep so you can feel better."

Chapter 8
Lola

woke up around nine, but Ethan was gone. He left a note on the pillow beside me that read:

> LOLA,
> I STAYED AS LONG AS I COULD, BUT I HAD A MEETING TO ATTEND. I DIDN'T WANT TO WAKE YOU. TEXT ME IF YOU FEEL LIKE GOING OUT, AND I WILL PICK YOU UP AT SIX
> ETHAN.

He's so sweet. Walking into the kitchen, I see my clothes from last night hanging up in the laundry area, cleaned and pressed. *Who is this man? He took care of my clothes like a pro.* I eat some toast, and by noon, I'm starting to feel better when I hear my phone chime.

ETHAN
Are you up yet, sleepyhead?

Yes

How are you feeling?

Much better. Thank you.

Do you feel like going out to dinner?

Yes, I would like that.

Pick you up at six.

I will be ready. Could we pick up my car afterward?

Look in your garage.

How did my car get here?

I had someone drive it back for you

Thank you

See you tonight.

Until then

Ethan picks me up right on time. He's holding his hand behind his back.

"I have a present for you," he says in a singsong voice. He pulls out my shoes that I left in his car last night.

"My babies!" I squeal, taking them from him. "I love these shoes. They were the first expensive thing I bought myself when I got promoted."

"They look good on you. Will you wear them tonight?"

"Of course."

We drive to the restaurant in silence. I don't have the words to say how embarrassed I am about last night. He takes my hand in his and leads me to the table.

"Are you okay?"

"Yeah, just embarrassed," I say, looking down at the table and rubbing my fingers over the smooth fabric of the tablecloth.

"Hey, look at me." I raise my eyes to him. "Don't be. Everybody parties too much at least once in their life."

"I know, but I *threw up* on you. That's a whole new level of embarrassment."

"I survived," he says, holding his arms out.

"Thank you for taking care of me. I don't know how I would have gotten home. Or who else I would have puked on?" We laugh. He's just so easy to be with.

"You were partying pretty hard with your team."

"We were so excited to win the contract. We've worked our asses off the last month preparing. And to find out we didn't get beat out by Brandish-Martinelli *again* felt amazing!"

"I'm happy for you," he says.

"Thank you. And thank you for cleaning and pressing my clothes. I am *very* impressed."

"Why are you impressed? You don't think I could press your clothes?" he asks, confused.

"No, it's not that I didn't think you *couldn't* do it. Why *would* you do it?"

"I have three older sisters, so I guess it just came automatically." He laughs.

"I forgot you had three sisters. No wonder you're so sweet."

"Yeah, they would kick my ass if I was a dick to someone as nice as you." He's making me blush.

"What are their names?"

"Lilliana, Maria, and Guilia."

"Those are all Italian names."

"They sure are."

"How did you get Ethan?

"Well, actually, my name is Rocco Ethan."

"Ethan is your last name?"

"No, it's my middle name."

"Well, what's your last name?"

"Do I have to?" He scrunches up his face like he's in pain.

"What's that supposed to mean? Why won't you tell me your name?"

"Because once I do, you'll hate me forever, and I really like you,

Lola. I want to get to know you better. Please don't make me."

"You would rather start whatever this is on a lie?"

"Not a lie, just not the whole truth."

"Please, I like you too. I won't hold it against you, I promise."

"Sure, you won't." He rolls his eyes.

"Please, Ethan." I give him the big puppy dog eyes.

"Fine… It's Martinelli."

"WHAT?!" *What the fuck! Martinelli? Really?*

His index finger shoots out at me. "You said you wouldn't hold it against me!" There's a long silence between us while I think about what the hell I'm going to say next.

"You knew last night my team was the one that won the contract with Mahdavia? And you stayed?"

"Yes, you were *so* happy, and I was happy for you. I couldn't tell you your team beat out my team for the contract because I knew you would have left your friends to console me. I didn't want that. I wanted you to celebrate and have fun."

"Are the Martinellis really like I've heard they are?"

"What do you mean?"

"That they do whatever it takes to win a deal. They lie, cheat, and steal to get what they want?" His shoulders roll forward, and he stares at his plate. "Are you like that, Ethan?" There's a long silence.

"Well?" I ask again.

"I'm not like them," he says so quietly I can barely hear him. He almost sounds ashamed.

"What does that mean?" I say more patiently, thinking maybe I should hear him out.

"I'm not like my father. That's *his* way of doing business. I head the advertising company. I try to be fair and work with the facts. I don't scrub the numbers and promise things I can't deliver. That's why we lost to you. You had the better deal, and you won fair and square." He sits up straighter and squares his shoulders and continues, "I'm not saying that Saturday morning my father didn't lay into me pretty hard for losing, but I took everything he dished out and stood by my decision to do business *my* way."

"Oh." I'm starting to feel bad for the way I'm treating him.

"I don't want to be like him. I want to run a legal business."

"I'm sorry."

"For what?"

"For jumping to conclusions like you said I would."

He pauses. "You know, I'm glad you won the contract, right? I can't wait to see the outcome."

"Thank you."

"Why did you stay last night?"

"I couldn't leave you. I knew you had a lot to drink, and I didn't want you to drive home," he says. "But when you were out there dancing, you looked so goddamn sexy. I couldn't stop looking at you. The way you moved your hips drove me insane. But as soon as I took you in my arms on the dance floor, I knew you were too far gone, and I needed to get you out of there."

"I should be happy you were there to protect me," I say with a coy smile.

"Yes, you should be. Because any other man may not have been able to control himself like I did." He has that chivalrous man voice going on again.

"What were you going to do to me if I wasn't drunk, Ethan?" My body is reacting to him in a way it never has for a man.

"I wanted to take you in my arms and kiss you."

"And..."

"Take you back to my house and make love to you long and slow. But I couldn't do that because you were drunk. I won't take advantage of a woman. I wanted it to be real, not clouded with alcohol."

"Thank you." I move in closer and touch his arm. "Can you tell me more about what you wanted to do to me last night?"

"How about I show you?" he says with a dirty smile.

"Yes, please."

He motions to our server. "Check, please."

Chapter 9
Ethan

As I drive back to my place, my mind drifts back to the meeting this morning with my father. He was so angry.

"Sit!" he demands.

"Yes, sir." Dropping down into the burgundy leather chair in front of his desk, I begin to speak, "Father, I know you're mad..."

He cuts me off with his hand in front of my face and yells, "Quiet!"

"Yes, sir."

"I am going to speak, and you are going to listen, Rocco," he shouts in his thick Italian accent. Nodding my head, I lower my eyes. I hate it when he calls me Rocco.

"I put you in charge of the advertising agency because you went to college. You are more than qualified to do the job and have a passion for the business. But you did not win the Mahdavia account. You let Kingsley and Masters take it right out from under you."

"Father—"

"I said quiet!" he rages.

"I know you have this crazy idea that you can do business differently than this family has for fifty years. I have tried to be patient with you, Rocco, but my patience is wearing thin. I want you beside me as *my second. But if you insist on running the advertising company, you must bring in the money, Son."*

"I do bring in the money."

"But not enough!" he blares.

"I want this side of the company to be legit. We need to change with the times, Father. I want a better life for my future family. I don't want to have to look over my shoulder everywhere I go, like you do. I don't want to fear getting arrested around every corner. Why can't this be mine? Why can't I make it what I've dreamed of?"

"Because it will fail. And my only son cannot fail!" he says, gritting his teeth.

"It won't fail just because it's different. It doesn't have to be illegal to succeed. Please, Father, let me have this. Please let me be free. I want a chance at a life with a girl I met."

"What girl?"

"Her name is Lola, and I like her. I want a chance with her, please. I cannot bring a woman into this life." The silence seems to go on forever.

He finally speaks. "I will give you until the end of the year, Rocco. Turn a bigger profit, and the company is yours to do with what you want."

"Thank you—" He puts out a hand for me to stop talking again.

"But if you don't... You belong to me. You will give up this legal business bullshit *and be my second. You will finish your training and do business my way."*

"Yes, Father."

"You have six months."

"Thank you, sir."

Something taps my leg. "Ethan, are you in there? Are you okay?" Lola asks.

"Yeah... yes... I'm sorry."

"Where did you go?"

"Just remembering the conversation I had with my father this morning. It's nothing."

"Do you want to talk about it?"

"Not right now. Tonight is for us. Just us." I bring Lola's hand to my lips and kiss it.

"You know I'll listen if you want to talk," she says.

"I know you will. I'm just not ready yet."

We drive to my apartment downtown and park in the reserved section of the parking garage. I open her door and take her hand.

"You said you lived on the outskirts of town."

"I couldn't tell you I lived in a penthouse downtown. You would have wondered who I was and started asking questions."

"I have *a lot* of questions."

"I know you do, and I will answer all of them. I promise."

The elevator doors open, and we step inside. Pinning her between the wall and my chest, I kiss her sweet lips.

She pulls me in close to her body. "Tell me, Mr. Martinelli, what did you say you wanted to do to me last night?" I kiss her again, only harder and deeper, until the elevator doors open into the penthouse. We both gasp for air, and I pull away and take her by the hand, leading her inside.

Chapter 10
Lola

Ethan kissed me so hard in the elevator, I saw stars. I want him so much. I have never felt like this before. All I know is I want him.

"Welcome to my home," he says as he ushers me inside.

"Wow. This is amazing," I say as my mouth gapes. "I've never been in a penthouse before." My entire house could fit in his living room. It has the largest open-concept area I've ever seen. A luxurious white kitchen with two large islands is off to the right. Beautiful high-backed cloth chairs line both sides of one. One must be for eating and the other for cooking. The countertops are marble, and the cabinets are white with black pulls. Straight ahead is a wall with a stone fireplace and what has to be a sixty-five-inch television above it.

"This must be where you hang out with the guys, watching football on the weekends?" I say, pointing at the TV.

"I don't watch a lot of football, but we do play games on the island when my sisters bring my nieces and nephews over," he says with a soft smile. He's a family man. I like that about him. A twelve-foot wall of windows takes up the entire left side of the room. I'm drawn to the skyline.

"This view is gorgeous. I bet the sunsets are breathtaking."

"They are. We only have about fifteen minutes until the sun sets. Would you like a drink while we wait?"

"That would be great, thanks," I say as I sit on a giant, soft white sofa that faces the windows. He hands me a scotch on the rocks and sits down beside me.

"I hope Macallan is okay. It's my favorite."

"As long as it's not tequila, I'll be fine." We laugh, and he wraps his arm around my shoulders. I lay my head on his chest and watched the sunset over the river.

"It's *so* beautiful up here."

"Not as beautiful as you are," he whispers, turning my chin toward him with one finger.

"Ethan." That's all I can say before he kisses me again.

"I want to know every little thing about you, Lola," he murmurs. "I want to hear those soft little sounds you made while you slept last night again. I want to hear you moan my name when I make you come."

"Ethan, I want you so much. I know this is fast... but I don't care."

He takes me by the hand, and I stand from the couch. After lifting me into his arms, he carries me bridal style to his bedroom.

The room is large, dark, and mysterious. A Wyoming king bed is against the far wall, with a high-backed upholstered headboard. Large nightstands flank both sides. The furniture is matte black, and another twelve-foot wall of windows has a different view.

"There are no curtains in these rooms. How do you keep people from looking in?" I ask shyly.

"First, we're sixty stories up, and there are no buildings near us, and second..." Ethan walks over to the nightstand and presses a button on a remote. All the windows blacken. There is zero light in the room. I can't see my hand in front of my face.

"Ethan?" I gasp. Suddenly, I feel his body pressing into my back. His hot breath is on my shoulder as he wraps his body around mine and holds me close. I can feel his hard erection against me.

"It took everything in me not to touch you last night the way I wanted to." He lightly brushes my hair behind my shoulder.

"I wanted to kiss you." He kisses me behind my ear.

"I wanted to lick you." He places slow, methodical little licks up and down my neck.

"I wanted to taste every inch of you," he says, turning me to face him.

His tongue swipes over my lips, and I open for him. Our kisses are hot and desperate. His left hand moves to cup my face, and his right pulls me closer to him. I feel like the darkness is consuming us. With one more click of the remote, a soft light in the corner turns on, and my breath hitches.

"Ethan…it's been a long time for me."

"How long?"

"About ten months and I've only ever been with two people," I answer timidly. "But I've never felt like this before."

"I feel it too. I want to take my time with you. I want to learn every inch of your body. It's been three months for me, and I'm clean, but we can wait if you want to?"

"No, please don't stop."

"Are you on birth control?"

"Yes."

He guides me over to stand at the foot of the bed. Staring at me with those melty dark eyes, he begins to unbutton my blouse.

"When I was undressing you last night, I tried not to look. I wanted to be the gentleman you deserved, but tonight, I want to see every inch of you." My shirt drops to the floor. He kisses his way down my neck and over my chest. He unhooks my bra and tosses it on the floor near my shirt. His strong hands cup my breasts, caressing and kneading them.

Dropping to his knees as if he is worshipping me, he groans, "Lola, I need you so much." A moan escapes my lips when he rolls my nipples between his fingers. "That's right, baby girl. I want to hear every sound you make." He sucks my nipples into his mouth one at a time until they peak, and my pussy clenches, then he kisses down to the waistband of my skirt. He reaches around and unzips it, letting it pool at my feet.

I'm standing in front of him now in just my red lace panties and high heels. He runs his hands up and down the back of my legs and groans. Then everything stops as fast as it started.

I open my eyes. He has his eyes closed and is taking deep breaths.

"Is everything all right?" I ask. He looks like he's having some kind of attack.

"Yeah, just give me a second, or I'm gonna come just from touching you."

I rub my thighs together to quell the wetness between my legs. "I know what you mean." I smile.

"Those shoes. Those fucking shoes. They turn me on so much," he grits.

"Please," I beg as he curls his fingers around the band of my panties and pulls them down my legs.

"Sit," he says, and I do as I'm told.

"You're so beautiful."

He cups my cheeks in his hands and kisses me. He runs his hands up my thighs and spreads them wide as he slides a finger through my folds. "You are so fucking wet for me," he says. He lifts his finger to his tongue and licks it clean. "And you taste so goddamn sweet."

My stomach does a little flip at the sight of him sucking my arousal from his finger. He takes one of my legs in his hands and runs his tongue down my calf, sending chills down my spine. After reaching for my shoe, he pulls it from my foot and places tiny kisses on each of my toes. I've never had anyone do this to me before. The sensation makes me squirm to find friction for my needy clit. He lifts my other leg and repeats the motion, and I'm not sure how much more I can take. It feels so erotic.

"Ethan," I rasp, leaning back on my elbows. He has a wild look in his eyes as he sinks his head between my legs, burying his face in my wet heat. I thrust my hips up to him, but he places a hand on my stomach to hold me firmly where he wants me. I lie back and relax into the mattress.

He places long, languished licks through my center before he plunges his tongue into my core. My body rocks at his presence, trying to open wider for him. He circles his tongue just inside my entrance, and my legs begin to shake. He replaces his tongue with a finger as he explores my clit with his mouth, sucking and flicking the sensitive bud. I'm writhing under his touch when he dips a second finger inside me, and my first orgasm of the night explodes.

He continues to tease and lick while I ride out the sensations. The feeling is so intense, it is almost unbearable. A sigh of contentment flows from my lips as I sit up and reach for him.

"Ethan, I need you inside me." His face flushes as I reach for his belt, unfastening it and sliding it with a swish from its loops. After I unzip his fly, I release his cock from its confines, and the sight of his long, thick cock takes my breath away. His is definitely the largest I've ever seen. I take him in my hand tightly and run my tongue along his shaft. The taste of his precum fills my senses. My eyes connect with his as I take his dick deep in my throat. A guttural growl comes from this throat. I have him in my mouth for only a moment when he pulls away from me.

"Baby girl, you have to stop," he says with a heavy sigh. "If you're not careful, that perfect mouth of yours is going to make me come, and I want to come inside your hot pussy tonight." I smile, knowing *I* did that to him. I made him ready to explode for me. I wipe my mouth with the back of my hand and scoot up on the bed, making room for him between my legs.

I hear a condom wrapper being ripped open, and in a short time, his body hovers above me. Our foreheads connect as he notches the head of his cock to my entrance. He allows me a moment to adjust to his crown before he pushes into me farther. There is a twinge of pain mixed with pleasure at his intrusion.

"Ethan," I say with a wince.

"I'm sorry, I forget sometimes."

"How big you are?" I smile.

"Yeah, I'm sorry. Did I hurt you?"

"No, just go slow." I wrap my legs around his waist as my pussy adjusts to his size. He presses inside me a little at a time until he's fully seated. I open my eyes to find him looking at me with concern. A smile escapes my lips when I realize he's waiting for a cue from me to move.

"I need you to move, Ethan. Please."

"Yes, ma'am." He presses a chaste kiss to my lips and begins to stroke in and out slowly.

"Lola."

"Hmm?"

"I need you." He thrusts faster. "I want you." He pumps harder. "I think I'm falling in love with you." Our orgasms detonate around us, consuming all the air in the room as we combust.

Did he say what I think he just said?

Chapter 11
Ethan

As I hold Lola in my arms while she sleeps, I know I'm going to have to tell her who I am. Who my father is. Tell her how I'm trying to be free of that life. She needs to know she could be in danger by being with me.

Stroking her arm gently with my fingers, I lie here, remembering the evening we had tonight, and I want more. This has been the greatest night I've ever shared with a woman. I think it's because I want to take care of her. To please her. Make love to her. It wasn't just sex. It was so much more. I've never cared enough about a woman to have those kinds of feelings. I don't ever want to be without her in my life. I can't explain it. I know it's too fast, but I *am* falling in love with her.

When I wake up, she isn't beside me. A sense of dread fills the pit of my stomach that she's gone. I stand from the bed, pull on my boxers, and check the bathroom first. She's not there, so I go toward the kitchen. I'm relieved to find her standing in the dark in front of the windows in the living room. She's wrapped in the sheet from my bed. I come up behind her, wrap my arms around her, and bury my face in her warm neck.

"What are you thinking about so hard, sweetheart?" I whisper.

"Did you mean what you said?"

"What specifically are you talking about?" I want to hear her say the words.

"That you're falling in love with me?"

"Yes, I meant every word. But we need to talk. I need to tell you who I am."

"What do you mean? Who *are* you, Ethan?"

"I told you my whole name."

"Rocco Ethan Martinelli. I remember," she says.

"I'm the only son of Antonio Martinelli." Her mouth hangs open, and I know she realizes who I really am.

"*The* Antonio Martinelli?"

"Yes, I'm sorry."

"Why are you sorry? You can't help who your father is."

"I know, but he's the biggest crime boss in the city. I want you to know I don't believe in the same things and living the same life that he does. I never have. I'm doing everything I can to get away from it."

"Ethan, what are you talking about? You work for an advertising company."

"I do, but he's trying to take it away from me and make me part of his world. I had a meeting with him this morning. That's why I had to leave before you woke up. He was pissed I lost the contract to your company. He said I'm not making *enough* money, and I have six months to bring in some big clients or he'll take it all from me. If that happens, I'll have to accept his way of life. I will be forced to finish training and become his second."

"What happens if you *do* sign some big clients in six months?"

"Then he *says* he'll accept me and leave me alone. Let me live my life the way I want to live." I walk over to the fireplace and turn it on. After throwing some blankets and pillows from the couch on the floor for us, I gesture for her to lie down. We cuddle in front of the fire as I continue.

"I'm his only son, and he wants me to take over The Martinelli Organization for him when he's gone. But I don't want a life of crime. I don't want to look over my shoulder constantly, wondering who's going to try to kill me today. I don't want my future wife and children to endure that either," I say, holding her tighter.

"I can't imagine what your life has been like, but I can understand why you don't want to live that way," she says.

"I hated all the security guards when I was growing up. I couldn't do anything alone. When there was a threat against the family, my sisters and I would have to go to a safe house and hide until the threat was eliminated. Sometimes it would last days and other times weeks. My mother had to have security just to go to the store. It was no way to live."

Watching the flames flickering, Lola is the first to break the silence. "Why don't you like the name Rocco?"

Letting out a deep breath, I say, "Because it takes me back to a time when I didn't like myself very much. I was fifteen the first time my father forced me to take care of business."

"What do you mean by that?"

"I'm sorry. That is the term we use when we kill someone," he explains.

"What?" Her hand covers her mouth.

"I told you; I've been trained my whole life to take over for him. My mother tried to keep me away from The Organization for as long as she could, but my father wouldn't relent. Part of my training was 'taking care of business.'"

We park in front of a warehouse. It looks big and empty. I follow the guards and my father down a gravel path to a heavy metal door in the back. Scanning the room, I see a man strapped to a chair. He's bloody and bruised. Father points at the man. "Rocco, this is what happens when you fuck with the Martinellis. Isn't it, Valentino?" The man tries to lift his head to no avail.

"What did he do?" I ask quietly and swallow hard.

"He thought he could rack up a big gambling debt, then run from us."

"What are you going to do to him?"

"You're going to take care of business."

"Me?" I swallow hard.

"Yes, you. It's time you learn what it means to be a Martinelli in this town."

"But I—"

He cuts me off. "You can and you will."

"I don't know how…" Panic takes over my body.

"Put the gun to his head and pull the trigger. Simple. Don't think about it. Just do it and walk away. The faster, the better."

"But I don't want to," I lean in to him and whisper.

"You don't have a choice, boy. Do it!" He pushes the gun into my hand and turns me toward the man with a nudge. My steps are slow and measured as I approach him.

"Please don't do this, kid," the man slurs. I look back at my father but continue walking toward the man. Everyone is staring at me. My hand shakes as I hold the gun tightly. I stop on the right side of the man and look at my father for guidance. Please don't make me do this. *My eyes plead with him.* Please let it be a joke.

"Now put the gun up to his temple." I raise the gun and hold it there. The man's head hangs low as he cries, snot running from his nose. "Pull the trigger." I look at Father and back to the gun at the man's temple, and I take a deep breath, close my eyes, and squeeze the trigger.

BANG.

There's blood on me. There's blood on the floor. There's blood on the wall. My body shakes, but I don't cry. He'll kill me if I do. I take in a deep breath, raise my chin, and walk toward my father. After handing the gun to him, I keep walking. As soon as I exit the building and am out of his sight, I throw up the contents of my stomach into the bushes and head for the car. That was the day I started hating Rocco Martinelli.

"Oh my God. You were *fifteen*." Lola pulls me in tight. "Was that the end of your training?"

"No, there was so much more."

"More shootings?" she asks.

"No, he seemed satisfied I could use the gun effectively, so we moved on to torture."

"I can't believe he would do this to you." Her voice comes out low and weak.

"Harry was the enforcer back then. I think he was secretly a serial killer because he could torture a man with a Q-tip. He taught me to do terrible things to get someone to talk. If they talked quickly, their death would be swift. But if they were determined not to tell him what he wanted to know, he would find, let's say, *creative ways* to get what he wanted from them before killing them."

"Oh my God, Ethan." She has tears in her eyes for that teenage boy. "Do I want to know what you learned?"

"No, baby, you don't. You'd have nightmares, and you could never look at me the same way again."

"How were you able to handle that at a young age?"

"I didn't do a very good job of it."

"What do you mean?"

"I went to school during the day but never got close to anyone. I couldn't let anyone know what my father was making me do. I wanted to play football, but he wouldn't let me. He didn't want me to have any friends. I had to go to The Organization after school to have lessons with him. My father owns strip clubs and brothels. He would send me there to have sex as a reward for a good week of training. *Fucking makes you a man,* he would say. I would take all my frustrations out on the girls I would fuck."

"What do you mean by *taking out your frustrations* on them?"

"I would…"

"You would what?" She placed her hand in mine.

"I would fuck them hard and sometimes… hurt them."

"How, Ethan?"

"I would slap them around. Sometimes worse."

"Oh." Her hand slides out of mine, and she rolls to her side away from me.

"You have to understand." I turn her back to look at me and pull her hands into mine. My voice pleads forgiveness for something that had nothing to do with her. "I had no control over my life. I was so young and was being forced to become a monster, so I behaved like a monster. I was so ashamed of what I was becoming, and how I acted and treated those women. When my mother died, I spiraled out of control, and so did my father.

"What happened to your mother?" she asks.

"She got cancer and died when I was seventeen. My father changed.

Her illness was out of his control, and there was nothing he could do to save her. He brought in specialists from all over the country and took her to research clinics all over the world. There was nothing anyone could do. He blamed himself for her death."

"It sounds like he loved her very much."

"He did. But when she died, part of him died with her. He became vengeful and angry. He seemed to take it all out on me."

"Why you?"

"My sisters were all older. Lilliana was married, and he didn't have control over her anymore. Maria was being courted by her future husband. Those arrangements were already in place. Guilia left town as soon as she graduated from high school and built a life in Europe.

I was only seventeen and still in school. He could control me. He had always trained me, but it became more intense. When I started to push back and tell him I wanted to go to college, he would beat the shit out of me."

"I want to go to college. I want a career of my own. Why don't you hear me?" I beg as we circle each other in the boxing ring.

"I do hear you, Rocco, but you are my only son. You are my only male heir. You must learn the business so you can take over for me."

"But I don't want to take over The Organization. I want to make something of my own."

"You are going to do as I say. Do you hear *me!" he screams as he throws a punch to my head with his left.*

"No, Father! I won't!" I say as I shake off the hit and move right.

"You will do as I say or suffer the consequences." He throws a punch to my stomach.

Grunting out in pain, I beg, "Father, please."

"You." PUNCH.

"Will." PUNCH.

"Do." PUNCH.

"As." PUNCH.

"I." PUNCH.

"Say!" PUNCH.

As I lie on the mat in the fetal position, he has the last word before he leaves me to think about everything he has done. "You need to learn right now, Son, I get what I want. I never lose."

Shaking me out of my memory, Lola asks, "But you went to college, so how did that happen?"

"My sisters intervened after he beat me up that day. They reminded him my mother's dream was for one of her children to go to college. I was her last chance. They knew my mother was his weakness in life and death. Knowing education was what she wanted, he finally agreed to let me go to college and get my degree. But I had to promise to come back and work for him. I agreed because I thought I could get him to change his mind.

"Leaving here was the best thing that ever happened to me. I got away from him and his expectations. I concentrated on the *good.* I got to be myself for the first time and didn't have to look over my shoulder. It gave me time to find out what was important to me and to learn to stand up for what I believed in. I made friends who knew nothing about my family. I went to parties and football games. I volunteered in the community at a drug recovery group on the outskirts of town. Helping people healed my heart. I pushed the devil down and locked him away deep inside me."

"What did you do about the guards? Didn't you still have to have them?"

"I had one guard, Jerry. We agreed he would keep his distance from me, and I wouldn't tell my father about his gambling debts. By the time I graduated, his debts were paid, and I knew I didn't want to take over for Father, ever. I've been fighting for my freedom ever since. I came to work at Brandish-Martinelli and worked my way up the ladder. Granted, it was probably faster than most, but I did learn all the areas of the business. When I got to the level I am now, I found out he was trying to control it too."

"How?"

"By sending clients our way who needed to launder money."

"Isn't Brandish your partner? Don't they have a say in this?" she asks, sitting cross-legged in front of me.

"Brandish *was* my partner until my father bought him out, right under my nose. He keeps the name as a kind of *cover*. If I turn a profit in the next six months, it all becomes mine."

"Then you need to turn a profit," she says so matter-of-factly like that's the easiest thing in the world to do.

"We *do* make a profit. A big profit. But he keeps saying it's not enough by his standards."

"Are his standards going to keep changing so you can never get away?"

"I hope not."

"Did he tell you specifically how much profit you need to pull in before he sets you free?"

"No."

"Maybe you need to go back to him and make him be more specific. So he can't keep changing the rules."

"My father doesn't really *play* by the rules. Am I too trusting to think he would do the *right* thing because I'm his son?"

"Maybe. You need to have another meeting with him and propose more specific guidelines. A contract maybe?"

"I knew I wanted to keep you around." Taking her into my arms, I say, "You help me be a better man. You calm me." Her back tenses. "Lola...Are you afraid of me?"

"No, I'm not afraid of you. I don't know what it will be like if I ever see that side of you," she says tentatively.

"What side of me?"

"The evil side you buried deep inside."

"I don't ever want to show you that part of myself."

"You are putting so much pressure on yourself by burying so much deep inside. If something triggers you, it may all flow out of your control, then what will you do?"

Cupping her cheek, I say, "I could never hurt you, Lola. No matter what happens."

Lola and I stay up discussing strategies and plans until close to dawn.

Chapter 12
Ethan

I took the contract Lola and I created last night to my father's office this morning. She truly is amazing. She had some great ideas, and we worked well together, brainstorming and feeding off one another. I walked past Sheila's desk. She looks up at me and shakes her head.

Knocking lightly on the door and poking my head inside, I say, "Good morning, Father."

"What can I do for you, Son?" he says, not looking up from his work. He waves his hand for me to come inside.

"I would like to discuss something with you about the advertising agency."

He stands up from his chair and rounds the desk. Slapping me on the shoulder, he says, "Good! You've come to your senses. You're going to come be my second."

"No, sir. I've drawn up a contract between us regarding the agency."

"You what?" His thick Italian accent fills the room.

"Yes, I think we should have some guidelines to follow for the next six months to gauge my progress with the business."

"Gauge your progress?" His brows scrunch together, and he sounds confused.

"Yes, to hold us *both* accountable to the six-month deal."

He lets out an exasperated breath and sits back in his leather chair. "Show me what you have." After running his hand through his black hair, he puts on his reading glasses. I lay the agreement on his dark mahogany desk and slide it over to him.

"You don't trust me to keep my end of the bargain?"

"It's not like that. I think that if we have clear rules to follow, whoever loses won't be upset."

"I will *not* lose! You seem to forget who the hell *I am,* Son. I'm your father. I am your Don!" He pushes the papers back across his desk and stares at me, trying to calm down. "I will play your game until the end of the year, but you will ultimately do as I say and be my second!"

"No, I will win fair and square, and you'll set me free. Free to be with Lola and live my life without the family business." He slams his fist on the desk.

"Never! Who is this *Lola,* and what bullshit is she feeding you? You're turning into her little bitch!"

"She's not feeding me anything! She works in advertising also, and we get along very well. I want the freedom to have a *real* relationship with her. She's... different."

"I'm not keeping you from seeing this girl."

"But you *are*. She can never be safe if she's part of this family. We'll always be looking over our shoulders. I don't want to live like that anymore!"

"Listen to me," he says, stopping to take a deep, cleansing breath. "You are a *Martinelli*. There will always be someone who wants what you have. Someone who'll try to take it away. You must accept this. It's part of who we are."

"No. I refuse. If people know my business is legitimate, it will be different for me. I know it will be."

"But it won't, Son. They don't care who they hurt as long as they get what they want. And if that means taking someone you love to control you, they will do it."

"Then I'll leave. Leave this town, leave this family. I'll take Lola, and we'll go somewhere no one will try to hurt us."

"Son..." He pauses but does not complete his thought because there's a knock on the door.

"*What!*" he bellows, and Sheila, his assistant, enters the room.

"I'm sorry to bother you, sir, but the Acosta brothers are here for their appointment, and they seem quite agitated."

"Fine. Son, I'll sign your damn agreement," he says while signing his name on the dotted line and handing me the papers. "If you feel you need it. But you need to know that I don't want you to leave. You are my *only* son. I need you to continue my legacy. Your sisters need you. Please don't do anything rash. We'll talk about this more, I promise."

I don't want to argue anymore. Bowing my head in respect, I say, "Thank you for signing. I *will* make you proud, Father."

"I know you will, Son." Leaving the room, I come face-to-face with the Acosta brothers in the lounge area. We've known each other for years, but I don't stop to talk to them. I nod in their direction as I head out.

"Nico. Freddy."

"Rocco," they reply in unison. God, how I hate that name.

Chapter 13
Lola

'm sitting in my office when my phone chimes.

ETHAN

Are you there?

How did your meeting go?

A typical conversation with my father, but he signed it.

I'm so happy for you. Maybe the contract will help.

I'm not so sure. But it's worth a try.

Why don't you come over tonight? I'll make you dinner, and we can talk.

Okay, what time?

7

Until then

I leave the office right at five. That's a big feat for me, but I made it happen. I get home, change into my lavender sweatpants with FIERCE written on the ass with the matching sweatshirt that is two sizes too big, and start making dinner. I decided on spaghetti with meatballs, with my mom's *special* sauce. Ethan knocks and lets himself in.

"You know, you really need to keep the door locked."

"I know, but I knew you were coming, so I left it unlocked."

"I would feel better if you kept them locked all the time. You don't know who's out there creeping around."

"No one is after me, Ethan. But I'll try to do better for you." He walks up behind me and puts his arms around me while I'm stirring the sauce.

"God, that smells amazing. Can I have a taste?"

"Sure," I say as I take a teaspoon and dip into the sauce. Turning around, I offer it up to his lips.

"Mmm, that's delicious. But I meant, can I taste *you*?" I get tingles in my stomach, and my cheeks blush. I turn back to the sauce. He pushes my hair back and sinks his lips into the crook of my neck. Kissing… Licking… Sucking.

"Ethan," I moan out. "Let me turn this off." I turn off the burner, take the pan from the heat, and set it aside.

"Don't you want to eat dinner first? Build up your strength?" I ask.

"You can be my dinner tonight." He turns me around to look at him and plants a passionate kiss on my lips, making me desperate for more of him. His hands are on my back, then under my shirt, moving, caressing, and stroking me. He moves down to my sweatpants.

"Fierce, huh?" He chuckles.

"I am fierce. Grrrr," I say, holding my hands up like claws.

"We'll see about that," he says as he hooks his fingers into each side of the pants and pulls them down. I have no bra or panties underneath my clothes. He whistles.

"Are you *trying* to kill me, baby girl?" I smile, and he drops to his knees before me.

"Ethan. I need…" My voice comes out raspy and broken.

"What do you need, baby? Use your words. What do you want me to do to you?"

"I want you to touch me," I beg.

"Where? Here?" He runs his hands down my back.

"Yes."

"Here?" His hands grab my ass cheeks, and I giggle.

"Yes."

"Here?" His hands trail down my thighs.

"Y-Y-Yes." I can barely speak.

"Or how about here?" Ethan moves his mouth to my mound and blows softly over it.

"Yes... Everywhere... Please," I plead.

He lowers one finger to my pussy and runs it through my folds. He then holds his finger up to show me the wetness I already know is gathering.

"Fuck, baby girl, how are you always wet and ready for me?"

"Fuck me, please," I cry out.

"Not before I have my taste."

He hoists me up to sit on the island, and I lie back, spreading my legs wide and planting my feet on the marble. I can barely contain my anticipation for what I know is coming. He lowers his mouth to my slit and begins to ravage me. The fervor he eats my pussy with is unmeasurable. When he pulls my swollen clit into his mouth and sucks, my orgasm flows over me like waves crashing against the shore. I arch my back up from the island. My hands that played with his hair now grip it tightly, pulling his mouth into my center as far as it will go.

When I come down from my euphoria, I open my eyes, and Ethan is looking up at me from between my thighs. His eyes are locked on me. He rises from his place between my legs with a devilish grin on his face.

Without words, he scoops me off the island and carries me to my bedroom. Setting me on the side of the bed, he lifts my sweatshirt over my head, then takes my breasts in his hands. He begins to knead them and pinches my nipples between his fingertips. My pussy clenches when he lowers to suck one into his mouth and nibbles. I moan with the need to feel him inside me. My hands move to his belt and remove it. He doesn't stop me this time. An urgency overtakes me as I unbutton and unzip his pants. The need to taste him is all-consuming.

"I need you in my mouth, E," I pant. After pushing his black jeans down with his boxer briefs, I sink to my knees before him this time. The precum on his tip shines up at me as I lean forward to lick it. His taste is so sweet as I circle my tongue over his tip, slowly easing him into my mouth deeper and deeper until he touches the back of my throat, and I gag. Ethan's groans are deep and low. Like a rumble of thunder as it approaches in the night. I run my hands up the backs of his legs, pushing him deeper into my mouth. He places his hands in my hair, and the piston action starts. He wraps my curls tighter in his fists. As quickly as the movement began, it all came to a screeching halt. Son of a bitch, not again!

"What's wrong?" I ask, trying to catch my breath.

"Are you sure you want to do this? I don't want to hurt you?"

"Oh my God, Ethan, I had you in my mouth. Of course, I want to do this. You won't hurt me. Please don't stop this time." I'm close to begging now. "I want to make you feel good. The way you make me feel good." I open my mouth and stick out my tongue, my eyes requesting him to slip inside. I wait, determined to suck him off tonight.

He lets out a soft sigh and places the head of his cock on my tongue, and I resume pleasuring him. It's not long until he's punching his hips forward into my throat. An occasional tear falls down my cheek when the thrust gets harder. I allow him to use my mouth, taking everything he needs from me. Tears roll down my face. No woman has probably ever tried to control Ethan *fucking* Martinelli, but I will have my way tonight.

Gripping his base, I use my tongue to swirl and suck his hard cock. Sucking and pumping with my tight fist, I make him buck wildly. His body becomes rigid, and ribbons of cum release into my throat. With each swirl of my tongue, his whole body jerks as if electric shocks are surging from my tongue into his cock. I look up at him. Cum drips off my chin, and I break into a big smile.

"Oh. My. God. That was incredible. Where did you learn to suck cock like that, baby girl?"

"Sometimes giving head is just as good as sex with the right person. I get off on making you come," I say.

"Get up off your knees. I should be bowing down to my *fierce* queen," he says with a smirk. I giggle shyly as he picks up his black T-shirt off the floor. I put my hands up, and he pulls it over my head. My ass peeks out when I bend over, but that makes it even more fun when I wiggle it in his direction.

"Let's take a break for dinner, and then we can go for round two," he declares with a sly grin.

Chapter 14
Antonio

"I want you to find out who the fuck she is," I say to the private detective I hired to investigate Lola, who stands at attention in my office. "I want to know where she works, what she does in her spare time, who her friends are, who her family is, what venues she frequents, what she fucking had for breakfast! I want everything. Do you understand?"

"Yes, Mr. Martinelli. I understand. When do you want a report, sir?" the private eye asks.

"Yesterday, dammit!" I yell, slamming my fist on the desk.

"Yes, sir, I understand. I will get right on it."

He exits the office and closes the door. Looking at the ceiling, I speak to my beloved wife, "Lucia, my darling, I miss you so much." I fall back into my chair, taking our wedding picture from my desk. Staring into it, I remember the day it was taken like it was yesterday, and there is a stabbing pain in my chest.

Our wedding day was the happiest day of our lives.

"You are stunning, my darling. I can't take my eyes off you in that dress," I say as I hold her on the dance floor.

"You look pretty good yourself, Mr. Martinelli," she says in her soft Italian accent. Her hand reaches up to straighten my collar.

"I don't hold a candle to you, my love." I press my lips to hers while we dance our first dance in front of our guests.

"I can't wait for you to be pregnant with our sons."

"Sons, as in plural? How many are we talking?"

"At least four. We must have someone to take over our empire, my darling, so we can grow old together." I place more kisses on her lips.

"What if we have girls?" she asks.

"Then we will keep trying until God gives us a boy."

"We will be so happy, Antonio. I want them all to attend college and give us many grandchildren."

"Of course, my darling. Many little ones will be running around the mansion, who will love their grandmama and grandpapa very much."

"We are getting ahead of ourselves. Let's raise our children first before we count grandchildren," she says with a chuckle.

"Of course, my love. Whatever your heart desires." I hold her tightly in my arms as we sway to the music.

Sheila beeps the intercom, snapping me out of my memory. Replacing the picture on my desk, I wipe the tear from my cheek and bark, "What?"

"Mr. Scarpelli called to say he'll have to reschedule his two o'clock appointment for tomorrow."

"Fine, thank you. I do not want to be disturbed for an hour."

"Yes, sir."

I pick up the picture of our family. Lucia and I sit in high-backed chairs while she holds Rocco in her arms, and I hold two-year-old Guilia on my lap. Six-year-old Lilliana stands by my side, and four-year-old Maria is by her mother's side.

Talking to the heavens again, I say, "My darling, you would know what to do about Rocco. You had a way with him that I don't have. I want him to be happy, but I need him to take over."

"Rocco, sweetheart, come to Mommy." His little body toddles down the hallway to the kitchen. "Is Momma's boy hungry?" she asks him sweetly. He nods.

"You're going to make that boy weak. I need him to be strong," I say.

"He will be strong, Antonio, but he is just a child. Responsibility

comes later. Let him enjoy being a boy." She waves me away with her hand.

"He needs to start learning his place in this family. He will rule my empire one day."

"He will go to college first and then rule your empire. Education, Antonio. I want them all to have the education we never had in the old world. I want them to have everything we did not." She speaks with such passion.

"Yes, my darling," I say, patting Rocco on the head.

Setting the photo back on my desk, I pick up the last picture. It's of Lucia. It was taken only months before her death. She's thin and frail but smiling with our children surrounding her—exactly where she liked to be, in the middle of the chaos.

"Antonio."

"Darling. I'm here. What can I get you?" I take her hand in mine and raise it to my lips.

"I love you so much, my love, but I'm tired. I can't live with this pain any longer," she rasps.

"Please, my love. I can't lose you." Tears well in my eyes as I beg her to stay.

"Please promise me Rocco will go to college. I always wanted them to go to college." She's trying to catch her breath to speak.

"Yes, my love. I promise. You get better, and you'll see him go to college. You must fight, Lucia. For us, for our family, please," I beg, holding her hand to my cheek as I weep.

"Antonio, I can't. Please, you must let me go," she says, coughing weakly. "Please." Her frail, outstretched hand points across the room. "Take the medication in that vial and inject it into my arm."

"No! I will not!"

"Yes, please. You... must," she says with her last bit of strength. "You must let me go."

"I can't lose you, my darling. You're my world. My everything. I-I can't live without you." I cry into her chest as I drape myself across her body. She places her hand on my head and runs her fingers through my hair to comfort my shaking form. She uses her hand to raise my chin to look up at her. Wiping my tears away with her thumb,

she says, "It will all be okay. You will find another to love. I want you to be happy."

"No… never. There is only you, my love."

"Antonio, I cannot go on like this. I need peace. The pain is too much, and I can no longer bear it. As much as I beg God for death, it eludes me." Her eyes are full of tears as she continues. "Please, help me. I want to leave this earth my way. In your arms, just the two of us." Looking deep into her eyes, I see the pain in them. I know what I must do for my wife. Taking a deep breath, I rise from beside her and cross the room, retrieving the vial and needle. I fill the syringe with fluid and tap it. I lie on the bed and pull her into my arms.

"I love you, my darling," I say as I lift her chin to kiss her sweet lips for the final time.

"I love you, Antonio. Thank you."

"Yes, my darling. Anything for you."

After injecting the fluid into her IV, I hold her tightly to my chest. The medication takes over, and her eyes fall closed. Her breathing becomes shallow, and her chest stops rising.

"No!" I scream as I rock her lifeless body. "Forgive me, Father, for I have sinned."

Chapter 15
Lola

'm sitting in my office, looking over contracts, when a text rings out

ETHAN

> We did it! We landed the Canon
> Brothers account!

> I am so happy for you, E!

> 4.5 million dollars, baby! I'm on my way
> to being free.

The terms of the agreement with his father included obtaining three top clients by the end of the year and profits of at least twelve million dollars.

> I know you will do it. Let's celebrate.

> You bet we will. I'll pick you up at eight.

> Where are we going?

> I got reservations for Mariah's.

> Holy shit, Mariah's! I don't know if I
> have anything to wear there.

> I took care of that.

Like magic, there's a knock on my door. I look up to see a delivery-man standing at the entryway to my office. Amelia is hot on his heels, telling him he can't just barge in on me.

"It's okay, Amelia," I say, waving for him to come in and put the big box on my round meeting table. After grabbing my purse, I give him a tip.

"What do you think it is?" she coos, coming in behind me and looking curiously over my shoulder.

"I have no idea what it is, but it's from Ethan."

"Oh, I bet it will be amazing, whatever it is," she says, clapping her hands and giving a little bounce of excitement. At twenty-two years old, Amelia is younger than I am and has the enthusiasm of a teenager. She's petite at five foot four. She has long blond hair and there is always a bounce in her step and a smile on her face. She's the only person I know who can find the bright side in any situation. We've had some good conversations over the past few months, and I hope we can be friends. She knows I'm dating Ethan, but that's about it right now.

I take the big red bow from the huge white box. Slowly, I lift the lid and pull out the most exquisite black velvet strapless Tom Ford gown.

"It's so beautiful," I say.

"There's another box inside," Amelia whispers, pointing as if whatever was inside would bite her. It looks like a shoebox. I look at Amelia, and she smiles back at me. Together, we peer inside. It's a pair of the most stunning embellished black velvet Manolo Blahnik pumps I have ever seen in my life.

"Oh. My. God." I pick up my phone and dial Ethan.

"I knew you would call me back," he says with a smile in his voice.

"What did you do? Ethan, this is too much."

"Do you like them? Do they fit?"

"I just opened the box. I haven't tried them on yet."

"Put the shoes on for me while I'm on the phone," he pleads.

"Okay, hang on."

"No wait! Put the phone up to your lips. I want to hear everything." Amelia sets the box of shoes on my desk in front of me. I reach my hand inside, pulling out the right shoe. I kick off the pumps I'm wearing and slide my foot inside. An unexpected moan escapes my lips. I didn't see that coming, but they are so comfortable.

"That's right, baby. I can't wait to see your feet in those shoes." Ethan sighs.

"These are the most amazing shoes I have *ever* seen. Thank you, Ethan. But you shouldn't have."

"Only the best for my girl. We are going to celebrate tonight. And before I forget, a style team will be at your house at six to help you get ready. So no staying late at work tonight."

"You're making me feel like a princess, Ethan."

"You are a princess, Lola. You're *my* princess. See you at eight."

"Until then," I say and hang up the phone.

I rush out of work right at five o'clock. Amelia shoos me out the door. The style team shows up just before six. There are three of them. They paint my fingernails and toenails, fix my hair, and do my make-up. They even help me get into the dress. I stand before the full-length mirror in my bedroom, and I cannot believe my eyes. I do feel like a princess.

Ethan rings the bell instead of coming right in like he always does. I answer, and he's standing at the door in a black Tom Ford tuxedo, looking too handsome for his own good. He's holding a giant bouquet. The types of flowers are ones I have never even seen before.

"For you, milady," he says as he lays them in my arms.

"Oh, Ethan," I say in a breathless whisper. "They're gorgeous."

"Not as gorgeous as you are. Step back and let me see you." He gestures for me to go into the living room. After laying the flowers on the coffee table, I proceed to give him a little twirl.

"Wow."

"You did an amazing job picking everything out," I say.

"I do have three sisters. They helped a little." He chuckles.

"These shoes are so comfortable."

"Yes! The shoes, let me see them," he chimes. Pulling up my dress,

I stick out my leg through the slit and show him the shoes. "You have the sexiest legs I have *ever* seen. I can't wait to fuck you with those shoes on later." That makes me blush as I turn and pick up the flowers and go hunting in the cabinets for a vase big enough to fit them. When we exit the front door, I see a sleek black Escalade with black-out windows waiting for us. Ethan helps me inside, and we are off to the ball. Dinner, that is.

Chapter 16
Antonio

"You have got to be *fucking* kidding me!" My voice bounces off the walls in my office.

"No, sir. She's related to Barry Patterson," my private eye reports, locked at attention.

"That was years ago. I didn't know he had any children."

"By the time you killed him and the years that went by before you found his wife, Lola was an adult."

"Tell me about her."

"Lola Marie Patterson, single, age twenty-five. Five foot seven inches tall, 120 pounds. Brown hair and blue eyes. Her father was Barry Patterson. He died when she was twelve years old from suffocation. He was terminally ill with pancreatic cancer. He owed you $110,000 at the time of his death.

"Her mother was Janice Anne Patterson. She was a registered nurse who often took travel nurse positions nationwide, but eventually landed back here. She was hit by a vehicle outside Johnsonville Hospital more than a year ago.

"Lola started her degree at the local community college and transferred to Syracuse University for her last year to earn a degree in advertising. During her last year of college, she began working for

Kingsley and Masters as a social media coordinator. She later moved to account coordinator and public relations assistant and is now the head of advertising for the Northeast Region. She has $56,000 in student loan debt.

"She has never been arrested or had so much as a speeding ticket. She lives in a small Cape Cod outside of town, which has no security whatsoever. When she goes out, it seems to be only with her employees. She has no other family or good friends to speak of.

"She enjoys reading contemporary romance novels and shopping on the internet. She had a cheese omelet from Gerald's Deli for breakfast." He steps back, awaiting further instructions.

"Thank you, you may go."

Let's see how much she knows about her father's gambling debts and how her mother paid for it with her life. This might be what I need to get Rocco to come home. I think I need to pay Lola Marie Patterson a little visit. I reach for the intercom.

"Sheila, get me Nico and Freddy on the line. I have a job for them to do for me tonight."

"Yes, sir."

Chapter 17
Lola

"**A**melia!"

"Yes, Ms. Patterson."

"I told you to call me Lola."

"Yes, Lola."

"Where's that file for the Simpson campaign?"

"In the filing cabinet under S."

"I looked there. It's not there."

"Let me check."

Pulling open the cabinet drawer, she looks through the folders and hands me the file.

"Where was it?"

"It slid under some folders."

"Thank you so much. I don't know what I would do without you."

Today has been a crazy busy day. I've been in meeting after meeting. We lost the five-million-dollar Katz Pens account to Brandish-Martinelli. I wasn't upset because it's one step closer to Ethan being free of his father, but no one here needs to know that.

"Don't cry over spilled milk. We gotta keep moving forward," I say, trying to boost my team's morale.

It's eight o'clock before I get home, and I'm dead on my feet. After dragging my butt inside, I slide into the tub. I text Ethan and let him know I'm going straight to bed and will call him in the morning. While I'm relaxing in the hot water, I hear a thud in the living room.

"Hello… Ethan… Is that you?" He didn't answer my text. Maybe he's trying to surprise me. There's no response, so I rise from the tub, dry off, and put on my elephant sleep shorts and tank. Opening the door to the bathroom, I peer out. Nothing *seems* out of place.

It's just my imagination. I try to shake off the uneasy feeling in my belly and head to the refrigerator for a drink. While I'm peering inside, I catch sight of a shadow on the door. Before I can speak, a bag is thrown over my head, and everything goes dark.

When I wake up, I still have the bag on my head. I'm tied to a chair by my wrists and ankles, and I feel groggy and lightheaded. I don't know how long I've been out of it, but my neck is stiff from my head hanging down. I'm trying to listen to my surroundings to figure out where I am, but it does no good. The bag on my head is making me panic. I try to take in slow, steady breaths. My wrists are starting to hurt from the ropes, and I wish I could stretch out my legs.

"Ah. You're finally awake," a man with a deep Italian accent says. I lift my head even though I cannot see anything through the bag.

"Who are you? What do you want from me?"

"You're going to give me some information, and then I'll let you go. Simple."

"What information? I don't know anything."

"I haven't asked you any questions yet, so how do you know you don't know anything?"

The voice is right, so I stay quiet.

"I want to know what you remember about Barry Patterson?" he asks in a slow, determined voice.

"He was my dad. He died when I was twelve."

"Mr. Patterson owed me a great deal of money, and he died before I collected it."

"Why did he owe you money?"

"Because he had a problem with the ponies. He liked to bet on losers."

I didn't know my father bet on horse races. "Why would he tell me that? I was just a kid."

"Maybe you overheard something or saw him arguing with some-one. I know it's been a long time, but I need to know."

"I don't know anything," I snap

"How about your mother?"

"What about my mother?" I hiss.

"Did you overhear her talking to your father about someone coming after him to collect? Did she leave you a large sum of money when she died?"

"No, my mother didn't have a large sum of money," I say, annoyed. "My mother worked herself to the bone to provide for us, taking any nursing position she could get. She was hit by a car leaving work a little more than a year ago."

"Yes, I know," he states.

"What do you mean, you know?"

"You see, your father left with an unpaid debt—"

"He didn't *leave*. He died of cancer."

He continues, "I had to collect somehow. Your mother eluded us for many years until she showed up working at the hospital downtown. Someone had to pay for your father's debt."

"You... You killed my mother?"

"I wouldn't say it like that, my dear. More like she fulfilled your father's contract. But now I find out she had a child...You."

"What do I have to do with it? I didn't know any of this."

"Your mother never said a word to you?"

"No, why would she? I was twelve when my father died." We did move around a lot over the years. I just thought it was because she was moving to find work. Maybe we *were* running? No. It can't be true. Running from this man? But why would she move us back here if there was a threat? "I don't have any money." I lift my chin and say through the bag.

"No, but you have something else I want." He's standing behind me now. I can feel his hot cigar breath on my neck as he speaks. "You are dating Rocco Martinelli." My breath hitches, and for a moment, my mind spins.

"Yeah, so?" I ask abruptly, trying to sound stronger than I am. I'm glad he cannot see the terror on my face.

"I want it to stop." He pops the P on the end of the word.

"But why?"

"I have my reasons. Break up with him and never tell him about our little conversation, and I will leave you alone. But if you breathe one word or see him again, I will kill you like I did your parents."

"Wait? What? You killed them both?"

"Do you think your father died peacefully in his sleep?" He laughs. I open my mouth to speak, but before I can, he calls out, "Nico!" and everything goes black.

The following morning, I wake up in bed, lying on my back with the covers tucked neatly under my chin. When I open my eyes and look around, I wonder if it was all just a scary dream. I lift the covers and look underneath, feeling relieved to see I am still wearing my elephant shorts and tank top. I sit up and wince with pain when I see the rope marks on my wrists. *Oh no, it can't be real.* I throw off the covers, grab my ankles, and wince at the irritation from the rope burns there too. *No. This can't be happening. Ethan.* I burst into tears at the thought of having to tell the only man I've ever loved goodbye.

Chapter 18
Ethan

Why won't she answer my text messages? Did I do something wrong? I haven't heard a word from Lo in three days. At first, I thought she was working on a big contract, so I let her have her space. When she gets busy at work, she sometimes forgets to respond. But this has been too long.

> Lo, whatever I did, I'm sorry.

> Please, you have to talk to me.

> Just tell me what I did, and I will fix it.

> Please, baby. I'm sorry.

> Why are you doing this?

> I'm coming to your house. We need to talk.

I hold an enormous bouquet in one hand and a bottle of scotch in the other. When I get to her house, I knock on the door. Nothing. I knock again. Nothing. I pound on the door. Nothing. I try the knob, and for the first time, the fucker is actually locked.

"What the fuck!" I lay the flowers against the front door and open the scotch. Taking a swig from the bottle, I start around the house to the patio. When I look through the patio door and the windows on the back side of the house, everything is dark inside, and there's no sign of Lola. I take another big drink from the bottle and sit on the love seat to watch our sunset. I'm determined to wait until she comes home, no matter when that might be.

"Ethan, Ethan, wake up." Someone is shaking me. When I open my eyes, it's Lola.

"Lola!" I slur excitedly.

"What are you doing here? You have to leave," she whisper-yells.

"I don't think I could do that even if I wanted to, which I don't," I say defiantly, holding up the empty bottle of scotch. "I would have shared it with you, but you never came home. Why, Lola? Why won't you talk to me?"

"I can't, Ethan. We can't see each other anymore. How long have you been here?"

"I don't know. I had to watch *our* sunset alone," I whine.

"Give me your keys," she says, holding her hand out.

"They're in my jacket pocket." She rummages through my pockets, pulls out my keys, and leaves. I get off the love seat, stumble through the patio door into the living room, and flop down on the couch. She moves my car into her garage and puts down the door. Standing in the middle of the living room, she has her hands on her hips.

"What am I going to do with you?"

Everything goes black.

Chapter 19
Lola

When I come back into the house after moving Ethan's car, I find him sound asleep on my couch. I stand here looking at his handsome face. Why? Why is this happening to us? I just found him, and I have to let him go. He is never going to understand.

I cover him with a blanket and press a kiss to his lips. After making sure all the doors are locked tight, I go to bed.

I shake him awake at eight in the morning. "Ethan, Ethan. You have to get up. You *need to* leave."

"Huh... What happened?" he asks, trying to stretch out on my little couch.

"You drank an entire bottle of scotch. That's what happened."

"I was waiting for you to come home. I watched our sunset *without* you. I must've gotten carried away drinking," he says, running his hand through his hair and down his face.

"You. Need. To. Go," I say, pulling on his arm. Panic seeps in once more.

"No, Lola. Please, whatever I did, I will undo it. I'm *sorry*." He sits up on the couch, grabbing my hand. "Please."

Softly, I say, "Ethan, you didn't *do* anything. It's me. I can't do this. It's too much. You have to forget about me."

"But I love you, Lola." His eyes are shining with tears he doesn't let escape.

"And I love you, Ethan, but we can never be. I am *so* sorry." I'm trying to be strong. But this is the hardest thing I've ever had to do. I was insane to think I could just stop texting him, and he would go away.

"You are the woman I have waited my whole life for. Please don't do this."

"Oh, Ethan." My eyes are brimming with tears because this is breaking my heart. I don't want to lose him either, but I'm terrified. How do I know they won't hurt him? I don't know who those people are. No, I have to let him go. Pulling on his hand, I get him up from the sofa and lead him to the garage. After pushing the button to lift the garage door, I kiss him on the cheek and raise my hand for him to go. He gets in his car, backs out of the garage, and pulls away. As I watch the garage door go back down, I can't believe I just let the love of my life go.

Chapter 20
Ethan

illiana is my eldest sister. She married Alessandro Pagola in an arranged marriage. They seem to have grown to care for each other. These kinds of marriages don't always have favorable results, but he's been good to her. They've had three kids together: Marco is five, Damian is three, and little Lucia is one. She is named after our mother. We nicknamed her Lucky.

Before Lil had to marry Alessandro, she loved fashion. She wanted to be a designer, but all that was put on hold to begin her life with him. She opens the door in fuzzy pink pajamas, with her hair pulled back in a sloppy bun on top of her head. She takes one look at me and pulls me inside.

"Ethan, oh my God, who died? You look awful."

"No one died, Lil. My heart is broken, but thanks." She pulls me in for a tight hug.

"Sit down and tell me everything." She grabs her phone and sends a text to my sisters. *Get over here now. Something has happened with Ethan.*

"I love her so much, Lil," I say, laying my head on her shoulder.

"I know you do, Rocky. Tell me what happened."

"I have no idea." I throw my hands up. "One minute, we were out to dinner celebrating a big win for the company, and the next, she never wants to see me again."

"Well, what did she say?"

"She said she loves me. But she can't do *this* anymore." I fling my index finger back and forth between us.

"You smell like a distillery. Are you okay?" She wrinkles her nose at me.

"I drank an entire bottle of scotch last night while I waited for her to come home."

"Rocky…" The lecture is cut off by a knock on the door. Maria and Guilia push their way inside.

"Little brother, what happened?" Guilia says with sad, pouty lips. Gilly (pronounced Jilly) is the youngest of the three girls. She's two years older than I am and the rebel of the family. Regardless of what my father says or wants, Gilly lives life on her own terms. When she graduated from high school, she left to backpack around Europe or some shit. She posts videos on TikTok and YouTube of her travels and makes enough money to live how she wants. She has been gone for years and is back home for a brief visit. She has deep-blue eyes, and today, she has pink hair. She loves anything to do with hair and makeup and is always the life of the party. We are only two years apart, so she was always up in my business when we were in school.

"That girl broke his heart," Lil says.

"Her name is Lola," I clarify.

"I'm so sorry, baby brother. We brought ice cream," Maria chimes in. She's the middle sister. She's been married for two years to Giovanni Bertanoni. He's eight years older than she is, and you guessed it, it was an arranged marriage. They have a baby boy named Riccardo, after her husband's father, but we call him Baby Ricky. She's the shortest of the girls with brown hair cut off at her shoulders. She's an introvert who likes to read and cook. She goes with the flow better than any of us. We call her MeMe.

"I don't feel much like ice cream, but thanks." I scrunch up my nose.

"He drank a whole bottle of scotch last night," Lil whispers over her shoulder.

"I understand," Gilly yells from the kitchen, then whispers to MeMe, "More for us."

"I heard that." She passes out bowls of ice cream to each of them and sits.

I continue, "I thought she was the one, ya know? We have so much in common. I love the way her nose crinkles up when she laughs, and how her hair swishes around her shoulders when she takes her bun out. I thought I had it all, and now it's gone, and I don't understand why." Putting their arms around me, MeMe and Lil squeeze me tightly.

"It's gonna be okay, Rocky," they say in unison. My sisters are the only ones who can call me Rocky.

"How is it ever going to be okay? I thought she was it for me. I know she felt it too. I just wish I knew why she did it."

"I hate to say this, but do you think Father had anything to do with it?" Lil asks quietly.

"She's never met him. I kept her away from him for this reason."

"Maybe you need to try to talk to her again, once you both have had a chance to think about it," MeMe says.

"I've tried, but I think she blocked me."

There have been times when I hated being the baby brother. When we were kids, they would torture me—dressing me up like a girl, putting makeup and nail polish on me. Momma would laugh, but she always helped me to take it off before Father got home. I was supposed to grow up to be a powerful Mafia boss, and I stood there dressed for a tea party. She always said, *Out of all my children, you feel things the deepest.* I guess because I was the youngest, and they all mothered me. Father hated it and said it would make me weak. But now that we have all grown up, it *is* nice to always have someone in your corner. They fight for me, and I fight for them. Hell, I would kill for them. The only difference between them and me is that they got away from our father, and I didn't.

Lying in Lil's spare bedroom looking up at the ceiling, I remember Lola's eyes. Her lips. Her touch. If I can't have Lola, then I give up. I don't care if Father wins. I have no reason left to fight for my freedom anymore. I should just do what he says and accept my fate. I will take my place as his second.

Chapter 21
Antonio

The phone rings three times before she answers.

"I thought I told you to tell Rocco you couldn't see him anymore?" I snarled into the phone. There's a long silence from the other end of the line, and she finally speaks.

"I tried to ignore him, but he came to my house. He was drunk. I couldn't let him drive. He slept on the couch, and the following morning, I told him I couldn't see him again. I won't see him again."

"You better not, or it will be the end of both of you."

"Please don't hurt him. I'll do whatever you want... I swear." I slam the phone down on her just as Sheila knocks on my door.

"What, goddammit!"

"Sir, Rocco is here to see you, and he doesn't look good," she says.

"Let him in." Rocco enters the room, and he's a mess. He hasn't shaved in days; his clothes are rumpled, and he has dark circles under his eyes.

"Son, what the hell happened to you?"

"She left me."

"Who?"

"Lola."

"What happened?

"She said she couldn't do *this* anymore." He does the finger thing between us.

"I *am* sorry, Son." Not really, but I try to look concerned. "Is there anything I can do for you?"

"I know it's only October, but I want to concede to our deal. I'll give up the advertising agency and be your second."

I've never seen my son so downtrodden, but I've won. That's all that matters.

"You won't regret this, Rocco. I'll teach you everything you need to know to take over the world."

I have my son back on my side. Let the training begin.

Chapter 22
Lola

I t's been weeks since I last saw Ethan in my home and told him I couldn't see him anymore. He texted me for days afterward. I finally had to block his number because I couldn't take it anymore. He broke my heart into pieces with all his questions and asking me to meet him. Today, when I came to work, I was called into Mr. Kingsley's office. His assistant, Carolyn, shows me in.

"Mr. Kingsley. Ms. Patterson is here to see you."

"Yes, yes, come in, Lola. Would you like some coffee?"

"No, sir. I'm fine. Thank you."

"You may go, Carolyn." He points for me to sit in the chair.

"Let me get straight to the point, Lola. Brandish-Martinelli is selling, and I want it."

"Sir?"

"I need you to write a proposal and get it on my desk ASAP."

"But, sir, why are they selling?"

"I guess the boy, Ricky, Rocky, or something, is stepping down, and his father wants to sell."

"Stepping down?" *Oh, Ethan, what are you doing?*

"Yes. Now I want you on this. Get your head in the game, Lola. I want this company. It will knock out fifty percent of our competition if we can merge with them."

"Yes, sir. I'm on it." I stand and leave the room. Walking down the hallway to my office, I pull out my phone, unblock Ethan's phone number, and text him.

> What the hell are you doing?

It only takes a few seconds for him to respond.

ETHAN

I guess you are still out there, after all.

> You can't do this.

I can do whatever the hell I want.

> You love that company.

But I loved you more.

> Ethan

If I can't have you, I don't want any of it.

> Don't talk like that. You still have six weeks to beat your father.

No, I already conceded. I'm going to work for him.

> Ethan, NO! You can't do that. You don't want to be like him.

I didn't want to be like him, but now I want everyone to feel the same pain I feel from losing you.

> You don't mean that.

> Yes, I do. You don't want me. I have nothing else.

> It wasn't because I didn't love you, Ethan.

> Then what was it, Lola? Tell me. Tell me anything.

> I can't. I'm sorry.

> Don't contact me again. I can't take it. You broke me.

> I'm sorry.

He never replied. I can't believe this is happening. I arrive at my office and start working on the proposal for the takeover.

I stay at work until ten o'clock, reviewing numbers and preparing our proposal to purchase Brandish-Martinelli.

The following morning, I find myself, proposal in hand, knocking on Mr. Kingsley's door.

"Come in," he says.

"I'm sorry, sir, but Carolyn wasn't at her desk."

"It's okay, come on in. What do you have for me?"

"I've prepared the proposal for your review. Please let me know if there's anything you would like changed." I set the folder on his desk and turn to leave.

"I trust you, Lola. The meeting is at ten in the morning."

"Sir?" I turn back around.

"I want you there. I want you to pitch the proposal to Brandish-Martinelli tomorrow."

"Oh, sir. I don't think that's such a good idea." Panic begins to spread through my body like wildfire.

"You are the best. And I need the best tomorrow. I'll see you at nine thirty in the lobby. The car will be there to pick us up."

"Yes, sir." I leave his office and start down the hallway toward mine. My brain spins with thoughts of tomorrow. What do I do if Ethan is there? Will his father be there? I don't know if I can do this. *I think I'm going to be sick.*

I spend half the night practicing the presentation in the middle of my living room floor. I'm as ready as I'll ever be. I pull my hair into a tight bun, put on my favorite tailored gray suit and cream silk shirt, and finish the look with my favorite Manolo pumps.

I get to work in plenty of time. Filling my Louis Vuitton briefcase with everything I need, I head for the lobby, talking to myself the whole way. *You can do this. Keep it together. If Ethan is there, just don't look at him. I am the ultimate professional. Mr. Kingsley is counting on me.* I exit the elevator and wait in the lobby. With the next ding of the elevator, Mr. Kingsley emerges. Without a word, I fall into step with him, and we head for the waiting car.

As we enter the Brandish-Martinelli boardroom, I scan the room for Ethan. I sigh in relief when he's nowhere to be found. *It's all going to be okay. He's not here.* A man with jet-black hair sits at the head of the long conference table. He has broad shoulders and an angry face. He looks like he's never smiled a day in his life. He's leaning to his side, talking to another man with salt-and-pepper hair and wearing black reading glasses. Our eyes meet for a moment, and I go back to preparing the presentation.

Mr. Kingsley shakes both of their hands and sits down at the table. When I'm ready, I clear my throat and look at Mr. Kingsley.

With a nod of his head, I begin. "Good morning, gentlemen. My name is Lola Patterson. I'm the head of advertising for the Northwest Region of Kingsley and Masters. Today, I will be presenting to you our proposal for the purchase of your company." The door slams, and all heads snap to see Ethan enter the room. My eyes connect with his, and he glares at me. He takes a seat on the other side of the man with the black hair.

Momentarily stunned, I take a deep breath and continue, "If you would please open your folders to page one, we can begin." The presentation continues as expected. The gentleman with salt-and-pepper hair is doing all the talking for them. I keep my cool and try not to look in Ethan's direction as I conclude my speech.

"Do you have any questions?"

The men talk among themselves, and finally, the man says, "Thank you, Ms. Patterson. Mr. Kingsley. We have a few more companies to hear from, as I'm sure you are aware. We will look over your proposal and get back to you by the end of the week." Mr. Kingsley shakes their hands, and I clean up, praying Ethan doesn't approach me.

Mr. Kingsley walks out the door first, stopping to hold the door for me. As I start to walk out, the angry man finally speaks.

"It was nice to see you again, Lola." I stop dead in my tracks, and chills run up my spine. I know that voice. I would know it anywhere. It was the man who spoke to me through the bag. It's him. My heart lurches through my chest, and I turn to look at him. Finally, putting a face to that deep Italian voice. If Mr. Kingsley wasn't there motioning me forward, I would've stayed frozen in my spot. Ethan looks at him and back at me, but I can't say a word. I try not to show the absolute terror that has invaded my soul as I continue walking out the door.

Chapter 23
Ethan

I cannot fucking believe Lola was there during the presentation this morning. She wouldn't even look at me. I wanted to chase her down the hallway. I wanted to ask her what the hell happened. But when I stood to leave, Father made me stay to discuss the proposal. By the time he finally let me out of the damn room, I was so full of rage that I wanted to hit something. I couldn't sit at my desk feeling like that, so I left and drove to the gym to spar with Jerry.

Jerry is older. He's maybe forty or fifty. Who knows? He was my bodyguard back at college. He has brown hair with hints of gray at the temples, and tattoos cover his arms and chest. He cleaned up his gambling debts and came to work for us, running the gym. He trains new recruits in self-defense, weapons, hand-to-hand combat, and anything we need. He's been my sparring partner for years, and when I need to work off some pent-up frustration, we box.

"Goddammit! What the fuck is wrong with you?" he yells, pushing me off him.

"Nothing," I say, spitting in the bucket in the corner. "Why?"

"'Cause you're hitting me like you fuckin' wanna kill me."

"It's just built-up frustrations, ya know."

"You need to get fucked, man." Jerry chuckles.

"Fuck you."

"Come out tonight with us, and we'll get you laid."

"I don't need your help to get laid, asshole."

"Then come out with us and have a few drinks. Unwind a little."

"I don't know."

"Come on, you'll feel better."

We spar a little longer. "Maybe you're right."

"Meet us at Scarlett's at ten."

"I'll be there."

Since getting back into The Organization full-time, my father insists on me having security and a driver to escort me everywhere. Nico and Freddy Acosta are my bodyguards now. I've known them for years. We went to the same high school, but I wouldn't exactly say we were friends. Father never let me play sports or have friends over. Freddy and Nico have become Antonio's go-to people for rounding up the deadbeats who owe The Organization money.

Freddy started as a bouncer with The Organization right out of high school. Antonio has invested a lot of time and energy in training Freddy and his younger brother, Nico.

Freddy is a little taller than I am but has at least fifty pounds of muscle on me. He's familiar with Scarlett's. It's a dance club with a private area in the back for *special* parties. He drops me off at the curb with Nico.

"I'll text you when I'm ready to leave."

"Yes, Boss."

We're ushered past the red velvet ropes and into the club. Jerry and a group of friends are seated in the VIP area at the back of the club.

"There he is, Mr. Mob Boss himself, Rocco Martinelli!" Jerry yells out, standing with his arms open wide and a drink in his hand. He gestures to the girl with a tray in her hand. "Get my man here a scotch."

"Yeah, yeah, so I made it here. What's so great about *this* place?" I ask.

"It's the private rooms, man. You can get whatever you want here." My father owns a lot of strip clubs, dance clubs, and bars. I used to frequent them when I was younger but haven't been to this one before.

"What do you mean, I can get whatever I want?"

"The girls back there will do and be whatever you want for the right price, ya know," he says, nudging my arm with his.

"I didn't come here for that, Jerry."

"I know you are all broken up about Lola." He puts his fists up to his eyes like he's crying. I shove him. "But it's time to let her go, man. You can live out your wildest fantasies with the girls here tonight. After a few more drinks, you'll change your mind."

I try to loosen up, and after a few more drinks, I think maybe Jerry is right. I see a blonde with killer legs on the edge of the dance floor.

"Go for it, man," he says, bumping my shoulder and giving me a little push. She's wearing a short red dress with a slit up her thigh, and she's wiggling her ass to the music. With one more hit of the amber liquid, I stride across the floor and hold out my hand. She looks up at me with green eyes and takes my hand.

"I've never seen you here before," she says as I guide us onto the dance floor.

"It's my first time."

"Well, we'll have to make it special for you tonight then, hand-some," she says with a sultry smile. She turns her back to my front and starts grinding her hips against my dick. I place my hands on her hips as she sways, and my dick hardens in my pants. She turns to face me and puts her arms around my neck.

"So what'll it be, honey?"

"I like it rough," I say with a stone-cold expression.

"Oh, baby, that's just how I like it," she croons.

"But I don't kiss."

"Huh?"

"I don't kiss."

"Okay, honey, whatever you want." She takes me by the hand and leads me toward a door in the back of the club. Visions of Lola come to mind. I won't defile our memories by kissing another woman.

Jerry is howling in the background. "Get it, Rocco!" I flip him off and follow her inside, down the hall, and to the last door on the right. We walk into a small room with a bed, table, lamp, and an adjoining bathroom.

The bed is covered with black satin sheets, and the headboard has hooks for restraints. The walls are backlit a deep red, and the thumping from the dance music pounds through the walls. She moves over to the bed and sits on the edge, crossing her legs and hiking her skirt up.

"So what's your name, honey?"

"They call me E."

"Well, E, why don't you come sit by me and let's get started?" She's older than me, but I'm not asking her age. There's an air of maturity about her like she's seen everything there is to see. Removing my jacket, I lay it over the chair, then I unbutton a few buttons on my shirt and pull it from my slacks.

"What do I call you?" I ask.

"Just call me J."

"Okay, J... suck my cock." She doesn't blink an eye as she stands up from the bed and walks toward me. She palms my crotch with her small hand and gives it a squeeze. After unbuttoning the rest of my shirt, she pushes it from my shoulders. Her hands guide their way over my shoulders and down my pecs.

"My God, you *are* gorgeous."

"I bet you say that to all the men," I say, smirking. She trails ardent kisses across my chest and down my torso to my pants. She removes my belt from its loops and tosses it on the bed.

"You can use that later if you want to." She giggles and gets back to work removing my clothes. When they're all discarded, she kneels before me and takes my cock in her hand, and strokes it firmly. My hands instinctively move to her hair and pull her head back, causing her eyes to connect to mine.

"No teeth," I spit out. She smiles slyly and sticks out her tongue, which beckons my cock inside.

She puts my crown into her hot mouth and sucks. Throwing my head back, I shut my eyes. She's not my Lola by any means, but she'll get the job done. She continues to lick and suck my cock while I fist her hair in my hands, pulling it tighter. I shove myself into the back of her throat, making her gag. She doesn't let up, and neither do I. Thrusting my hips upward, I chase my release. I pull my cock out of her mouth just in time to mark her face with my cum.

She licks her lips and smiles like the greedy little slut she is, and I motion for her to get on the bed. She uses her hand to wipe the cum down her face and rub it on her chest. She hikes her skirt up and slides her panties down her legs. Stepping out of them, she lies back on the pillows and spreads her legs wide for me. She puts her hand between her legs and rubs her clit, readying herself for me. Taking my dick in my hand, I stroke up and down my shaft. Once, twice, and the hardness returns.

"I'm going to fuck you so hard you see your dead relatives," I growl out through gritted teeth. I cover my cock with a condom and climb above her. Her fingers are all she's going to get because there will be no foreplay tonight.

I take her thighs in my hands and lift them to her chest for a better angle to go deep. Notching my throbbing dick at her entrance, I shove my way to her core in just one stroke. She lets out a yelp. Pulling back out, I thrust into her again, hard and deep, taking all my frustrations out on this pussy.

"Oh my God," she pants as I pound into her. She pulls me close like she's going to kiss me.

"NO!" I roar.

"Sorry, sorry, I forgot." She flinches as if I'm going to hit her, but I hammer into her pussy even harder for it. Fisting her hair in my left hand, I hear her whimper while my right hand holds her where I want her as I chase *my* release. The sounds of our bodies slapping together fill the room. My release comes. I roll off to catch my breath, not caring if she got hers. Minutes later, I'm putting my clothes back on.

"You don't have to go so soon, do ya, honey?"

"I need to go." The darkness is overwhelming me. I wanted to hurt her. I feel the old Rocco, the uncaring piece of shit I used to be, reemerging. The user and abuser of women, the man who took what he wanted with no consequences. The Mafia boss I've been pushing away all these years is clawing his way back up from the darkness. I need to get the hell out of here.

Monday morning, I am summoned to my father's office.

"You wanted to see me?" I flop down in the leather chair and throw my arms across the back of it.

"Yes, I have a job for you. I want you to go with Nico and Freddy to collect my money from Marc Yates."

"They know what they're doing. They don't need me."

"They haven't been successful in collecting my money from this guy. I want you to show them how it's done. Make it clear to Yates that *you* are in charge. If he doesn't give you the money, kill him."

"Kill him?"

"Yes, kill him. It will send a clear message to anyone else who doesn't want to pay that Rocco Martinelli is in charge and won't take shit from anybody."

"But it's just money," I say.

"Just money! Money is everything, Rocco. Haven't you figured that out yet?" he bellows.

"But—"

"No buts, boy! You will do as I say and take care of this matter for me. Money or he dies. I've given him enough chances." He reaches into his drawer, takes out a 9mm, and hands it to me. "Get out and don't come back until it's done."

"Yes, sir," I say, sliding the gun into the back of my pants and covering it with my suit jacket.

Nico, Freddy, and I scour the city looking for this idiot. I hope he pays because I don't want to have to do this. It's dusk now. The time of night when all the lowlife scum crawls out of their holes. Sure enough, he's on the street corner trying to convince a hooker to spend some time with him. We roll up on him, and his eyes widen as the window goes down.

"Get in," Freddy says.

"Nah, I'm good," he says, turning his back on us.

"I said GET IN!" Freddy bellows, reaching for the door handle.

"Okay, okay, I'm gettin' in." He opens the door and slides in the back seat with me. Pointing his thumb over his shoulder at me, he asks, "Who's this guy?"

"I'm Rocco Martinelli. I'm here to collect the money you owe Antonio Martinelli... my father." With my stern mask fixed tightly in place, I stare him down. His eyes grow wide, and his face loses all color as if all the blood drained from his body.

"I...I...I don't have it, but I will soon," he sputters.

"Wrong answer."

"Here, you can have what I have right now." He digs into his pockets and pulls out a little vial, half full of a white substance, and a few bills. I take the bills.

"You think fifty dollars will suffice Antonio Martinelli when you owe him thousands?" I ask with a dark laugh and throw it back in his face. I hear Nico and Freddy in the front seats chuckle under their breath.

"Please, it's all I have," he cries.

"Well, it's not good enough," I snarl. Grabbing him by the shirt, I pull him in close. "It's my understanding that these fine gentlemen have been trying to collect from you for *months,* and you keep putting them off. You cannot put me off. I'm your *last* chance. Do you understand me?"

"Yes... Yes...I understand. I'll go to my brother. Maybe he can give me the money," he begs as I toss him back into the seat.

"You have until eight tomorrow morning. Be in this exact spot with the money, or you're a dead man." Opening the door, I shove him out onto the curb.

"Oh, and don't try running because I *will* find you." I slam the door, and Nico drives off.

"Boss. What are we going to do until morning?" Nico asks.

"Let's go to Scarlett's."

Nico parks the Escalade at the curb in front of Scarlett's. The three of us go inside and are ushered to the VIP section. Scanning the room, I look for J. I spot her over by the bar and come up behind her.

"Evening," I croon into her neck, and she whips her head around.

"Hi, gorgeous." She smiles when she recognizes me.

"Are you *busy* tonight?" I ask, raising an eyebrow.

"I'm always free for *you,* honey," she says in her sultry tone.

"Can you find some company for my men over there?" I motion to Nico and Freddy.

"I think that can be arranged," she says. I pick up our drinks and make my way to the booth. J and two other girls head in our direction. J sits on my lap. She wraps her arms around my neck and plays with my hair. A brunette with big tits scoots in beside Nico, and his eyes grow wide, while a redhead with a tight little ass shimmies up to an uncomfortable Freddy.

"Boss. Mr. Martinelli wouldn't like us mixing business with pleasure like this," he says.

"*This* Mr. Martinelli is telling you it's okay tonight while we kill time. Just don't get so drunk that you can't take care of business in the morning." They both smile like I just gave the mice some cheese. I tap J on her leg to get up.

"You ladies take good care of my boys tonight," I say with a wink, and we walk toward the door to the private area. J ushers me into the room we had before, and I grab her from behind.

"What did you have in mind for tonight, sweetie?" she coos.

"I'm going to tie you to that bed and fuck you until you scream."

"Still no kissing?" She turns to loosen my tie.

"No kissing."

"Somebody must've hurt you real bad."

"No talking either, just fucking," I blurt out. She removes my suit jacket and lays it neatly over the back of the chair.

"I'll be keeping that," I say as I snatch my tie back from her. She giggles and continues undressing me. I reach for the zipper on the back of her dress, and it falls to the floor. Her tits are bare, and her nipples are hard.

"Get on the bed," I bark. Without another word, she does as she's told. Wrapping my tie around both wrists, I raise them above her head and attach them to one ring on the headboard. I run my hands over her body until I come to rest on her panties atop her clit. She shudders beneath my touch.

"Please touch me this time," she begs.

I drag her wet thong down her legs and toss it aside. Reaching out to touch her hot cunt, I find she's dripping wet for me. She spreads her legs wider, raising her hips for me to touch her more. I hold her thigh hard in my grasp, and she whimpers. I tease her, just touching her on the outside, not putting my fingers inside her sweet cunt.

"Please, E… I… need," she says breathlessly as I cut her off.

"What do you need?" I ask. Lola pops into my head, and I remember the night we said those words to each other. I try to shake that memory out of my head.

"I need your fingers inside me, please," she whines.

"You know I don't do easy and sweet."

"I know. Please, I need…" That's all she gets out before I ram my finger deep into her dripping cunt, and she screams out. Not sure if it's from pain or pleasure, but I don't care. I add my middle finger and pump them in and out of her pussy fast and hard, curling my fingers on her G-spot.

"E, please, not so hard."

"You can take it. I know you can."

I circle my thumb on her clit, and she erupts into an orgasm. Her mouth opens in the shape of an O, but no sound is coming out. Her abs are clenched so tight she lifts off the bed.

"Oh my God, that was so hot," she says, trying to catch her breath. I chuckle and slide on a condom. Climbing above her, I don't give her any time to recover before I plunge my rock-hard dick inside her cunt. With each pass, I thrust harder. As if the harder I fuck her, the more it will help me forget Lola. I have to forget her. This life is not for her. If I have to end a life tomorrow, it will take Lola away from me forever because the darkness will claim my soul, and Rocco will be back.

Gritting my teeth, I increase my pace and push farther into J, but I can still see Lola's face. I slam into her over and over, begging my brain to forget Lola. Harder… Harder… Harder…

"Stop!" J yells, and I'm shaken back to reality. She's pulling on her restrained arms, trying to get herself free. Snapping me out of my trance, I realize I'm torturing her with the thrusts of my cock.

"I… I… I'm sorry," I say.

"I like it hard, baby, but not *that* hard, okay?"

"Yeah… I'm sorry." I've had no release, but I pull out of J and remove the condom that only holds the precum from my tip. Unhooking her hands and removing the tie, I fall back onto the bed and throw my arm over my face, disgusted with myself.

"I *am* sorry," I rasp out.

J turns on her side. Leaning on her elbow, she says, "Who is she?"

"What?"

"Who. Is. She?" Saying it as if she could read my mind.

"Her name is Lola. How did you know?"

"I've been doing this for a long time, honey, and I know when a man is into me or just needs to fuck something. And you just need to fuck something... hard." She chuckles. "What happened?" I'm not sure why I feel like I can confide in this woman, but I do.

"We dated for a few months, and I fell for her completely. I think I fell in love with her the moment I saw her for the first time. I loved to spoil her, take care of her, and make love to her. I was different with her. I wanted to be a good man for her. Something or someone took her from me. All I have left now is hate."

"Why do you say they *took* her from you?"

"Because one minute we were celebrating and had the best night of our lives, and the next, she said she couldn't see me anymore. I know she loves me too, but something made her pull away from me."

"Have you seen her again?"

"Yes, once at a work meeting. She wouldn't even look at me."

"Honey, you have to find out what happened. Maybe there's a good reason for what she did?"

"Maybe, but it's too late because I gave up everything when I lost her. I can't bring her into this life, even if she does still love me."

"But you're still the same good man inside."

"After tomorrow, I think all the good I have left will be gone."

"What happens tomorrow?"

"I have to do a deed for my father. It will change everything." She looks at me with concern in her eyes.

"Get some sleep, honey. Tomorrow is a new day."

I meet up with Nico and Freddy in the empty club after waking up beside J. They both look satisfied, probably because they got off all night with those chicks. I pay our bill and tip J very well, and we leave to find Yates.

Pulling up to the curb, he's standing there waiting for us.

"Do you have it?" I roll down the window and ask.

"I tried, I really did, but my brother wouldn't speak to me," he blubbers.

"Gee, I wonder why? Probably because you're a worthless piece of shit, and he gave up on you too. Get in!"

"Please," he begs.

"I said get in!" I snap, opening the door wider. He climbs into the Escalade and doesn't say another word. Nico drives us to the warehouse on the outskirts of town. I haven't been here in years, but it still looks the same. A big empty warehouse where we bring people to die.

"No, please, you can't do this," he cries like a child.

My jaw is set, and my figurative mask is in place. I have *business* to take care of.

"I can, and I will. The people in this city are going to learn *not* to mess with Rocco Martinelli."

Nico is in front of him, and Freddy is behind him as we enter the warehouse. There's nowhere for him to go now but into the ground. A lone metal chair sits in the middle of the room, and they strap him to it.

"This is your last chance, Yates. Give us the money, or you die." I lift the 9mm out of the back of my pants and point it at his head. Remembering how I was taught. Don't think. Fast and simple.

"I don't have—"

BANG.

"Call the cleaners," I say to Nico and Freddy. "I'll wait in the car."

My mind takes me back to when I was fifteen. Exiting the warehouse, I want to vomit like I did that day, but I push it down and climb into the back of the Escalade. There's a heavy weight on my chest as the darkness surrounds me. I gave the devil the last piece of my soul without a fight. I truly am Antonio Martinelli's son. I can never have Lola back now, ever.

Chapter 24
Lola

Four months have passed since I saw Ethan at the board meeting. Our company won the bid for Brandish-Martinelli. I'm not sure if Ethan had anything to do with that, but Mr. Kingsley was beside himself. He was so happy, in fact, he saw fit to promote me to chief marketing officer. I have a large corner office now with an entire wall of windows. Amelia came with me as my assistant, and now she has an assistant to help her with all the additional work.

She and I went shopping to celebrate. I bought my first pair of Louis Vuitton shoes, and I bought Amelia a new bag as a thank-you for all her help these past months. She's the closest thing I have to a girlfriend to hang out with. She was very supportive when I broke up with Ethan, even though I couldn't tell her a lot of the details. Amelia knocks and lets herself into my office.

"Lola, you have to see this?" She practically vibrates as she reaches my desk.

"What has you all worked up, Amelia?" I say with my nose in my contracts.

"This. Look," she says, pointing at the gold-leaf invitation in her hand.

You and one guest
are cordially invited to a
night of pomp and circumstance at the 2025

Mystery Masked Ball
At the Goodman Museum of Art

To benefit
The Children's Hospital
Of Johnsonville

April 19th

"This is so exciting!" she squeals. She might as well be jumping up and down.

"You go then," I quip.

"No, you *have* to go. This is an enormous honor. Not just anybody gets invited to this party."

"What's so great about it?"

"You get to dress up in a ball gown and wear an elaborate bejeweled mask, and no one knows who you are. You can be whoever you want to be." She lowers her voice like someone might be listening to us. "I've heard rumors about rooms where you can have a one-night-only experience with a stranger." She's dancing around the room like she's freakin' Cinderella or something.

"One night only with a stranger, huh?" I question.

"Yeah, leave your mask on the whole time. Totally incognito." She waggles her eyebrows at me.

"Interesting… You can go."

"No, you *have* to go. But I'll go as your plus-one. Come on, it will be so much fun." She pulls me up from my desk and grabs my shoulders with intention. "You haven't been out in so long. You're working yourself to death up here. We could get our hair done, and you could wear your new Louis Vuitton shoes. You can drink ooh-la-la drinks, and maybe you'll meet someone new, and—"

I cut her off with my hand.

"Fine."

"I'm so excited. I'll set up a few appointments for dress shopping this weekend. We only have two weeks to prepare. That's not a lot of time."

"Okay, whatever."

Amelia has driven me crazy with dress shopping. If I hear her say *it has to be just the right dress* one more time, I'm going to scream.

April 19th comes around all too soon, and Amelia's preparations have paid off. We stand side by side in the mirror of my bathroom. My hair is fixed in a half-up and half-down do. I wear brown contact lenses to hide my eye color, and my dress is a sapphire-blue velvet corseted gown with gold jewels shining from the bodice. It feels like it weighs a ton from all the layers upon layers of material underneath.

My mask matches it perfectly, of course, and covers my entire face, except my eyes and lips. I thought it would be uncomfortable, but it's padded and is actually pretty plush and soft. My own mother wouldn't know who I am. That was Amelia's promise to me—one night that I could become someone else.

Amelia wears a shimmering red mermaid gown with hundreds of crystals that sparkle in the light. Her blond hair is in a long, soft braid that looks right out of *Romeo and Juliet,* and her mask complements her dress while allowing her bright-blue eyes to shine through.

Our limousine is promptly in front of my house at eight, and we are off to the ball. I guess I do *kinda* feel like Cinderella, after all. *Maybe it will be fun. I'll try to keep an open mind.*

After riding for about thirty minutes, we pull up in front of the museum. A man dressed in a tuxedo opens the door for me. I present the invitation, and he holds his hand out to help me from the limo, and then Amelia. We are led down a long red carpet to the museum entrance, where two more men hold open doors for us.

Servers with trays of champagne flutes mingle with the guests, and we each take one.

"This is so exciting," Amelia chirps.

"Yeah, it *is* pretty neat. I'm glad you made me come," I say as she gives me a side hug.

"I'm so glad. Now let's have some fun." Hors d'oeuvres circulate the room, tiny little drops of savory goodness from heaven. There's no proper dinner, so we try each thing they bring past us, quietly critiquing each choice and laughing. Last, they bring around petit fours that melt in your mouth. After filling up on the delicious little courses, we enter the area set up with a string quartet for dancing.

"Fancy," Amelia exhales.

"I wonder where the secret sex rooms are?" I ask, giggling under my breath.

"I hope I meet someone and get to find out." She sighs.

Chapter 25
Ethan

"Why do I have to go to this stupid thing again?" I bark.

"Because you need to represent our family," Antonio says.

"Why can't you go?"

"Because without your mother by my side, I have no desire to be around a group of people, let alone dance and mingle."

"But no one can see my face. How will they know I'm there representing the family if they don't know who I am?"

"Trust me, Son, you have the air of power and strength all around you. They'll know you're a Martinelli as soon as you enter the room."

My monkey suit has been tailored to every muscle. It's tight and uncomfortable. My body is leaner and has more muscle since I've been working out so hard. My chest is wider, and my neck is thicker. *Thank you, Jerry.* When my frustrations get too much, I go to Jerry, and we spar, lift weights, run, or get fucked. I was going to J for the latter, but I told her too much about my life, so I stopped seeking her out. I don't need a damn psychiatrist. I need a hard fuck. Unfortunately, the women I choose to have relations with cannot seem to handle me more than once. They say I'm too rough. I zone out during sex, trying so hard to forget Lola, and I guess I get carried away. No matter what I try, I can't get her out of my mind.

I've been sent on several missions in the past few months to collect from deadbeats who owe The Organization money. Whether it be for gambling debts, money laundering fees, or other reasons, Father insists it's important I show myself as the *enforcer* of the family to gain respect. When I take over, they will already fear me.

With each kill, I lose more and more of myself. I'm up to eighteen now. He wants me to become a heartless son of a bitch like he is, and I'm well on my way. The fury builds in me more and more each day.

Nico is the driver tonight, and he's happy he doesn't have to wear a tux. Freddy is my bodyguard, and he's dressed in a monkey suit like I am, complete with a mask. We enter the museum, and women in ball gowns are everywhere. Did I time-warp back to the fourteenth century? How did men wade their way through all that material to ever get a piece of ass?

"They aren't even going to feed us dinner? After all the money we donated this year," I say as I reach for one of the tiny hors d'oeuvres.

"Yeah, I'll have to eat a hundred of these little things to be filled up tonight," Freddy says in his deep voice. "You know, I've heard about parties like this."

"What are you talking about?" I raise my brow.

"People hook up with strangers for a quick fuck. It's supposed to be *mysterious*. You know, be someone else for one night."

"Interesting." I think tonight might end up being fun after all. We weave our way back through the crowd to find the event coordinator. We get all the details on the secret rooms. Freddy and I indulge in drinks and miniature food and make our way to the area with a string quartet playing in the corner. Not being able to see someone's face makes it easier to just pluck someone out of the crowd to fuck. I don't think anyone knows who I am, but I can't be too careful.

I scan the crowd for a wench I would like to fuck when I catch a glimpse of a red dress shimmering near the dance floor.

"Come on," I say, leading Freddy across the room past the dance floor. Standing beside the woman in the red dress is a woman in a dark-blue velvet gown. Her lips are painted with a lip color that shimmers in the lights. I'm mesmerized by her eyes, which are the color of milk chocolate. I reach out for her hand, and she places hers in mine. After guiding us out onto the dance floor, I put one arm around her waist and her hand in mine, and we begin to dance.

"Are you having a nice time this evening?" I lean forward and speak into her ear. She nods.

"Did you enjoy the food?" Again, she nods.

"Don't you talk?" I ask.

She points at her throat as if she cannot speak.

"You can speak, just not tonight?" She nods again. Well, this could be perfect. She can't scream.

"You know, I've heard about secret rooms in the back where I could do unspeakable things to you, and no one would ever know." Her eyes go wide, and she bows her head. Is she shy?

"Would you be interested in something like that with me tonight?" I ask. She raises her gaze to look at me and nods again. I look over at Freddy, who's slow dancing with *Red Dress*, and I motion to him with my head. He knows where I'll be. I guide us to the hallway off to the left, past the bathrooms, and through the brown door. I've already secured our special location, the third door on the left. I use the passkey and hear the click of the door opening.

"Are you still okay with this?" I ask. When she looks up at me with her big doe eyes and nods again gingerly, I push the door open.

The room is softly lit with flowing curtains around the balcony. This shit is like one of those romance novels MeMe reads. She walks into the center of the room and turns to look at me. I walk over to her and meet her gaze.

"I don't kiss. Is that okay?" I ask. She nods, but her eyes scrunch up like she's skeptical.

I turn her around to figure out how to remove this dress. There are all these strings crisscrossing her back. It looks like she's sewn into the damn thing.

"How do I get you out of this dress?" I ask. She turns back around and motions for me to go under the skirt. This is getting more entertaining by the minute. I sink to my knees and lift the front of her skirt. My eyes go directly to the four-inch Louis Vuitton heels she's wearing. My heart stops when I think of Lola and those damn shoes she always wore, and my cock hardens in my pants.

Chapter 26
Lola

Amelia and I linger near the dance floor until two tall, dark and handsome gentlemen approach us. *God, look at all those muscles.* I think I can see every single one through his clothes. He's so well-defined and masculine. He holds his hand out for me to dance, and I take it. His clean, woodsy scent is making my panties wet.

I told Amelia I was going to act like I couldn't talk if someone approached me. It would add to the *mystery* and another layer of defense to keep my identity private. I can't put my foot in my mouth if I'm not talking. I keep nodding with every question he asks. When he asks me if I would like to go to a secret room with him, my stomach drops. This is why I'm here—to have crazy sex with a stranger and help fuck Ethan Martinelli out of my head—so I nod.

When we enter the room, it's soft and romantic, just like what I envision in those smutty books I read. The lights are low, and quiet music plays in the background. There's even a balcony with billowing curtains letting in a soft breeze. He has no idea how to extricate me from this dress or, better yet, get me back into it when we are done, so I motion for him to go underneath. I raise the front of the dress, and he pauses. I think he's staring at my shoes. Ethan always liked my shoes. I shake the thoughts from my head. *I'm supposed to be forgetting Ethan.*

I sit on the edge of the bed and reach for my shoe, but he stops me. He grasps the back of my calf in one hand and tugs the shoe off with the other, kissing the top of my foot. My breath hitches. *That's two men who have a thing for feet.* I chuckle at the thought. He places my foot back on the floor. Picking up the other, he repeats the motion. I can't believe how sexual it feels to let him remove my shoes like that.

He runs his hands up the inside of my thighs to my panties. I lean back on my elbows and lift my hips so he can pull my panties free. After sliding them down my legs, he places them in his pocket.

"Just something to remember you by." His voice is so dark and menacing. I know I should fear him, but I don't.

"I'm clean. I was tested last week. Are you clean?" I nod.

"Do you want me to use a condom?" I nod.

"Are you a virgin?" I shake my head.

"Do you have a husband I need to know about?" I roll my eyes and shake my head again.

"A crazy, overprotective boyfriend?" I snicker and shake my head.

"No names." I shake my head.

"You're okay with rough?" I lift my shoulders to say I don't know.

"You've never had it rough?" I shake my head.

"I'll try not to hurt you then." My stomach sinks. *Hurt me? What the fuck?*

"If it gets to be too much and you want me to stop, tap my leg three times. Maybe… *smack* my leg three times. Sometimes I zone out. Do you understand?" I tentatively nod.

His warm palms push my legs apart, and I oblige and open my legs for him. He begins to make his way under my dress to my now bare pussy. I went out and splurged on a waxing session—*that hurt like a bitch*—just for this experience. I want him to see my landing strip, so I pull my dress up even higher. His eyes widen, and he runs a finger through my slit.

I pull my feet up onto the edge of the bed and lie back. He places one finger inside as if testing the waters, and I squirm under his touch. He adds a second finger and fucks my pussy with them while rubbing my clit with his thumb. I'm close to my release already. It's been months since I've had sex with Ethan.

"I don't usually do this with strangers, but... can I taste you?" I raise my hips, pushing him toward my center. His tongue laps at me. My mind reels as he sucks my clit and slides his finger inside me. I'm trying to let go, but I'm in my head and can't quite get there.

"I can tell you're nervous. Close your eyes and feel," he says with a grin. I do as I'm told and try to enjoy *this* moment. His tongue is relentless. He adds another finger and slams them into my pussy. My orgasm spreads over me like hot butter on a griddle. He continues eating my pussy through my orgasm, almost sending me into another.

Sitting up, I reach for his jacket, unbuttoning and pulling it from his shoulders. He stands, placing it on the chair. He removes his tie and throws it at me. I hold it in my hand and try to climb farther up on the bed. But my dress is so cumbersome that I huff out a breath in frustration. He smiles and comes closer to me. He lifts me, dress and all, and places my head on the pillows like I weigh nothing. He goes back to removing his clothes piece by glorious piece.

I'm so covered in all this fabric, and he's so bare. All he can see are my legs and pussy, but I can see all of him in the low light of the room. I can tell his cock is huge, and a surge of excitement runs through me. I want to touch him, to feel his skin against mine, but I'll have to accept that it won't be happening that way tonight. He takes the tie back from me.

"I'm going to tie your hands above your head." I shake my head frantically and start tapping his leg.

"Oh yeah, how can you tell me to stop if your hands are tied?" My eyes widen. He thinks about it for a second and tosses the tie aside.

"Another time, then." I let out my breath. *Thank God.* He unwraps a condom and rolls it down on his hard cock. He notches his thick head to my entrance and shoves his way inside.

"God, you are so tight. Are you sure you're not a virgin?" I shake my head and squint my eyes at him. I want to say *it's because you're so fucking big*, but I can't. He begins to thrust into me. It's not gentle. It's dark and determined. I raise my legs to make more room for him as he plunges into me deeper.

"You are so fucking tight on my cock," he grunts out as if he's in pain. I relax and take him all in. The sensation of his hard length filling me makes me so wet. He pulls out and back in again, ramming into me over and over. I didn't think I would like it, but the wild, animalistic feeling is freeing, and I find myself hungry for more.

His eyes glaze over as if in a trance, and he mumbles something about *forgetting*. He's thrusting into me at breakneck speed now. I try to match him thrust for thrust, but he's going so brutally fast that I stop trying and let him control all the motion. I'm no longer a participant. I'm along for the ride. My whole body is lost in the movements. With each thrust, my body rocks back and forth on the bed. My tits slide with the motion in my corset. I put my hand on the headboard to stop myself from banging my head. My mind is vacant, with only the need to come consuming it.

My orgasm crashes down around me like an erupting volcano, and his eyes fly open as if he can't believe this is happening. Like I'm the first woman who has ever come on his dick. I'm panting and trying not to say any of the words that want to spill from my mouth. My chest heaves, and I'm trying to catch my breath. When he throws his head back, his body stiffens, and his cock pulses inside me, filling the condom.

"Holy shit. You're the first woman to take my cock like that. Usually, they're tapping for me to stop or just lie there and hold on, but you... *came* for me." The confusion in his voice is confusing to me too. I raise my shoulders and wink, hoping he understands I did like it a lot. He pulls out and reaches out his hand to help me sit up.

"We should probably get going."

He ties a knot in the condom and throws it in the trash. He finds a towel and hands it to me. Offering his hand again, he helps me to the edge of the bed. He lifts my feet one at a time and replaces my shoes, then pulls me to stand. Dropping my dress in the front and smoothing it down with his hands, he says, "There. Just like new." I smile and nod in thanks. I look around the room once more to remember my one night of passion and start for the door, but he grabs my hand.

"Can I see you again?" I shake my head, my brows pinched.

"Why not?" I put up one finger. "It's just a one-time fling? I understand," he says. I open the door and lead us out into the ballroom. In the distance, I see Amelia sitting at a table with my guy's friend.

She's laughing and looks like she's having a good time. I achieved what I came here to do—have wild sex with a stranger—but before I give in and make it more than it was, I need to get the fuck out of here. I walk straight to the table and gesture for Amelia to come to the bathroom.

We make our way to the bathroom and lock the door. She immediately bombards me with questions.

"Oh my God, what was it like? Was it everything you wanted? Was he hung like a horse? Were his muscles as big as they looked? Was he good?"

"Amelia!" I snap, cutting her off.

"Sorry." Her mouth snaps shut.

"It was amazing. He was amazing. But he wants more, and I need to go," I say.

"I understand. My guy's name is Freddy. Let me get his number, and I'll leave with you."

"You can stay. You don't have to leave."

"No, that's okay. We came on this adventure together, and we'll leave it together. Just give me a minute," she says.

"Okay. I'll call for the limo and meet you at the door." She leaves the ladies' room, and I head for the entrance.

The driver drops us at my house, and we go inside.

"The Cinderellas are back from the ball," I say sadly, opening the door and turning on the lights. Finally removing my mask, I set it on the back of the couch.

"It was a great night though, wasn't it?" Amelia says all dreamy. "I had a nice time with Freddy, and you got your brains fucked out by Mr. Muscles."

"Yeah, it *was* pretty good," I say with a big smile. "Hey, before you leave, can you help me get out of the dress?"

"Sure."

"You know I got Freddy's number, right?" she says, winking at me. "If you ever decide you *want* to see Mr. Muscles again, I'm sure I can work it out."

"No thanks. It was just a one-time thing," I say, walking her to the front door.

"Well, if you change your mind…" She gives me a quick hug. "Thanks for tonight."

"Yeah, it was fun, after all," I say, not wanting to admit she was right all along.

"See you at work on Monday."

I close and lock the front door and step into the bathroom to take a quick shower. I dry off and put on my shorts with hearts on them, along with my Ohio State sweatshirt. When I climb under the covers, I replay the night in my mind. It was everything I wanted it to be and more.

Chapter 27
Antonio

"What do you mean, she saw him again? That bitch! I told her to stay away from him," I yell, slamming the phone down. I've had the private eye tailing Lola until I can be sure she's staying away from Rocco. *Son of a bitch!* I didn't want to hurt her for Rocco's sake, but now I'm going to have to teach her a little lesson.

"Sheila, I need Nico and Freddy," I yell into the intercom.

"Sir, they are out on assignment with Rocco."

"Dammit! Get me Jackson and Buddy, then." I don't wait for her to answer.

Ten minutes later, they're standing at attention in my office.

"I need you to go to this address. Drug the girl and take her to the warehouse. I want you to give her a little message for me. Tell her she violated our contract and this is her last chance. You know the drill. Rough her up a little, but don't kill her. When you're sure she's got the message, take her back home."

"Yes, Boss."

Chapter 28
Lola

I'm sitting on the back patio in my pajamas, watching the sunset and drinking a glass of chardonnay, when the doorbell rings. I weave my way through the house to the front door. Before my eyes adjust, I'm pushed backward with a hand over my face, and everything goes black.

When I wake, it's dark, and my hands are tied behind my back. My legs are free, but there is no room to kick. Thank fuck, there is no bag over my head this time. I hear the engine and feel the bumps of the gravel road. My head is killing me. I wish they would stop drugging me. I think back on what I might have done to deserve this. I didn't see Ethan. I don't have the money they want, so what the hell?

The car comes to a stop, and the trunk pops open. There stand two tall, menacing men looking down at me. One has blond hair with thick whiskers on his face. The other has jet-black hair pulled into a bun with a tattoo on his neck. I'm snatched under my arms and hauled out of the trunk. I stumble as I try to get my legs underneath me again.

"What do you want from me? I didn't *do* anything," I yell as I struggle to get free.

"Shut up, bitch!" Tattoo says.

"I don't have his money."

"I said shut the fuck up!" Tattoo yells. He's walking in front of me, and Blondie is to my back. They lead me down a gravel path to the back of the building that looks like an old warehouse. Tattoo opens the heavy metal door, and they push me inside. It's a big empty room with concrete floors and one metal chair in the middle of the space. There's dried blood on the surrounding floor. I squirm and kick until I connect with Tattoo's knee.

"You bitch!" He punches me in the stomach, and it takes my breath away. I'm gasping for air while they tie me to the chair. Looking around the room, I try to take in everything I see, but there isn't much. The windows are sprayed over, so there's hardly any light coming in except from the skylights in the ceiling.

"What do you want from me?" I ask. There's no answer this time. Just a blur as I'm slapped across the face. *Fuck, that hurt*! I take a deep breath and raise my chin to look at them.

"We have a message for you from the boss," Blondie finally speaks.

"What message?" My head is still groggy from being sedated, but I try to shake the ringing from my ears.

"You violated the rules of your contract when you saw Rocco."

"I haven't seen him," I say in confusion.

"Yes. You. Did," Tattoo growls.

"No, I didn't!" He slaps me again, and my head snaps to the side. The coppery taste of blood invades my mouth, sliding down my chin and dripping onto my shirt.

"The boss says you have, so stop lying," Blondie says.

"I. Did. Not. See. Him," I snap out. A fist flies into my cheek, and blood fills my mouth. I spit onto the floor in front of me and stare up into the face of the tattooed man.

He grabs me by the front of my shirt and brings his face close to mine. The smell of cigarettes fills my nostrils. "This is your last chance, girly. See him again, and we'll have no choice but to take you out," he says through gritted teeth. *Take me out?* I don't want another punch, so I pinch my lips closed before I say something stupid. He pushes me back and walks away. I can hear them talking in the corner.

"Can I play with this one?" Tattoo says.

"The boss said rough her up, not *play* with her," Blondie says.

"Aw, come on, man. She would look so good on my dick." He walks over to me and runs his hand through my hair and wraps it around his fist, pulling my head back to look up at him.

"I bet you're a wildcat in the sack."

My breathing becomes erratic, and I'm trying not to panic. This can't be happening. I didn't *do* anything.

I try to shake off the tattooed man. "Your boss says I was with Ethan…"

"Rocco!" Blondie yells from across the room.

"Fine… Rocco. Where did I supposedly see him?" I ask.

"That masked ball you went to last Saturday night."

"He wasn't there. I wasn't with anyone that night but…" All the air leaves my body. Oh my God. Oh my God. Oh my God. No! My Mr. Muscles was… Ethan? It couldn't be. I didn't see his face, but his body was *so* different, and he was so dark and menacing. I'm snapped back to reality when a hand runs up my thigh and begins to make its way to my pussy.

"No!" I beg as I struggle in the chair, trying to break these damn restraints.

"Aw, come on. We have time for a little taste of this sweet pussy, don't we?" His hand lands on my pussy and rubs hard.

"Hey!" Blondie yells at Tattoo, "Cut it out, man!" He dips his head down to look me in the eye. He's so close. His hot breath flows over my face.

"Fine… but if you see Rocco again, I *will* get what I want from you before I kill you."

Blondie stands in front of me, looking down at me.

"Did we make it clear to you to stay away from Rocco?"

"Yes."

"Good, that's what I needed to hear." I feel a pinch on my neck, and everything goes black.

I wake up on the couch back home. The thumping has returned to my head. I look around the room and wince from the pain in my face and stomach. I make my way to the bathroom and see a bloody mess. I run the bathwater and remove my stained clothes.

Looking in the mirror, I have bruises across my abdomen, marks on my wrists and ankles, a busted lip, and a black eye. As I sink into the tub, the water stings my body. I cannot believe Ethan was my mystery fuck. Did he know it was me? Surely not. I was covered from head to toe. I didn't know it was him. What am I going to do? This is such a nightmare.

Chapter 29
Ethan

'm in the Escalade with Nico and Freddy, headed to pick up a scumbag who owes The Organization money from the car wash business.

"Hey, Freddy, have you heard from Red Dress?" I ask.

"Yeah, we've texted a bit. Why?"

"Do you think she could hook me up with that girl I fucked at the party?"

"I don't know, Boss. Amelia said she wasn't interested."

"Amelia, huh? I wonder what my girl's name was."

"I don't know. She won't tell me."

"Ask again," I demand.

Freddy starts texting.

FREDDY

What is your friend's name again?

AMELIA

I never told you her name.

Can you tell me now?

No.

Why not?

Because she doesn't want to see him again.

He really wants to see her.

She just wanted a one-night stand.

Come on, please. For me.

No. I can't. She's my friend and my boss.

Where do you work again?

Kingsley and Masters

What do you do there?

I am a personal assistant.

It's okay. I understand. I'll call you tonight.

Ok

Freddy turns around so he can talk to me over the seat.

"She wouldn't tell me her name, but she's some bigwig at Kingsley and Masters."

"Kingsley and Masters?" My eyebrows pinch. It can't be...

We find McGrath pretty fast. Freddy grabs him off the street and throws him in the bench seat across from me. He's already had all the chances he's going to get.

———

"Look, man, I can get you the money. I just need more time," Mc-Grath begs as Freddy and Nico drag him up to the metal door of the warehouse.

"You've had all the chances you're going to get," I growl.

"Boss, we might have a problem," Nico chimes in.

"What?"

"The door wasn't closed."

"What the fuck," I spit, taking out my gun. "Keep a hold on this piece of shit. I'll check it out." I push past them and slowly open the door. There isn't much in the space, so it doesn't take long to clear it.

"It's clear. Get him in the chair," I bark. I pull Buddy's contact info up on my phone.

"Hey, man, were you at the warehouse recently?"

"Yeah, last night, why?"

"You didn't fuckin' close the door all the way."

"We had to carry that chick to the car. I guess I forgot to go back and close it. I'm sorry, Boss."

"What chick?" I ask. We don't take many women to the warehouse. Antonio can make them pay their debts in other ways.

"The sweetest bitch I've ever seen. Long dark hair and big blue eyes," Buddy croons.

"What did you do to her?"

"We roughed her up a bit and then took her home."

"Roughed her up…why?"

"I don't know. The boss said she violated some contract and wanted us to send her a message."

"A contract?"

"Yeah."

"What else?"

"That's it. I wanted to play with her, but Jackson wouldn't let me. Said the boss just wanted her roughed up, ya know."

"Thanks… Wait! Where did you take her when you were done?"

"We took her back to her house and left her on the couch."

"What's the address?"

"It was 102 Florence Way," Buddy says.

"What?" I can't comprehend what he just said. My vision darkens, and my head spins.

"It was 102 Florence Way… Boss, are you there?" There's a long pause while I try to wrap my head around what he said. That's Lola's address.

"Yeah, I'm here. Don't leave the door open again," I say and hang up.

Panic starts to settle into my body. I turn to McGrath. "Do you have the money?"

"No."

BANG!

We wait for the cleanup crew to arrive, then the three of us climb back into the Escalade.

"I want to go to Kingsley and Masters."

"Boss?" Nico asks.

"Park in the garage, and we'll take the elevator instead of going in the front door."

"Is everything okay?" Freddy asks.

"I sure hope so."

Nico does as he's told and parks in the garage. We get off the elevator on the twentieth floor and follow the signs to the office of the chief marketing officer. Amelia sees Freddy approaching.

"Freddy, what are you doing here?" She has worry in her voice.

I interject before Freddy can speak. "I'm here to see Lola."

"She's not here. She took the day off."

"Lola doesn't take *days* off," I growl.

"She said she wasn't feeling well. She's staying home the rest of the week."

"Text her," I demand, picking her phone up off the desk and shoving it toward her.

"What?"

"Text her. See how she's doing."

"Why?"

"Because I'm worried about her. I don't think she's sick."

"Okay," she says cautiously, but does as she's told.

AMELIA

You up?

LOLA

Yes.

How are you feeling?

Same.

I'm coming over there.

No. I need to rest.

Are you sure you're okay?

I'm fine. I need to go back to sleep.

I'll text you after work.

That won't be necessary. I'm good.

It will make me feel better to know you're okay.

Fine.

I'm reading the text messages over Amelia's shoulder.

"Something's wrong. I'm going over there." I point my finger at Amelia. "And don't you tip her off either."

"I won't because I'm going with you."

"We need to go. Now!" Amelia locks up the office, grabs her bag, and we head for the garage. Freddy drives, and I gesture for her to sit with him. Nico climbs in back with me.

"What's happening?" Amelia asks.

"I think someone hurt her," I say.

"Oh my God," she says, and her hand flies to her mouth.

The car is silent for a few miles before I ask, "Does she ever talk about me?"

"She misses you." Amelia's voice is quiet as if she's giving away a secret.

"Not so much that she didn't fuck a random stranger last weekend."

"Just so you know, that was to get *over* you. Wait? How did you know about that?"

"Because *I* was her random stranger."

"Nooo... You're Mr. Muscles?"

"Yes… Wait… What?"

"Never mind. Do you think she knows it was you?" she asks.

"I don't know, but we're about to find out."

"Did you know it was her?"

"I had no idea it was her," I say. "Freddy, park on the street parallel to hers, and we'll come in through the neighbor's backyard."

"Okay, Boss."

We all pile out of the car.

"Amelia, you lock yourself in the car."

"Like hell I will. I'm going with you!" I don't have time to stand here and argue with this woman.

"Stay behind Freddy." Freddy takes his arm and pushes her behind him protectively, and she disappears from view.

As I lurk through the neighbor's yard and onto Lola's patio, I don't see anything out of place. I pull the handle to the sliding door, and it's unlocked. Because *of course, it is*. I poke my head inside, and she's not on the couch or in the kitchen. She must be lying down, like she said.

I motion for them to wait, and I start down the hall, passing the laundry room and bathroom. Reaching her bedroom door, I hear her talking. No, she's struggling. I swing the door open, but there's no one else in the room. She lies under the covers asleep, and she's having a nightmare. I walk across the room and kneel by the bed. I slide the back of my fingers down her cheek, but she doesn't stir, so I shake her arm.

"Lola. Lola. Wake up, baby." Her eyes spring open, and she jumps across the bed, screaming.

"Get the hell out of here! I told you I won't see him again!" I spring to my feet with my hands out in front of me, trying to calm her.

"Lola. Baby, look at me. It's me, Ethan."

Her eyes focus on me. "Ethan?" She leaps into my arms, crying and holding on to me for dear life. Putting my hands on either side of her face, I pull her back to kiss her. When my eyes focus on the bruises, blood on her lip, and a black eye, my blood begins to boil.

"What the hell happened to you?" I grit out, pushing her back to get a better look.

"Don't look at me," she says, turning away and trying to hide her face. I take her by the arm and force her to look at me, and she winces.

"No! You're going to tell me what the fuck's going on. I can't take this anymore. Why did you stop seeing me? And what the hell do you have to do with my father?" All the color leaves her face, and she looks like she's about to pass out. I scoop her up in my arms and sit down on the side of the bed with her on my lap. I tap her cheeks with my hand lightly to bring her back to me.

"Boss, is everything okay?" Nico says, poking his head in the door.

"Yes, we're fine, Nico. Thanks."

"Nico?" That name seems to snap her out of it. She sits up stick straight, and points her finger at him.

"You were there that night."

"Yes, ma'am. I'm sorry," he says.

"What the fuck?" I stand and set her on the bed. In three strides, I have him pinned against the wall with my hand on his throat. "Nico! You fucking did this to her?"

"No, Boss, N-N-No, it wasn't me. It was Jackson and Buddy."

"What do you have to do with it?" I yell, squeezing his throat tighter.

"I was there the night your father sent us to bring her to the mansion. I didn't hurt her, I swear. None of us did *that* night," Nico says, trying to suck in enough air to speak.

"What do you mean, none of us? Who else was there?"

"It was the boss, Freddy, and me, that's all. There was no one else there that night," he says.

I release his throat, and he falls into a heap on the floor, trying to suck air into his lungs.

"He's telling the truth, Ethan. They didn't hurt me that night. They just drugged me, put a bag over my head, tied me to a chair, and threatened to kill me if I didn't stop seeing you forever."

My eyes burn with rage. My darkness is awake, and it needs to kill. I drag Nico to his feet and use the back of his shirt to throw him out of the room, then slam the door shut. I turn back to Lola.

"Tell me everything right the fuck now."

Chapter 30
Lola

"You can't be here, Ethan. He'll kill us both! Please. You have to go!" I'm close to hysterical now.

He pulls me into his arms.

"Shh, shh… it's going to be okay," he says softly, holding me to his chest and stroking my back. "Nothing will ever come between us again. Not even my father."

I tell him about both of my encounters with Antonio's men. Anger boils in his eyes when I tell him about Buddy hitting me and how he touched me. He's trying to keep himself contained, but a fury boils in the depths of his soul, waiting to be set free. I've never seen him with hate in his eyes. They have always been soft and caring with me. But this, this is outright hatred. I take his hands in mine and bring his gaze back to me, trying to calm him down.

"Ethan, were you my mystery lover?"

His eyes focus on me. "Yes."

"When did you know it was me?"

"Today, after Freddy texted Amelia."

"Amelia?"

"Yes, we were in your office when she texted you. That was when all the pieces fell into place. I never would've been the wiser if Buddy hadn't left the door to the warehouse open. When I called him, he told me they had taken a woman there to send her a message. He said they returned her to your address."

"Ethan, you have to go. Right now." Panic rushes through me once again when I remember his father's words. *I won't see him anymore! You better not, or it will be the end of you and him.*

"I'm not going *anywhere,* Lola. I love you. I've never stopped loving you." He kisses me, and I wince.

"Take off your clothes."

"What?"

"I want to see your injuries. I need to know if you need a doctor."

"I'll be fine."

"That son of a bitch punched you in the stomach. I need to see it." Before I can open my mouth to protest again, he pulls me to my feet and removes my shirt. The pain is like a knife to the gut, and I double over. I see the blackness in his eyes as he looks over my bruises. They are darker than they were earlier.

"Ethan—"

"Shh…" He cuts me off.

I blink, and he's on his knees before me, putting his hands on the back of my legs and pulling me into him. He kisses the bruises on my stomach as if his kisses will make them disappear. I run my fingers through his dark hair and brush it back from his eyes. My breathing slows, and relaxation floods my senses.

Rising to his feet, he says, "Stay here. I'll be right back. Don't move."

He returns a few moments later with a bottle of water.

"I sent Nico to get Ruck."

"Who's that?"

"Ruck is short for Ruckowski. He's our doctor."

"E, I don't n—"

"Ruck will assess your injuries and tell us what to do. I sent Amelia and Freddy in your car to get food. I hope that was okay." I nod. "Now, where were we?"

He grasps my pajama pants and lowers them down my legs. He looks me over and motions for me to sit on the bed. Taking my left leg in his hands, he kisses the rope marks on my ankle. He mimics it on my right. His powerful hands are slow and methodical as he checks every inch of my body for damage. When he reaches my hands sitting in my lap, he brings them to his lips one at a time, kissing the rope marks on each wrist.

"I'm so sorry they did this to you. I was afraid this would happen."

"It's not your fault, E."

"But it *is*. If I—" I put my finger to his lips to stop him.

"*You* didn't do this. Antonio did." I squeeze my eyes closed tight. "He killed my parents."

"What the fuck?"

"My father owed him money for gambling debts. He had cancer and was dying. They just helped it along. They searched for my mother for years, and when they finally found her, they killed her in front of the hospital and made it look like an accident. Antonio never knew they had a daughter until he started looking into your new *girlfriend*. He was going to kill me, but when he found out you had feelings for me, he made the deal instead."

"Tell me about the deal."

"It was simple. I stop seeing you, and I live. Somehow, he knew you were on my patio that night. He said if I saw you again, he would kill you too."

"He must be having you followed."

"If he's having me watched, then he knows you're here right now. Ethan, you *have* to go."

"No, because he'll send for you again. I can protect you, Lola. Nico parked the car on the back street, and we came in through the neighbor's backyard. I don't think anyone saw us. He's taken everything from me and turned me into a monster. I've done terrible things, Lola. Things I can never fix," he says, shaking his head.

He helps me back into my clothes. "He'll kill us, Ethan."

"I'll never let him hurt you again." His eyes are dark and haunting as he picks up his phone.

"Freddy, can you tell if anyone is following you?" There's a pause.

"Because I think someone from The Organization is keeping an eye on Lola. Watch for a tail." Hanging up, he takes me back into his arms and says, "You need to rest until everyone gets back. Come on, let's lie down." We lie on the bed, and he covers us with the duvet. He takes me into his arms, and I rest my head on his chest.

"Will he treat Amelia right?" I ask.

"Who?"

"Freddy."

"He has a good heart under that hard mask he wears. Can she handle what he does for a living?"

"What exactly does he do for The Organization?"

"Whatever is needed, no questions asked," he says bluntly. "He has been a loyal employee since high school graduation and has become my trusted confidant these past few months." He takes a strand of my hair in his fingers and twirls it.

"I'll talk to her. I don't know how serious she is about him," I say.

There's a slight pause in the conversation before he chuckles. "So you like it rough, huh?"

"Maybe."

"Did I hurt you that night?"

"No, you didn't hurt me. I didn't know I liked it rough until that night at the ball. What about you? You were so different. So dark and brooding."

"I guess I have been since I lost you. I didn't care about anything anymore. That's why I gave up my company and went to work for my father. I had nothing else to live for. There was no light without you, Lola," he says and places soft kisses on the top of my head. "I was using sex, any kind of sex, to try to forget. I was trying to fuck your memory out of me, I guess, but it never worked. When we hooked up at the ball, it was like I came to life again. You didn't speak a word, and I knew you were different. I was drawn to you. That shows me we are meant to be together. I never stopped loving you, Lola."

"I never stopped loving you. I haven't been with anyone else since you. I went to the masked ball that night intending to have a one-night stand. I thought if I could have *one* night of wild, crazy sex, you would get out of my head. But it didn't work. You were still in my head, and then I felt guilty. Like I cheated on you."

Chapter 31
Ethan

I took about an hour for Nico to return with Ruck. He's former military, very intimidating, and built like a brick house. He's a man of few words but a great doctor.

"Ruck, this is Lola. Some thugs beat her up. Can you please look her over and make sure she doesn't need to go to the hospital?"

"Ma'am." He nods at Lola. "I'm going to have to see the injuries," he says in his deep, husky voice.

"We don't have to do this. I'll be fine. He's just a worrywart," she says nervously.

"I think I hear Amelia. I'll go get her to stay with you." I point over my shoulder.

"Okay, if I have to," she concedes.

I was right; I did hear Freddy and Amelia come in through the garage with dinner. I take the bags from her.

"Amelia, Lola is in with the doctor. Would you mind staying with her to make her more comfortable, please?"

"Of course."

When she's gone, Freddy says in a hushed voice, "We *were* being followed, Boss, by Vito. He's parked down the block in a gray sedan. Do you want me to tell him to leave?"

"No, you and Nico stay here with the girls, and I'll take care of him."

I leave through the patio door, walk through the backyard, and around the block to come up behind Vito's car. He's looking down at his phone. Cocking my gun, I moved to his door and point it at his head.

"What the fuck are you doing here, Vito?" I snarl.

"Boss? What are *you* doing here?" His eyes grow wide with fear.

"That's no concern of yours. I'm going to ask you one more time, Vito. Why are you here?"

"Boss, the other Boss, ya know, your father Boss, sent me to keep an eye on that bitch Lola." I hit him with the butt of the gun in his face. Blood splatters across the steering wheel and dashboard. He screams out in pain, "What the fuck!"

"Don't you ever address her that way again. Do you understand me?"

"Yeah, yeah. That's what he called her. Sorry. Sorry."

"Now, you're going to leave and go get that nose looked at," I say, slapping my hand on his shoulder and squeezing hard until he cowers beneath my grip.

"What do I say when he asks me why I left my post?" he asks.

"I'll take care of him. And, Vito…"

"Boss?"

"If you ever see Miss Lola again, you will be there to *protect* her, not harm her. And you will treat her with *respect*. Do you understand me?"

"Yes, Boss." I go back inside, and Ruck is coming out of her room. "Well?" I ask.

"She's going to be okay. She'll be sore and bruised for a while, but I don't think the punch hurt her internally. Give her two of these painkillers every eight hours for the next couple of days and make her *rest*. If something changes, call me."

"Thanks, Ruck."

"She's a strong lady. I like her," he says with a slap on my back.

"I know. Me too."

The five of us spend time eating and talking. It almost seems… normal. But after a short while, I can tell Lola has had enough.

"Okay, everybody, Lola needs her rest. I think you should head out. You can check on her tomorrow."

"If you need me, just text me," Amelia says as she gently hugs Lola.

"I will. I promise."

Nico walks to the patio door and turns to address Lola.

"I'm sorry, Miss Lola. I was just following orders."

"I know, Nico, and you didn't hurt me."

Freddy stops in front of Lola next. "I'm sorry, Miss Lola. I was there that night too."

"I know, Freddy. You didn't hurt me either. It's over now." She put her hand on his forearm. "Let's start over."

"Thank you." He leads Amelia toward the sliding door.

"And, Freddy... take good care of my girl," Lola says.

"I will," he says as he puts his arm around Amelia and pulls her close. I lock the patio door and check the front door and all the windows while I'm at it. Lola's already in the bathroom when I enter the bedroom. I sit down on the bed and wait. She emerges and walks to stand between my legs. I place my face on her stomach and wrap my arms around her, breathing her in. I look up at her, and she places the softest kiss on my lips.

"I'm so sorry, Lola. I never wanted you involved in this life."

"I should've told you about your father. I should've trusted we could handle it together, but I was so afraid he would hurt you, hurt us." I stand and push back the covers.

"Have a seat." She sits on the side of the bed. "Take this medicine Ruck left for you. It will help with the pain." She does as she's told, then lies down. I cover her up and kiss her on the forehead. "I'm going to jump in the shower. I'll be quick. Promise." I hold a gun out to her. "Take my gun and put it under your pillow until I get back."

"Ethan..." she says, shaking her head.

"Just to make me feel better, please." After a tentative moment, she finally takes it.

I quickly take my shower and towel dry. When I come back into the bedroom, she has her eyes closed. I snuggle in behind her and pull her into my arms. I have Lola back. Now I have a father to kill, so we can finally be free.

Chapter 32
Lola

We have spent the past five days locked in our little cocoon at my house, watching sunsets and eating good food, but it's time to return to our lives. Ethan comes out of the bedroom and wraps his arms around me from behind.

"Good morning, sunshine. I could get used to having you all to myself," he says as he snuggles into my neck.

"Good morning," I say with a giggle. "I love being shacked up with you, but I'm *fine* now. I need to get back to work."

"You're not safe out there, Lo. When you're here, I can protect you."

"Ethan, I *have* to get back to work. Mr. Kingsley was already upset because I missed three days last week for being *sick*."

"Will you at least let Bennie escort you for a few days?"

"I don't know. A bodyguard, really?" she whines.

"You'll never know he's there. He can sit out in the lobby. I need to know you're safe. And Bennie is the best."

"Just until you settle things with Antonio?"

"Just until I settle things."

"Okay, I guess it will be okay."

Ethan calls Bennie, and he picks me up for work. Bennie is a beast of a man. He's probably in his fifties, but he's almost as tall as Freddy and has muscles coming out of everywhere. What is it with these men? They are all huge and have a shit ton of muscles. He has sandy-brown hair with a little gray at the temples. He's as polite as can be with his Brooklyn accent.

"Thank you for driving me, Bennie."

"It's my pleasure, Miss Lola."

"So…what are the rules?"

"The rules, Miss?"

"Yeah, I know Ethan told you to follow me around all day, but what else did he say?"

"He said to protect you against all harm, and if anything happens to you, I won't see tomorrow."

"Oh my."

Bennie parks the Escalade in an unmarked spot in the parking garage and escorts me to my office.

"Amelia, this is Bennie. He's going to be with us for a while," I try to say like it's no big deal. Amelia looks up and down at the giant filling the space and back at me. "Bennie, you can sit right there, and if you need anything, Amelia will be glad to help you." He nods his head and takes a spot by the door. Amelia follows me into my office and shuts the door.

"What the hell is going on?" she asks in hushed tones.

"Ethan thinks I need protection."

"Protection? That guy is huge!"

"Amelia, there's a lot you don't know. I'm not sure what Freddy has told you about his *line of work*, but Ethan's father is a powerful man, and he's coming after me."

"Why?"

"The long and short of it is my father owed him a large sum of money. He killed him and my mother and recently found out I exist. So now he's coming after me."

"Oh my God," she says as she drops into the chair across from my desk.

"Bennie is our protection. I want you to tell him if there's anyone or anything out of the ordinary going on at work. He'll take care of it."

"Yes, Lola."

"If you're going to keep seeing Freddy, you need to talk to him about what he does for a living."

"I will," she says quietly and turns to leave.

"And, Amelia…" She turns back around.

"Yes?"

"We're all going to be okay."

"Your first appointment will be here in fifteen."

"Great, thanks."

Fifteen minutes later, Amelia comes rushing into my office.

"Can you come out here, please? Bennie has Mr. Kingsley in a chokehold."

"What?!" Rushing out into the sitting area, I find Bennie with his hands on Mr. Kingsley.

"Oh my God, Bennie. No! That's my boss! He's allowed to see me whenever he wants." I pull the arm holding Mr. Kingsley, and it's like pulling on a steel bar. Bennie finally lets go.

"What's the meaning of this?" Mr. Kingsley bellows, straightening his jacket.

"I am *so* sorry, sir. This is Bennie," I try to say calmly. "He's here to watch over us for a few days."

"Watch over you? Why?" he asks.

"My boyfriend thinks I need a *little* protection. He won't get in the way again. You won't even know he's here."

"I better not!" As he leaves the office, he turns to say, "I almost forgot. I wanted to let you know the meeting with Caldwell and Sons has been moved to the conference room downstairs."

"Thank you. I'll be right there." I let out a huge sigh of relief when the door closes behind him.

"Bennie, please don't attack my boss again."

"I'm sorry, Miss Lola."

The rest of the day is better, and I arrive home promptly at 5:30. Ethan is there to welcome me, and he releases Bennie for the night.

"How was your day?" he asks, closing the door and locking it. He takes my bag from me and ushers me to the island for a drink.

"It was okay. Oh, except for the part where Bennie attacked my *boss.*"

"Why did he attack your boss?" He chuckles.

"I guess he thought he was a threat."

"Tomorrow will be better." He pulls me in close to his body and wraps his warm arms around me. "You'll get used to having him around, and he'll learn who he can and cannot trust."

"Ethan, how long do we have to do this?" I whine.

"Until I can get rid of my father."

Chapter 33
Ethan

"**W**here the *hell* have you been for five fucking days?" my father shouts at me as I walk into his office.

"I had some things to take care of," I answer and plop down in the chair in front of his desk. Throwing my arms across the back of the chair, I place my left foot on my right knee.

"What fucking things are more important than reporting back to *me*?

"I was busy," I say, a hint of teenage rebellion in my voice.

"With what?" He snaps.

"A little side project I'm working on."

"Oh my God, Rocco! The Organization always comes first, dammit! What happened with McGrath?"

"He was strung out on drugs and couldn't pay, so we took care of him at the warehouse. Cleanup crew did the rest."

"I had another job for you, but since you didn't answer your phone for a fuckin' week, I had to send Beckett and Rosco. Jackson and Buddy are AWOL too. Do you know anything about that?"

"I have no idea." I do, but I'll be damned if I tell him they spent a little time at the warehouse with Nico and Freddy after I found out what they did to Lola and will be indisposed for a few days because of their injuries. "I'm sure they'll show up in a few days. You know how they are when they go whoring around."

"I guess you're right."

"I'm tired of being the enforcer. I am ready to resume my training to be your second."

"Finally! I have been waiting all this time for you to come to your senses and take your rightful place in this family." He jumps to his feet and comes around the desk to bring me in for a hug. "Let's go over some books *if* you can spare a few hours today?" he snarks.

"Sure, I'm free." I need to learn everything I can so I can take this place from him and kill him like he deserves.

He proceeds to show me the altered books for some of the business interests, where he keeps everything hidden, and what to look for when making them look legit for the feds. This is the first time he has shown me that part of The Organization. I need to learn as much as I can, as fast as I can, to find his weaknesses and to take him down. When I walk out of his office a few hours later, my eyes meet Sheila's, and she gives me a nod. I have to get to Lola's house before she gets home.

After dinner, Lola and I sit on the love seat on the patio watching our sunset. "The steaks from Lowell's were delicious. How did you get them to deliver?" Lola asks.

"Only the best for my girl…Listen, I want to talk to you about something."

"Sure, what is it?" She turns her body and gives me her full attention.

"I would like you to come live at the penthouse with me." I put my hands out in defense. "Just let me explain before you get upset." She huffs and crosses her arms over her chest. "There is zero, I mean *zero* security here. I am lucky if you remember to lock the doors." She rolls her eyes at me. "I would feel better if you were with me, and I could have constant security on you. I need this, Lola."

She takes a deep, cleansing breath.

"Ethan, this is what you said he did to you as a kid. You were constantly surrounded by security. You had no freedom. Remember what you said about your poor mother? She couldn't even go to the store alone. Now you are doing it to me."

"I know, and I'm sorry. Once I take care of Antonio, you *will* have your freedom back. I promise."

"How long will that be, E? A week, a month, a year?"

"I'm not quite sure. I'm putting together a plan now." He crosses the room and takes my hands. "I can't sleep at night at your house because I'm afraid if I doze off, they'll attack us and take you from me again. I need this, Lola."

She's quiet for a moment. Concentration takes over her face.

"Fine." There's defeat in her voice. "How can I say no to you?"

"Thank you, baby. I love you so much," I say, pulling her body to mine and hugging her tightly.

"I love you too."

She packs a few bags, and Bennie picks us up and takes us home to the penthouse.

"Let's get you unpacked so we can watch our sunset."

Wine in hand, we're sitting on the white couch in the living room, watching the stunning sunset. My arm is around her, and her head is on my chest. "E," she whispers.

"Mm-hmm?"

"Why haven't you touched me?"

"I didn't know if you were ready or not. You've been having nightmares every night, and you were covered in bruises. Not to mention, Ruck told me to make sure you got lots of rest. I don't want to pressure you into something you're not ready for."

"Oh." There's a long pause.

"E."

"Mm-hmm?"

"I'm ready."

"Thank fuck." I take our glasses, set them on the end table, and pull her onto my lap. "I love you so much."

"I love you too."

She puts her arms around my neck and giggles.

"What's so funny?" I ask.

"Remember that night in the museum?"

"Yeah."

"You were going to tie my hands above my head, but I couldn't speak, so you said *next time*."

"Yeah."

"Can we do that tonight?"

"Hell yes!" With that, I pick her up and take her to our bedroom.

She's naked and sprawled across our bed. One arm is tied to the headboard on the right, and the other arm is attached to the left. I didn't tie her legs down because I want them wrapped around my waist when I fuck her.

"We didn't talk about safe words before because you *couldn't talk*, but I think you should pick one now."

"Hmm. I choose… snickerdoodle."

"That's a weird word."

"That's the idea, right?"

"I guess so. Snickerdoodle it is, then."

"I want you to fuck me hard like you did that night."

"Your wish is my command. But first, I get dessert." Climbing between her legs, I breathe in her sweet scent. "Oh Lord, I've missed you. Your smell, your taste, this perfect pink pussy," I say, licking slowly through her folds. "I'm going to drive you insane before I let you come and fuck you hard." She moans, rocking her hips up and down. My licks are slow and deep, lingering at her entrance before plunging my tongue inside. She moans when I run it back and forth just inside her opening. When I feel her tense, I pull back. She sighs like I just burst her bubble. I smile and chuckle deviously under my breath. She probably has no clue what I'm doing,

I go back to that pretty little clit of hers and nibble and lick it. Edging is a delicate balance of ebb and flow—building her just to the brink and pulling her back before she falls. When I get her there for the third time, she blurts out, "What the hell is happening? Why won't you let me come?"

The smirk on my face must be dirty as hell because she gives me the evil eye. "I'm edging you, baby. Don't you like it?"

"No, I need to come, Ethan." She almost sounds mad. "You've never denied me my orgasm before."

"Oh, you'll come harder than you ever have before when I'm done with you." I go back to the job at hand with the intent to make her have a glorious orgasm. I assault her pussy with groans as I suck her needy clit into my mouth and insert a finger into her warm center.

She's panting and bucking when I add another finger, thrusting them harder until I can hear the sounds of her wetness filling the room.

"Come for me now, baby. I won't pull away, I promise." She explodes on my face, and my fingers are drenched as her juices are set free. The shock waves roll through her body, and she shudders each time I lightly lick her clit.

"Now you're just teasing me."

"Mm-hmm," I hum.

"Paybacks are a bitch, you know." She smiles.

"I'm not done yet," I say, grinning up from between those hot legs. I lick my lips, tasting her sweet release on my tongue. I pull my fingers into my mouth one at a time and suck them clean. Her eyes are glued to mine.

I move up her body and land on her mouth, and she ravages me. Our tongues intertwine, and I suck her bottom lip into my mouth and bite. She's pulling on her restraints, trying to get closer to me. Moans of need leave her mouth and fall into mine.

"Let's make it a little more exciting for you, shall we?" I say as I reach under her pillow.

"More exciting. What the fuck?"

I pull out a blindfold and run it across her skin as goose bumps form. She shudders when I secure it over her eyes.

"Are you okay, baby girl?"

"Yes, I'm fine. Please *fuck me,* Ethan. I want your hard cock buried deep inside me." Those are the sweetest words I've ever heard. I remove my clothes and free my aching cock, then kneel before that gorgeous pussy like I'm praying to the goddess in front of me. I pull her legs around my waist and notch my head at her entrance.

"Ethan."

"I'm going to take you bare. Is that okay?"

"Fuck. Now. Ethan." Without any hesitation, I thrust my cock deep inside her and hold it there, feeling her pussy clamp around me. A loud guttural moan comes from Lola's chest, and her hips buck up into me.

Chapter 34
Lola

My eyes are blindfolded now. It's another new experience to add to the list with Ethan. Having my vision removed makes me feel more vulnerable, and my body is on high alert. Every lick and touch sends me spiraling into an abyss of pleasure. He gives me a little bit of his length and begins to rock his hips slowly. It feels like his cock is pulsing as he rotates his hips in a circular motion. He's hitting my G-spot in the most amazing way.

"More. E, please, I need more. I want it all. Deeper."

"You're just my needy little slut, aren't you?"

"Yes."

"Say it."

"I'm your needy little slut." In one hard thrust, he's deep inside me. My walls are crying out for more. I groan his name in a voice I've never heard come out of my mouth before. It's hungry and loud.

"I'm going to fuck you so hard," he growls out as he quickens the pace.

"Oh shit, Ethan!" I can feel every part of my body shifting on the mattress beneath me as we rock up and down on the bed. My second orgasm barrels over me like an avalanche, taking away all my air. My mouth is open, but no sounds are coming out. I'm lost deep in the sensations Ethan is giving me.

"Breathe for me, Lola," he says as he tweaks my nipple. The pain pulls me back to reality.

"Oh Fuck," I scream as he continues to bang my pussy through my orgasm.

"I want another. Come on my cock again."

"I don't know if I can," I pant out. "It's too much. They're so intense."

"You can do it." He repositions us with one of my legs on his shoulder, causing him to go deeper still.

"Ethan!"

"You got this. Take my cock, Lola." He plunges in over and over. We're sweaty, and our breaths are ragged as the tingling sensation in my core begins. I've never come so much in my whole life.

"Shit!"

"Come for me, baby," he says as we both fall over the brink into the darkness of our lust together.

Chapter 35
Sasha

enter Don's Pub on Main. It's sketchy at best. Sitting off to the side so I can see the door, I wait. I'm dressed in black leather shorts, a long-sleeved red silk shirt with black embroidered trim, and black thigh-high boots. My makeup is dark and heavy, and my long black hair is braided loosely in a Dutch braid, with pieces framing my face. It makes it easier to put my helmet on. He enters the pub just like she said he would. All alone, looking for someone to hook up with. His eyes search the bar until they fall on me.

Walking over to the bar, he says, "Is anyone sitting here?"

"Just you, honey," I coo.

"I'll have a beer and bring the lady another," he says, gesturing to the bartender.

"Jack Daniel's," I say

"Jack Daniel's," he tells the bartender. The bartender pours our drinks in front of us.

"Thank you," I say with a fake smile.

"What's your name, pretty lady?"

"Sasha," I say with a sultry smile.

"I like that name. It's very sexy," he croons.

"What's yours?"

"Jack Richards." Bingo, he *is* my man.

"Nice to meet you, Jack." His name makes me want to say it long and drawn out—Jaaaack. We make small talk at the bar for a while. I pump him full of drinks, waiting for him to make his move and ask me to leave with him.

"So… Sasha, wanna get out of here?" he slurs. And there it is. Dumbass, this is why I am going to blow your fuckin' brains out. Because you can't keep your dick in your pants.

"Sure, let me get my coat." I reach for my leather jacket. When I pull it on, I make sure my gun is where I left it in the inside pocket.

"Where do you want to go?" he asks.

"There's a motel down the street. We can walk."

"Sounds like fun." He throws his arm around me, and we walk toward the little motel at the end of the street.

He rents a room for two hours. What a gentleman. We head up the stairs, and as soon as we enter the room, he pushes me against the door. He wastes no time running his hands all over my body and trying to kiss me with his slimy mouth. Reaching into my jacket, I pull out my gun and point it at his head.

"What the fuck!" he shouts. I push him back, now aiming it at his chest.

"Well, Jack, Julianna is done with your shit. She's tired of you messing around with all your whores behind her back." His eyes are wide, and there's a surprised look on his face as if he thought she was clueless.

"Yeah, she knows *everything*. All about your sluts, and the drugs, and the debts you racked up to the Martinellis. All of it."

"She wouldn't do this. Not my Julianna."

"Yes, *your* Julianna wants you dead, you piece of shit. Now, I have a job to do, so pull out a chair and have a seat." I keep the gun trained on him. He's a good boy and does as he's told.

"Please, I'll give you whatever you want. Please don't do this," he begs as my phone rings.

"Dammit! I gotta take this." I click the button and put my phone up to my ear while Jack lets out a sigh of relief. Maybe he thinks it's Julianna changing her mind. I lower the gun to his stomach while I talk.

"Hello."

"What the hell are you doing, Sasha?" the boss's voice booms through the phone.

"I'm a little busy right now," I say in a singsong voice.

"Where are you?"

"I'm in the middle of a job."

"Did you get the papers I needed copied yet?"

"I almost had them copied this morning, but he returned a little earlier than expected."

"How much longer do you think it will take?" he asks.

"It's tricky, but I *will* get them. I just need another day or two."

"Fine, the sooner the better. Who are you with?"

"Jack Richards."

"You know he owes The Organization money, don't you?"

"Yeah, I know, but my client paid me to take care of him first."

"Antonio is going to be fucking pissed that you got to him first."

"I'm sorry I beat you to it." I laugh.

"What are you going to do about his wife?" he asks.

"The wife has nothing to do with it. She just found out what he was doing and contacted me."

"Are you sure?"

"Yeah, she's innocent."

"We'll call it closed then."

"Thanks for leaving her out of it, boss."

"He's one fucked-up individual."

"I know, right?" I say with a smile. "Bye."

Pocketing my phone, I say, "Sorry about the little interruption. Now back to you, Jack." I roll his name off my tongue. "It's not up to me." I aim the gun back between his eyes. "Julianna wants you gone. You understand that, don't you?"

"No, no, please, I can pay you to *not* kill me."

"Now, Jack, you're already in debt. Who are you going to borrow money from?"

"I don't know. I… I… I will get it for you."

"We know you won't, so let's get this over with." He's blubbering like an idiot and begging me not to shoot.

"You've been a baad boy. Any last words, Jaack?" I singsong. I wait.

One...

Two...

Three...

BANG.

He took too long.

Chapter 36
Antonio

I t's Saturday morning. Rocco, Freddy, and Nico are at the mansion, and we're discussing a strategy for taking out a drug dealer who has moved into our area. My phone rings.

"What?" I bark.

"Boss, we have a problem," Vito says.

"What the fuck now?" I say, wiping my hand down my face.

"Jack Richards is dead. Gunshot to the head."

"What the hell?"

"Cleaning lady found him in that old motel off Main Street this morning."

"Who did it? Who the fuck took out Jack Richards?"

"I have no idea. It wasn't any of us," Vito says.

"Find out who killed him, dammit!" I slam down the phone.

"That was Vito. He was supposed to be keeping track of Jack Richards, and the cops found him dead in a motel off Main Street. Shot in the head."

"Did he owe someone else money?" Rocco asks.

"I don't fuckin know. Shit! There's some fucker out there who's one step ahead of us. Taking out people who owe us money before we even get close to collecting. Let's talk about Ricci and get the fuck out of here. What do you have?" I ask. Rocco begins the briefing.

"Well, we know he sold drugs laced with fentanyl at the local high school. There were five deaths, and ten ended up in the hospital when a kid named Matthew Barber had an impromptu party at his house one weekend. He was lucky."

Nico continues, "He was lucky because he was trying to stay halfway sober, so his house wasn't destroyed that night. I went to talk to him in the hospital. He said he bought it from a guy who matched Ricci's description. He wears all black, has a scar on his right cheek, and a tattoo of a rose on the top of his hand. He works out of the alley behind John's Deli."

"We need to take care of him. Drugs are one thing, but tainted drugs are another. The three of you go and have a little talk with Ricci. See if you can talk him into better business practices. Follow him. I want to know who his principal supplier is. And keep your ears open around town for our mystery assassin too."

Chapter 37
Ethan

We find Ricci with very little effort. He was right where the kid said he would be. Nico parks the Escalade, and we exit the vehicle. We are all dressed in black from head to toe. We couldn't look more menacing if we tried. I check my gun in the back of my pants. We communicate without even speaking. Freddy goes first, then Nico, and I bring up the rear.

"Hey, Ricci, how ya doin'?" Freddy asks as we get closer. He steps to the right.

"I don't have any beef with you guys. What do you want from me?" Ricci says, backing up.

"Ah, we just wanted to have a little chat with you," Nico says, stepping to the left.

"We hear you're selling drugs laced with fentanyl," I say. When he sees me, he stops dead in his tracks.

"Rocco. Nah, man, it wasn't me."

"If it wasn't you, who then?" I ask.

"Just some guy."

Walking up slowly behind him, Freddy says, "Some guy, huh? Well, we want to meet *some guy*."

"He doesn't go out much."

"Oh really? You can call him and tell him Rocco Martinelli wants to meet him." I chuckle.

"Why?" I raise my eyebrows at him. Did he just fucking ask *me* why? "I... I... I mean, what would you like to know?" Ricci sputters.

"Why does he want to hurt so many people?" Freddy speaks dark and menacingly over his shoulder.

"Man, I... I... I don't know anything about that. I go pick up the stuff, sell it, take the money back, and get more. It's a well-oiled machine," he sputters out.

"Well, someone is putting sugar in the gas tank of your well-oiled machine, and it's about to explode. If he keeps killing off customers, we'll have to take care of him," Nico says, cracking his knuckles.

"Please, I'll tell him what you said. Just let me go."

"We just came to talk, Ricci," I croon, walking up to pin him between Freddy and me. "If it continues, we'll be back. And it won't be to talk. Do you understand?"

"Yes, yes, I understand."

We all step away and leave him with his thoughts. After we load back in the Escalade, Nico drives down the street and parks in the alley. We wait to see if Ricci takes the bait. About thirty minutes later, he's all packed up and walking down the street. Freddy gets out and follows him on foot. He walks a few blocks and turns into "Your Special Day Bridal Shop" on the corner of Smith and Wayne.

"I'm going around back to check it out," Freddy says into his earpiece.

We lose sight of him for a few minutes. He walks back to the car.

"Well?" I ask.

"He went to the back and talked with a man. Big fat guy, with black, greasy hair, and a mustache. He had a couple of thugs with him. Maybe they run their business out of the shop. Good cover, I guess."

"Did he look familiar?"

"No, Boss, I've never seen him before. There are some windows in the basement. I tried to look in, but they were covered with cardboard. They could make it down there, but the space is pretty small," Freddy says.

"Thanks, Freddy, you did good. Let's go back and tell Antonio what we learned and see how he wants to proceed."

The next day, Antonio sends Sheila to the bridal salon to act like she's looking for a wedding dress. The owner is very chatty and tells her the greasy guy in the back is Eliseo DeLuca.

"He hasn't been in the country very long, but he has taken over my shop. He stinks it up with his cigars and scares all my customers away," the owner says.

"I know some people who may be able to help. Just try to stay away from him, and I'll see what I can do," Sheila says.

Chapter 38
Sasha

I t's Sunday night, and I've wasted my entire fuckin' weekend looking for this piece of shit. His name is Ricci, and he works for a scumbag named DeLuca. DeLuca is a greasy, fat pig, and I'll take care of him later. I've been staking out John's Deli, but there's been no sign of Ricci. He sold some tainted drugs to my clients' kid, and they want revenge. I'm here to provide that service for them. Sitting in my car, I've waited and waited, and my thoughts take me down a path I've been trying to forget. A time when I was living on the street, living fix to fix. Doing whatever it took to get a hit.

"Listen, I just need a hit, Jonah, please," I say.

"You owe me too much money, Sasha. I can't give you any more."

"What can I do to make you change your mind?" I saunter up to him and nibble on his ear.

"Sasha! I can't," he says, shoving me away. "Go find Henry. Maybe he can help you."

"Fine," I blurt out in defeat. Walking down the street, I see Henry on the corner.

"Henry, hey. Do you have a little fix for a long-lost friend?" I ask.

"What've you got in mind?" He wiggles his eyebrows at me.

"I'll do whatever you want. I just need a hit to get me through, please," I say, cozying up to his side.

"Come with me." He takes me by the hand and leads me into the alley. We stop at the dead end behind the dumpsters. "Get on your knees."

I do as he says, and I look up at him. "You get my dick off, and I'll give you a bump."

I reach up, unbutton his pants, and lower his zipper. I push them and his boxers down around his ankles and take his cock into my hand.

Shit! There's Ricci. Shaking me out of my daydream—or nightmare more like it—I get out of my beat-up Ford Escape and follow him down the alley.

"Hey, Ricci. How ya been?" I ask, slowly approaching him. My gun digs into my back. I'm dressed in black leather pants, a black tank top, combat boots, a blond bob wig, and red lipstick.

"Do I know you?" He squints, trying to figure out who I am.

"No, but I know you," I say, pointing at him.

"Who are you and what do you want, bitch?"

"Oh, such nasty language. I'm actually here for someone else."

"Who?"

"Mr. and Mrs. Lopez," I say, stopping about six feet away from him.

"Who the fuck is that?" He shifts from side to side.

"Parents of one of the teens you killed at the party a few weeks back."

He pauses and just stares at me before he says, "I didn't kill no one."

"You sold the drugs to that boy who had the party, didn't you?"

"Well, yeah, but I didn't make anyone take them."

"But you knew they were laced, didn't you? You knew someone was going to get hurt." I raise my chin.

"No, I didn't. I didn't want to hurt anyone. It was…"

"Who was it, Ricci? DeLuca? Was he the one who orchestrated it?"

"I didn't say that. You ain't gonna make me no snitch."

"I'm going to make you dead, whether you *snitch* or not, so you might as well just tell me."

"Fuck you, lady." He points his dirty finger at me.

"No, not today, but I am going to fuck *you* up."

He laughs in my face. "You ain't gonna do shit to me, bitch." Before he can flinch, I grab his outstretched hand, spin him around so his back is to my front, and point my gun at his head.

"What was that you said, Ricci?" I whisper in his ear. "Tell me, you motherfucker, was it DeLuca? He ordered you to sell those drugs to those kids, didn't he?" I tighten my arm around his throat.

"Yes! Yes! Now let me go!" he chokes out.

"Sorry, but I can't do that. I have a job to complete, and I wasted my whole fuckin' weekend on your ass already. Any last words?"

One…

Two…

Three…

BANG.

Chapter 39
Antonio

"**S**on of a fuckin bitch! What the hell is happening? Sheila!" My voice thunders through the room.

Sheila lets herself into my office. "Did you call for me, Mr. Martinelli?" She doesn't seem fazed by my behavior.

"Get me Rocco and all my captains in here now!" Sheila backs out of the room and leaves. In thirty minutes, I have Rocco, Jackson, Buddy, Nico, Freddy, Vito, Roscoe, and Beckett standing at attention in my office. I sit behind my desk, leaning back in my leather chair. Scotch in hand, I'm trying to slow my heartbeat before I speak.

"I would like someone to tell me who the fuck is killing everyone?"

"Sir?" Rocco asks.

"Ricci is dead. Did any of you kill him after I told you not to?"

"No," they all answer in unison.

"Well, someone fucking killed him in the alley behind John's Deli. Bullet through his head, just like Jack Richards."

"Maybe there's someone new in town we don't know about, sir," Freddy speaks up.

"I want to know who the fuck it is. If they get to DeLuca before we do, there will be hell to pay. Do you understand me?" I beat my fist on the table. "I want you to use all those technology resources I paid so much goddamn money for and figure this shit out. Then I want you to bring this guy to me."

"Yes, Boss," they all say and file out. Rocco stays behind.

"Why do you think they're after the same people we are? Maybe it's just a coincidence," he asks.

"I don't know what the fuck's happening. They could be targeting us next. We need to find this guy. Go to Daniel and have him check all the cameras in the area to see if he can get a picture of this fucker."

"The cameras were all disabled at the motel where Jack was killed. We already checked them, but I'll have him search the ones in the alley."

"And you need to put some sergeants on that damn bridal shop around the clock. I want eyes on DeLuca. I want to know what the hell he's up to. And for fuck's sake, find out who this new assassin is and who they're working for."

"Will do," Rocco says as he leaves my office.

Chapter 40
Ethan

I t's after two in the morning when I walk into the penthouse. I need to be with Lola. To lie with her in my arms to make this shit go away, even if it's only for a few hours. Going over to the floor-to-ceiling windows to look out over the city, I recall an earlier phone conversation.

"You need to back off for a little while," I say.

"Why? Because it's making Daddy crazy?" she says with a snark.

"Not just that, but I need you alive to do your job, not dead because he figures out who you are."

"No one will know who I am. I've never been seen."

"You better hope not, or our entire plan will be shit."

"I have jobs to do too. I have people to help and a reputation to build. It's because of you I do what I do. It just so happens my missions involve people The Organization is watching as well. My next job isn't even in the city. It's three hours away. He'll never be able to put it together," she says.

"Don't you fucking touch DeLuca," I snap.

"Why not?"

"Because Antonio wants him for himself. And... he'll lose his shit if you kill him first." There's laughing on the other end of the phone.

"I won't kill DeLuca." She chuckles.
"Did you get those copies yet?" I ask.
"Yeah, they're ready."
"You sure you copied everything?"
"Yeah, I got it all."
"I'll get them tomorrow morning."
"Okay, Boss."

I turn around to find Lola asleep on the couch facing the windows. I didn't notice her before in the dark. She's so small, lying on the giant couch. She's on her side, cuddling the throw blanket, as if she was looking out the window when she fell asleep. As I stare at her in the light of the moon, she looks so peaceful and sweet. She's wearing those damn bunny shorts and a tank top.

Her breathing is low and even. I scoop her limp body up, and I sit down on the couch, holding her in my lap. Brushing her long brown hair from her face, I kiss her soft cheek.

"Hi," she whispers

"Hi. I'm sorry I woke you, but I needed you in my arms."

"I tried to wait up for you." She yawns.

"I know, baby. I'm sorry. It took longer than planned."

"I'm glad you're home," she coos, cuddling into my neck.

"Me too." I stroke her back in slow circles.

"Mmm, you can do that all night," she says, a little moan coming from her chest.

"You keep making those sexy noises, and I'll be carrying you to our bed and having my way with you."

"Promise?"

"I love you so much, Lola," I say, hugging her tightly.

She leans up and places her hands on my cheeks and gingerly kisses my lips.

"I love you too, E. What's wrong?"

"Just a long day."

"Tell me."

"It's just a part of my plan to take down my father. It's causing me to run around putting out a lot of fires, so he doesn't find out what I'm doing."

"Can't we just leave? Start a new life somewhere he won't find us," she says with a little whine.

"You know it doesn't matter where we go, he'll find us. I want to be *free*. I don't want to run."

"Ethan, I don't understand something."

"What, baby girl?"

"When you take care of Antonio, you'll be in charge, right?"

"Yes."

"What if you become just like him?"

"I won't."

"You already said you've done things you regret."

"I have. Taking a life isn't something I ever wanted to do."

"Then how will that all just disappear when you take over?"

"I have a plan. I'm going to keep all the parts of The Organization that are legit and dissolve everything else. If I no longer have things people want, they'll leave me alone."

"I hope so."

"When all this is over, I'm going to get down on one knee with the biggest ring I can find and ask you to be my wife. I want to have a family with you. Build a life together."

"What if I want to continue my career before we have children?"

"You can do whatever makes you happy, my love. I'll buy Kingsley and Masters, and you can run the whole damn show."

"What if I told you I'd like to do volunteer work?" Pushing her back, I look into her eyes to see if this is real. Her gaze never falters. Volunteer. She wants to help others.

"That would be amazing. Where do you want to help? We can make that happen right now. Why wait?"

"I remembered you telling me about the rehab center you helped at in college. I think a battered women's shelter or homeless shelter might be where my passion lies, but I'm not sure yet."

"Let me know what you decide, and we'll make it happen."

"I'll do some research."

"Now, what can I do to help *you*?" She waggles her eyebrows.

"Well, to be honest, I would love to keep you in the penthouse out of harm's way until this is over."

"Ethan…" She sighs and puts her hands on her hips.

"But I know you don't want to do that. Just don't do anything crazy, and make sure Bennie is always with you when you go out."

"I promise to be a good girl," she says with a devious smirk on her lips.

"Oh, you're my *good girl,* all right." Standing from the couch with her in my arms, I throw her over my shoulder, smack her on the ass, and carry her to our bed.

Chapter 41
Sasha

It seems like all I do is sit around and wait. Wait for these idiots to show their faces so I can take them out. Tonight's assignment is Bill. Bill Johnson. What a fucking boring name. Bill's wife is a woman scorned. It seems Bill cheated on said wife with some bitches at the local strip joint. One night, he used the wrong credit card to pay his bill, and she found out he was there.

Vicky Johnson has balls. She dressed in disguise and went to the club all on her own. She sat in the back and watched her husband paw all over the strippers. He got a lap dance from one and then took another to the back room, where she could only assume they had sex.

She's paying me twenty-five thousand dollars to take him out, so she can pocket the insurance money and move on with her life. I don't care what she does as long as she pays me. So here I sit, waiting for Billy Boy to walk into the strip joint. My mind wanders while I wait.

"Where am I?" I'm groggy, and my vision is blurry.

"You're at St. Mary's Hospital. You overdosed," a male voice says from behind me. I try to turn around to see who it is, but a firm hand on my shoulder holds me in place.

"I gotta go."

"No, you need help. Will you let me help you, Sasha?"

"Who are you?" All I can see of this man is his leg and the hand on my shoulder.

"I'm someone who can change your whole life."

"Why would you want to help me?"

"Because I see something in you, Sasha. You are so much more than the drugs. You have potential."

Thinking about how shit my life is. How tired I am at just trying to survive. I say, "What do I have to do?"

"First, you need to go to rehab and get clean. Then I'll turn you into the most badass assassin this town has ever seen."

Bill pays the entrance fee and goes into the club. I exit my car, walk around to the back of the building, and enter as if I did it every night. I remove my coat and place it on a shelf by the door.

I'm dressed in a red thong and bra set with six-inch clear heels. My hair is down in waves over my shoulders, and my makeup is heavy with smoky eye shadow and red lipstick. Coming up behind him, touching his shoulder, I say, "Hi ya, honey. How ya doin' tonight?"

"Wow... Hi." His eyes are wide, and I think he likes what he sees. "I've never seen you here before."

"This is my first night." I move to stand in front of him and lean over, squeezing my breasts together. His eyes about pop out of his head. "Can I interest you in a lap dance?"

"Sure, th... th... that would be great," he blabbers.

He puts a wad of money in my thong, and I proceed to rub myself all over his lap. I straddle him and push his face into my tits, and he almost drools. I turn around with my back to his front and sit on his lap again, then lean back on his shoulder. I can feel his hard cock on my ass while I rub into him to the beat of the music.

"Would you like to go to a back room for a *private* dance?" Seductively, I coo into his ear. "Just the two of us." He doesn't even speak; he just shakes his head emphatically. I take him by the hand, through a black door, and down the hallway to the first room on the left. After ushering him inside, I lock the door behind us. Not that anyone will hear him screaming with all the music thrumming through the walls, anyway. It's a BDSM playroom, and the red lights are dim. His eyes scan all the equipment hanging on the walls and the sex furniture sitting around.

"Have you ever used this room before, honey?" I say, running my hands up and down his arms.

"N-N-No," he stutters out.

"Oh, don't be nervous, baby. I'll make you feel *real* good." I was here earlier in the day and paid the owner to let me have this room for the evening. I have some items planted to use on our little man.

"Let's get you out of these silly clothes." I lift his shirt over his head, then push his pants and briefs down his legs. His cock is hard as a fucking rock, standing at attention for me.

"We'll start with the Berkley Horse," I say, holding out my hand and directing him to the center of the room. He kneels behind it and waits.

"I've never done anything like this before."

"I think you're gonna like it *a lot*. Now, lean over the horse with your ass in the air." He smiles and does as he's told. I tie his hands to the rings on either side of the horse with pieces of rope I chose from the wall. This guy is an idiot to allow someone he doesn't know to tie him down. I could do anything to him, which is exactly what I'm going to do. After placing leather straps around his thighs, I secure them to the rings on the bench. Perusing the devices hanging on the wall, I land on a red paddle with a black handle.

I walk all around him, tapping the paddle on the palm of my hand, watching his anticipation grow with every beat. He tries to follow me with his eyes but can only move his head from side to side. I stand behind him and strike his ass with the paddle, and he yelps. His left ass cheek turns red, and I can see the slight shape of the paddle.

"Don't I have to pick a safe word or something?" he asks as he winces.

"Nah, that won't be necessary." I strike his right cheek.

"Hey! That really hurts. Are you supposed to do it that hard?"

"Don't you like it, honey?" I ask as I hit him with the paddle again.

He wiggles in his restraints, trying to get free. "I don't think I like this. Let me go!"

"Oh, I don't think that's gonna happen, baby," I say, taking a handful of his hair in my fist and forcing his face to look up at me. "You see, your wife wants me to give you a message."

"My wife? What are you talking about?" he spits out.

"Yes, you see, Vicky, dear sweet Vicky, found out you're cheating on her with the strippers in this club." *Smack.*

"I don't know what you're talking about." Panic fills his voice.

"Vicky told me you used the household credit card to buy time with these whores." *Smack.*

"The household card? Shit."

"Yeah, I'm sure that was an accident, but anywho," I say, waving the paddle around like it doesn't matter. "Vicky saw the charges. You lied and told her you had to work late at the office one night. She dressed in a disguise and followed you here. She saw everything, Billy Boy. You let those girls bump and grind all over you with your tongue down their throats, and then you went to a back room with a redhead." *Smack. Smack.*

"We didn't do anything." The muscles in his back tighten, and he struggles in his restraints.

"Yeah, you just talked, right?" *Smack.* I laugh in his face. He really is a *terrible* liar.

"I'm here to make sure you never hurt my girl, Vicky, again." I hit him as hard as I can. His ass is red, and I'm sure it burns like hell.

"Please. I'll do anything. Just let me go." He's still struggling to get free as I continue to talk.

"She left it up to me to decide how to take you out, so here are some ideas I had."

"Take me out? You're crazy, bitch!"

"Let's see, I could shoot you like all the others." *Smack.*

"Others?" he says under his breath.

"Or I could get creative with *you*. I could shoot you full of drugs, so it looks like you overdosed on the horse. Ooo or better yet, make you look like you had a heart attack in the throes of your punishment." *Smack, smack.*

"I'm sorry. I'm sorry. I'll never come here again. I swear!"

"Promises aren't good enough, Billy Boy. You'll just go somewhere else." *Smack, smack, smack.*

"Fuck. You. Bitch!" Tears run down his cheeks. "No, I won't do it again, I swear."

"I think I've made my decision."

"N... N... No... I'll give you whatever you want!"

"It's not what I want, honey. It's what Vicky wants."

"I'll give her whatever she wants."

"Too late." I put the needle in his neck and push the plunger. Bill falls limp on the horse. I put the lid back on the needle, then casually walk out of the room and close the door behind me. I retrieve my coat from the shelf by the back door. As I head for my car, I dial Vicky Johnson.

"It's done," I say.

"Are you sure he's gone?" Vicky asks.

"It went just like you planned it."

"Thank you so much."

"Happy to help. Just wire the money. I'll wait."

A few moments later, I hear a ding.

"Got it. Thanks for doing business," I say.

I get lost in my thoughts on the drive home.

"Come on, girl, you can hit harder than that! Put all your weight into the punch." I'm in the boxing ring at the gym sparring with Jerry.

"I'm not a girl!" I yell, throwing an uppercut. "I'm twenty-three years old, you geezer." I do as he says, and I finally connect, causing him to step back and rub his jaw.

"Better, better. Go work the heavy bag for twenty, then meet me in the weight room."

I'm getting stronger and faster every day. Exactly what my mystery man promised. Jerry is a talented trainer. He's been training me for nine months now. I had zero strength when I first left rehab, but he taught me what to eat, how to train, and how to take care of myself. No one has ever devoted this much time to me before.

I fought everything after I got out of rehab. It's hard to have people telling you what to do. It took me a while, but I finally understood they were just trying to help me. I did drugs to escape—escape my shitty life, shitty parents, shitty boyfriends, shitty job, shitty environment. I guess I never thought I would have the power to fix any of it. Thanks to Jerry and my mystery man, I have people who care about what happens to me.

These people are investing their time and resources into turning me into the best assassin I can be. I want to make a difference. I want to help women who can't help themselves. If that means getting rid of their cheating husband or abusive boyfriend, fine by me. Once I can defend myself with my hands, Jerry says we'll move on to other techniques. Like all the ways to take someone out, how to stalk my prey under the cover of darkness, and how to leave no trace.

Three months later...

"*I'm so proud of you, girl, woman, I mean, Sasha.*" *Jerry smiles.*

"*Thanks, Jerry.*" *He envelops me in a big bear hug.*

"*I was skeptical when the boss brought you to me, but he saw something in you. You proved him right. You're the best damn shot I've ever seen.*"

"*I had a great teacher.*"

"*Sasha,*" *a voice behind me says. I turn to see Rocco Martinelli holding his hand out to me.* "*Congratulations, I knew you could do it.*" *I put my hand in his to shake.*

"*You're the man who came to the hospital. I would know your voice anywhere.*"

"*Yes.*"

"*Why did you do all of this for me?*"

"*Because I knew you had the potential to be so much more if you just had a little help.*"

"*Thank you.*"

"*I want you to make a difference for the women of this town. But I also want to make sure you and I have an understanding,*" *he says.*

"*What kind of understanding?*"

"*I want to be sure that you'll be on board if I need you to do jobs for me.*"

"*Of course, Mr. Martinelli, anything you need. Ever.*"

"*My father tasked me with finding him a new personal assistant. I need you to plant yourself in his office. You need to disguise yourself. He can never get a glimpse of Sasha. Gain his trust. Keep your eyes and ears open for anything I can use against him. When the time comes, I want you to be the one to take him out. But I will give that order when the time is right.*"

"Anything. I'll be forever in your debt for saving my life."

"I'll leave you with Jerry. He'll get you all set up. Congratulations again."

Jerry steps forward.

"Here's your first assignment. It's a lady whose husband has been beating her. She just got out of the hospital for the fifth time, and she wants him gone. You can take care of that piece of shit for her, right?"

"Oh, I'll take care of him all right." I give him a devilish smirk. He hands me a burner phone.

"The rest of the assignments will come via text from an unknown number to this phone. Payments will be deposited into your account once the jobs are completed unless you make other arrangements. You're on your own, kid, girl, dammit, Sasha. Go save the world."

I pull into the parking garage at my apartment and park. Knowing I'm helping people gives me purpose. Even though my methods are a little unorthodox, I have worth and value now. I'm looking forward to my biggest assignment yet...Taking out Antonio Martinelli.

Chapter 42
Ethan

Antonio has us meeting in his office this morning.

"I want to have a sit-down with DeLuca," he says.

"Do you think that's a good idea, Boss?" Freddy asks and then rethinks what he said when Antonio's eyebrows rise to him. "I mean, it might put a target on your back."

"Thanks for your concern, Freddy." He looks at him like he's crazy. "But I think I have it handled. Sheila!" he booms.

"Yes, sir," she says, entering the room.

"I need reservations for four at Lowell's Steakhouse. I want to be seated in the center of the room."

"Who will be the four?" I ask.

"You, me, DeLuca, and his right hand." He points at Nico. "Go request their presence at, let's say… six tonight."

"Yes, Boss." Nico leaves the room with Sheila.

"What do you want me to do, Boss?" Freddy asks.

"You just make sure some of our lesser-known guys are having dinner there tonight for backup. Just in case he tries to pull something stupid. Oh, and make sure Sheila reserves tables around the room for them. And, Freddy, make sure the car is ready to go."

"On it." He leaves the room, addressing Sheila.

"And what do you want me to do at the meeting?" I ask.

"Don't say a word. You're the muscle. My right hand. He needs to see your menacing face, and hopefully, he'll get the message."

I leave the office and go back to the penthouse. Lola's at work, so I pull out my dark-blue Armani suit for tonight and lay it on the bed. After crossing the room, I sit down on one of the white sofas by the windows and text Lola.

> I won't be home for dinner tonight.

LOLA
> Okay.

> Having a dinner meeting with Antonio.

> Will I see you after?

> Yes. Hopefully, it won't take too long.

> Until then.

> Until then.

I'm the first to arrive. I take one quick scan, zeroing in on the three tables of our guys spread around the room.

"Bring him in," I say to Freddy in my earpiece. He escorts him into the restaurant. I take over and lead him to the table in the center of the room. He's dressed in a dark-gray suit. His jet-black hair is slicked back, and four Cuban cigars stick out of the front pocket of his jacket. He wears his usual grumpy scowl.

It's just a few minutes, and DeLuca and his second enter the restaurant. I'm sure they were watching us from the street. The maître d' escorts them to the table, and after quick pleasantries, we all sit.

We stare at one another until finally, DeLuca says in a deep Italian accent, "So why did you bring me here? I'm a busy man, you know."

"Oh, I know you're a busy man. Busy killing innocent people," Antonio says.

"You don't know what you're talking about."

Antonio leans forward. His deep Italian voice mimics DeLuca's. "I know your *products* are contaminated."

"Not all of them, just a select few." DeLuca's lip curls.

"And I can't seem to figure out why you would want to eliminate so many paying customers."

"I have enemies, just like you do, Antonio. Sometimes you have to clean out the riffraff."

"How are high school kids at a party riffraff?"

"Maybe it wasn't the high school kids I was after. Maybe it was their scumbag father who owed me money. Who would've known he would send his son to pick up the *items?*" He looks around the room and lowers his voice. "And that the kid would serve it up at his party. Not my problem."

The two men are engrossed in their conversation, and I'm scanning the room when I see Lola and Amelia enter the dining area. My breath hitches. What in the hell are they doing here? I can't acknowledge them in any way. The hostess ushers them past our table. I lock eyes with her, and she lowers her head and walks on past. I need to get her the hell out of here. When I look over at DeLuca, his eyes are wide, and a dirty smile comes over his face as he watches the girls walk by.

"I would like to believe we could come to some sort of agreement so those types of products do not end up on my streets again," Antonio says.

"Well, I can't promise you that," DeLuca says, waving for his security guard to come over to the table. That gesture puts me on edge, and my hand moves toward my gun. He says something into his ear, and the guy nods and leaves. "Would you know anything about who took out my best guy, Ricci, behind John's Deli?"

"I heard about that. I sure don't. But I'll let you know if I hear anything. Now let's eat," Antonio says.

He waves the server over, and we place our orders. Our food is out in the blink of an eye. You wouldn't want to keep men like us waiting. As they are engrossed in their meal, I excuse myself to make a phone call when I see Lola heading for the ladies' room. She walks in, and I push the door open before she can close it.

"What the hell are you doing here?" I whisper-shout, checking to be sure the stalls are empty.

"You said you were at a dinner meeting. I didn't know it was here. What are we going to do? Do you think he saw me?" Lola sputters out.

"I don't think so. If he did, he didn't show any expression. But DeLuca sure liked what he saw. Where's Bennie?"

"He's waiting in the car."

"I want him to take you straight to the penthouse, do you hear me?"

"What about Amelia?"

"Take her with you. Freddy can take her home after he takes me to the penthouse."

"But she doesn't know I live there yet."

"Well, I guess tonight she'll be getting an education."

"She only knows your father is after me, and that's why I have Bennie following me everywhere."

"Try not to give her any more information than you have to."

"I won't," she says as I pull her into my arms.

"Hmm, we're in here all alone. We should take advantage of it." I push her hair behind her ear and place kisses on her neck. Putting her hands on my chest, she pushes me away.

"You need to get out of here so you don't raise suspicion."

"I know. But I've missed you today," I whine.

"Ethan," she scolds.

"Fine, but you're going to pay for making me wait." I give her a smack on the ass.

"I think I can handle that," she says with a devious grin. I take her face in my hands one last time and kiss her hard. I motion for her to lock the door behind me and return to the table. The two men are discussing grandchildren and finishing their coffee. Antonio reaches into his pocket and hands all of us a cigar. That's his signal we're leaving.

Standing, he says, "DeLuca."

"Martinelli." He reaches out his hand to shake, and Antonio obliges, then we exit the restaurant. When we're on the street, I search for Bennie. Our eyes connect, and his mouth flies open. I escort my father into the car, walk to the other side, and get in.

As Freddy pulls the car away from the curb, Father speaks, "How long do you think you were going to hide her from me, Son?"

"I don't know what you mean."

"Bullshit. You know what I'm talking about. The girl."

"What girl?"

"Dammit, Rocco, Lola, *that girl.*" He raises his voice in frustration with me, pointing his thumb over his shoulder toward the restaurant. I sit here in silence for a moment. This is it. My moment to set the record straight and make my stand.

"I know about your little deal with her, and it's over. She's mine, and you can't do anything to stop it." My voice comes out demanding and harsh.

"Don't you speak to me like that!" His brows pinch together, and he scrunches up his face.

"I'm done hiding. I love her. And we're going to be together and you're going to leave her the hell alone!"

"She's going to hurt you, Rocco."

"The only thing she did to hurt me, *you caused*, by scaring her into leaving me."

"I had to. She was making you weak, just like your mother did."

"*Don't* talk about Mother that way."

"She coddled you as a child, and it made you have all these *feelings*," he says, waving his hands around.

"Just because I'm not as heartless as you are doesn't mean I can't be a good leader."

"Heartless. Is that what you think of me? I loved your mother with my whole soul, and when she died, she took a piece of me with her." His voice is quieter now. Broken.

"I know you loved Mother. But you changed when she died. You became so angry and unfeeling. Like you were going to take it out on the whole world. You sure took it out on me," I mumble, staring out the window.

"Because you don't *listen* to me."

"No, I don't blindly do what you say and play by your rules. I have my *own* mind, Father. And I want to live my life, *my way.*"

"You're in too deep with this girl, Rocco. You can't escape this life, which means she'll have to live with it. Can this girl handle our way of life?"

"I hope so because I'm not letting her go again."

"I'm sorry I had the boys rough her up."

"That wasn't right, and you know it."

"I had to do something to keep her away from you."

"You didn't have to hurt her. What Buddy tried to do to her was uncalled for."

"What did Buddy do to her?"

"He wanted to *play* with her."

"I didn't tell him to do that. You have to believe me, Son." I look into his eyes and believe he's telling the truth. My father doesn't hurt women for sport.

"I believe you."

"What happened to Jackson and Buddy after that night?" he asks.

"I had to teach them a little lesson. No one hurts my woman."

"You *are* your father's son, after all. If you love her, you'll do whatever it takes to protect her.

"I would die for her."

I finally break the silence. "I'm the one who broke Vito's nose." We burst out laughing.

Chapter 43
Lola

Bennie drives Amelia and me straight to the penthouse. He puts us on the elevator and stands guard in the garage, waiting for Ethan to arrive.

"Holy shit! Look at this place!" Amelia yells, coming into the penthouse with her mouth hanging open. She walks straight to the windows that look out over the city. "Do you know what you're getting yourself into, Lola?" She's worried. I know she is. "These people are killers."

"Ethan is different. He doesn't want the same things his father does."

"Just be careful."

"Bennie is here to keep us safe. Besides, I live in a damn fortress now," I say, throwing my arms out wide. "C'mon, let's have a drink." We stand by the island with our glasses of wine. "So have you and Freddy talked?" I ask.

"Yeah. He told me what he does in a nutshell."

"What do you see in him? He always looks so mean."

"He has a lot on his mind. But he's sweet with me."

"You're not afraid of him?" I ask.

"No. He's a teddy bear under all those muscles. He doesn't talk much, but I make up for it." She laughs.

"It doesn't bother you that he's so much older than you?"

"No. He makes me feel safe and protected, and he knows so much more than I do in the bedroom, if you know what I mean. He doesn't make me feel stupid or less than."

"I'm glad he's good to you. Do you love him?"

"I'm not going there. He doesn't talk about his feelings, ever. If I try to get him to tell me about his past or his feelings, he shuts down. So I decided I'm just going to have fun. If he ever tells me he has feelings for me, that's great. But if he doesn't, then I'll have to deal with it."

"How long can you go on that way? Loving him and him not loving you back?"

"I guess we're going to find out."

"Besides, you haven't been dating that long for *love*, anyway." I won't tell her I knew I loved Ethan the moment I saw him at Anthony's that day.

"I do like it when he throws me over his shoulder and carries me to bed." Her innocent little giggles fill the space. The elevator door opens, and Freddy and Ethan step into the room. Their large forms command the space. They cross the room and pull us in for hugs.

Freddy whispers something in Amelia's ear. She lets out a little giggle and says, "Well, this has been fun, but we gotta go." She gives me a wink. "See you tomorrow at work."

When the elevator door slides closed, I say, "I know what they're doing tonight." I'm giggling now. In one swift movement, Ethan throws me over his shoulder and starts toward the bedroom.

"Probably the same thing we're about to do," he says as he smacks my ass.

We're lying in bed afterward. I'm cuddled up in Ethan's arms, and he's stroking my shoulder.

"You didn't say if your father saw me or not."

"Oh, he saw you all right." I sit up and turn to him.

"If I had known you were there, I wouldn't have suggested the restaurant to Amelia. What did he say? I'm *so* sorry." I always talk a mile a minute when I get anxious. Ethan takes my hands in his to calm me.

"Lola, it's okay. We talked in the car on the way to the mansion, and he agreed to leave you alone. He's worried you're not strong enough for this life. But I assured him you're the strongest woman I've ever known, and you can take care of yourself. Which reminds me, I want you to meet with Jerry."

"The trainer at the gym?"

"Yes. He can teach you some self-defense techniques."

"Do you think I need that if your father is done kidnapping me?"

"Yes, it might not be him next time."

"Next time?"

"Lola, I told you that you could become a target just because you're involved with us now."

"I know, but I was hoping it wasn't as bad as it sounded."

"You need to be prepared and keep the damn security, okay?"

"Okay. I like Bennie. I trust him."

"That's why I put him in charge of your security. He might look like a grandpa, but he can beat anyone's ass. Did Amelia talk to Freddy yet?" he asks.

"Yeah, she said they talked, and they're going to take it slow. Will she be a target too?"

"Maybe not as much as you are."

"What do you mean by that?"

"He's not high on the food chain yet."

"Yet?"

"Yes, I want him as my right hand when I take over. *Then* she'll need more protection."

"This is so intense," I say under my breath.

"I know what else is intense." He wiggles his eyebrows at me and pulls me to lie on top of him.

For the next few weeks, I go to the gym and train with Jerry. He teaches me how to get out of different holds and how to defend myself.

"Take out whatever you can reach. Their eyes, ears, nose, throat, knees, ankles, top of the foot, and best of all, their nuts, if you get a chance," Jerry instructs.

"Do you think I'll ever need to use this stuff?" I ask, punching the heavy bag.

"I don't know, girly, but Rocco wants you to be ready, just in case. It can't hurt, right?"

"I guess not." Jerry is an excellent trainer. I like how he talks openly to me and answers all my questions.

"Today, when we're done here, I'm taking you to the gun range. I'm going to teach you everything you ever wanted to know about guns and more."

We take the elevator to the basement, to a state-of-the-art gun range. Nico stands to the right as I walk in the door. He has on headphones and is shooting at targets. To the left is a beautiful woman with straight, long black hair hitting her target in the head over and over.

"Wow, she's really good," I whisper to Jerry.

"She's my best student." He waves her over to us.

"Sasha, this is Lola. Lola, this is Sasha." She stares at me and seems uncomfortable.

"Have we met?" I ask her.

"No, I don't think so. It's nice to meet you. I'm sorry. I'm on my way out," she says as she rushes off.

Jerry spends all afternoon teaching me how to hold different types of weapons. How to load, unload, aim, shoot, clean, and take them apart.

"Which one feels best in your hand?" he asks.

"I think I like the Glock the best."

"A Glock it is, then. I'll tell Rocco that's what you want." A gun. I'm getting a gun?

"Oh, I don't need a gun."

"Yes, you do, and you handle it very well. You'll be just fine." I smile weakly as we head out.

Ethan and I are having dinner that evening.

"Jerry said you did a great job at the gun range today. Said you're a natural." He's beaming with pride.

"It was fun, I guess. Do I really need a gun of my own?"

"I think you should have your own weapon. One you feel comfortable using. You don't have to carry it around with you every day. But the more you're around guns, the less you'll be afraid of them."

"I guess," I say, shrugging.

It's been a few weeks since my training with Jerry ended, and Antonio found out we're still together. I'm at the little coffee shop a few blocks from work with Amelia. Bennie is sitting at a table adjacent to us. There have been no problems, so I've just gone on with my normal routine, except for the fact I have a *giant* following me around. I get up to use the bathroom, and Bennie stands.

"It's okay, Bennie. I'm just going to the restroom. I have my phone," I say, waving it in the air.

"Yes, Miss Lola." I can feel his eyes on me as I walk the fifteen feet to the bathroom.

I enter, and someone's in the first stall, so I go to the second. I'm doing my business when I hear a voice speaking to me from the other side of the wall.

"They know who your boyfriend is," the female voice says quietly. *What the hell?* Is she talking to me?

"Rocco. They know you're his, and they're coming for you," she says, exiting her stall. I'm trying to look through the crack, but all I see is curly red hair and lots of it.

"Why? What do I have to do with anything?" I ask.

"You're *his*. That's all that matters to them. They'll hurt you to get what they want from him. Trust me, I know. This is a warning from one woman to another." She leaves the room. I hurry and rush out into the coffee shop. Nervously, I search all around, but I don't see the red-haired woman anywhere. Bennie jumps up and comes over to me.

"Miss Lola? What's wrong?" He takes me by the forearm and leads me back to the table with Amelia. We sit in the booth, and I tell them what the woman said. "We need to leave. Now," Bennie says. We immediately leave the coffee shop and get into the Escalade. Bennie is on the phone in the front seat, but I can't hear the conversation. Amelia is sitting beside me. Her eyes are wide, but she doesn't say a word. When we arrive at the office, Ethan is waiting by the front door.

"I got her now, Bennie. See you tomorrow." He takes me by the hand and rushes me into his vehicle, and we pull away, leaving poor Amelia standing on the curb.

"Ethan, what are you doing? I have work to finish, and you just left Amelia standing there." Panic takes over my whole body.

"That was a *threat,* Lola. I'm taking you back to the penthouse, where you'll be safe. This is what I've been afraid of all along. Some-one trying to take you to get to me."

"It wasn't a threat. She was trying to *warn* me…"

"Of… A… Threat," he clarifies. "I'm sorry about Amelia, but Ben-nie will wait with her until Freddy gets there." I'm silent the rest of the way to the penthouse. Ethan parks in his spot, and I can see Jackson, Buddy, and Vito at various stations in the garage.

Ethan takes his gun out of the glove compartment, checks it, and puts it in the back of his pants as Jackson approaches my door.

"I called in extra security until we find out who the threat was from," he says as Jackson opens my door. He holds out a hand to help me out.

"Miss Lola," Jackson says. I take his hand, and he helps me out of the vehicle.

"Thank you."

Ethan comes to my side of the car, and he pulls me tight into his side. "Ethan, you're starting to scare me," I whisper as we walk toward the elevator.

"Good, you should be scared. You don't understand what's happen-ing, but this is serious. Let's get inside." He motions for me to enter the waiting elevator and turns to Jackson. "Did you check the penthouse?"

"Yes, Boss, it's all clear."

"We aren't going anywhere tonight. Keep your head on a swivel, just in case. And under no circumstances do I want Buddy alone with Lola. I don't trust him after what he pulled at the warehouse."

"Yes, Boss," he says as the elevator doors close. The elevator is private and only stops at the penthouse, so we are secure in our own little bubble now. I stand here staring at the mirrored wall while my mind swirls with possibilities. How can this be happening?

As soon as we get inside, Ethan goes to work. He gets my gun and ammo out of the safe and lays it on the table. Then he pulls a black backpack from the bottom of the closet. *I didn't know that was there.*

His eyes connect with mine. "This is your go bag. Put in a change of clothes, extra medicines, and anything else you might need for a couple of days," he instructs.

"Why do I need that?"

"In case we need to go to the safe house."

"Safe house?" That's the last straw. My brain can't take any more, and it just explodes. Tears stream from my eyes. Ethan stops what he's doing and strides over to me. Taking me into his arms, he holds me tightly.

"We are *safe* here. It's going to be okay. We'll find out who the threat was from and eliminate them." I squeeze him tighter.

"Do you think someone can get to us in here?" I ask.

"Only if they're stupid, but we need to be prepared." He pulls me back, wipes my tears from my cheeks, and kisses my forehead. "Put those few things in your go bag, and then why don't you take a nice hot bath?"

"Okay. I'll text Amelia to apologize for leaving her so abruptly, then tell her I'll see her on Monday."

"That sounds good," he says, placing a kiss on the top of my head.

I stayed in the penthouse all weekend. Ethan left twice to go to the mansion to talk to Daniel about the red-haired woman. He hadn't come up with anything except that she exited the coffee shop and got in a black van. I'm on edge the whole time Ethan's gone, but thankfully, I have my work computer to keep my mind busy.

It's Sunday evening, and I'm on the giant couch by the window, working on the Bookman Proposal, when my computer seems to glitch. Then it all goes black.

"Ethan, I think there's something wrong with the internet," I holler across the penthouse.

A male voice comes through my computer.

"We are coming for you, Lola. You cannot escape us. Rocco Martinelli will pay the price."

I drop the computer onto the couch and run toward the bathroom, screaming for Ethan. He comes rushing out of the bathroom, and I'm pointing at the computer.

"What the hell is wrong?"

"The computer. It-it-it's talking to me." His eyes widen, and he cautiously walks over and picks up the laptop. "Ah, Rocco, nice to see you. Put the phone in your hand down on the floor, please." Ethan looks just as dumbfounded as I am. He drops the phone to the floor and flips the laptop over and back like he's trying to see who's talking to him.

"Who are you? What do you want?" Ethan yells. Somehow, they can see us. Maybe if I black out the windows. I grab the remote control, and they all go dark.

"Good try, Lola, but I can still see you," the voice singsongs through the speaker. I hide behind Ethan and hold the back of his shirt.

"We don't like being threatened by The Organization. We live by our own rules. If you don't back off, we'll take your little Lola there and have our way with her. Do you understand?"

"We have a lot of enemies. Who do you work for?" Ethan asks.

"You'll have to figure that one out for yourself, Rocco. Remember what I said." The voice is gone, and my work pops back up on the screen. I'm holding on to Ethan for dear life.

"How could they see us?" I cry as he turns me around to face him, and I bury myself in his chest.

"I don't know. I'll have Daniel check the computer. It had to be through the camera. Maybe he can trace it somehow. I've already had the penthouse swept for cameras and microphones, but I'll call Freddy and have him do it again and take Daniel the laptop." I'm clinging to him and won't let go. He picks me up and sits me on his lap on the couch. I bury myself in his chest. I feel like a child, but this is the only thing that makes me feel safe.

"I see why you were so scared as a kid."

"You can't ever let them know you're afraid. That's what they want. You remember the things Jerry taught you, right?"

"I think so."

"Good. Run through them in your head. Try to prepare yourself in case you have to use them or the gun. I want you to start carrying it with you when you are out of this house."

"But I have Bennie."

"Things happen, Lo, just like when you were in the bathroom. I trust Bennie, but he's not invincible. He's just one person. He can't be everywhere. You must be aware of your surroundings."

"Okay, I'll put the gun in my work bag in the bedroom."

He holds me close. I use the remote to turn the windows back on, and we watch our sunset.

"Let's go to bed. I've had enough for today," I say.

"You go. I'll be there as soon as Freddy comes and sweeps the penthouse and takes your laptop."

We wake up like normal on Monday morning, and I get ready for work. Dressed in a navy-blue wrap dress and high heels, I pull my hair back in a bun and apply soft makeup for the day.

"Are you sure you don't want to stay home today?" Ethan asks.

"I'll be *fine*," I say, pulling him toward me for a kiss. "I have a couple of meetings today I have to attend. I won't be alone."

"Listen," he says in his serious voice. I turn to look at him. "If you feel that tingle in the pit of your stomach that tells you something isn't right, you tell Bennie and get the hell out of there."

I give him a quick kiss and run my palm down his handsome face. "I'll be fine. What are your plans for the day?"

"I'm going to see my father."

Chapter 44
Ethan

We're in my father's office at The Organization. I filled him in on everything that's been happening. We have a meeting with the heads of our car dealerships and the construction business. Sheila has lunch brought in for us, and we're sitting at the table eating.

"You need to get rid of that girl, Rocco," he says, digging into his corned beef sandwich.

"Look, we've been over this shit. Lola stays."

"She's only causing trouble. You're spending so much time protecting her that you're neglecting your duties."

"What the fuck are you talking about?"

"You're supposed to be finding out who the assassin is."

"They're a mystery. We've only hit dead ends looking for him. They haven't taken out any more of our clients, so I think it was just a fluke."

"There are no flukes, *boy*. You need to keep working on it."

"I will." I know who the fuck the assassin is, and *she* works for me. The longer I can keep him in the dark, the better for everyone concerned.

I'm standing in the office at the gym watching Sasha train with

Jerry on the monitors. I don't want her to know who I am just yet. I need her to focus on her training. She's made so much progress in the past six months, but now she needs to perfect her skills.

"Hit me harder!" Jerry barks at her. She leans back on her right leg and uses all her power to propel her glove into his face. "That's better, but I want more. Think about a memory that infuriates you. Someone you want to punish and hit me, dammit!"

She's tired and covered in sweat. Her face is flushed, and her hair falls out of the ponytail on the top of her head. They've been at it for a while now, but I don't miss the determination on her face. Jerry has really pissed her off. She hits him as hard as she can in the gut with her right and then an upper cut with her left. Jerry falls to the mat. Shaking the cobwebs out of his head, he smiles widely.

"That's what I'm talking about. Great job! Hit the showers," he says as she bounces out of the ring. Jerry slowly makes his way to his feet. He looks at me through the camera and nods his head. I know we have a killer on our hands if she can channel that rage.

"Are you listening to me, Rocco!" Antonio snaps me out of my thoughts.

"Yeah, I'm listening, and I told you Lola stays."

"Not her, the assassin!"

"I'll keep looking."

Chapter 45
Lola

It's Friday evening, and I'm at the penthouse alone. Ethan is meeting with the captains and will be home when he's done. The usual three guards are downstairs: Jackson, Vito, and Buddy. I take a bath, put on my baby-blue sweatpants and oversized hoodie, and watch our sunset alone.

Afterward, I grab some ice cream out of the freezer and hunker down under the blankets in bed and turn on Netflix. I'm watching a movie when there's a banging on my bedroom door. What the hell? I keep it locked because the elevator opens into the living room. I'm afraid if someone got to the elevator, they could get to me.

"Miss Lola, it's me, Buddy."

"You're not supposed to be in the penthouse, Buddy," I yell through the locked bedroom door.

"There's an emergency. Jackson sent me up here to get you and take you to Rocco." What do I do? Should I trust him? I pick up my cell and try to call Ethan, but the call goes straight to voicemail. I quickly leave him a message:

Ethan, Buddy says there's a threat, and he's bringing me to you. I'll see you soon. Until then.

"Let me change my clothes."

"There's no time, Miss Lola, we have to go NOW." I have that feeling in the pit of my stomach that Ethan was talking about. I go to the closet, grab my gun from the go bag, and put it in the pocket of my sweatpants. I grab my switchblade and tuck it into the front pocket of my hoodie. I push the hoodie down to cover my pocket and open the door. Buddy stands there, alone, and he looks nervous. He ushers me to the elevator.

When the elevator reaches the parking garage, I look for Jackson and Vito, but I don't see them. Overwhelming panic consumes me. This isn't right.

"Oh, I forgot my purse," I try to say calmly and turn to get back on the elevator, but Buddy is on to me. He clutches my upper arm and pulls me back just as the elevator doors close.

"You won't need your purse where you're going," he says. I look over to the right and see a pair of legs lying on the ground by a car. I squint, and I think it's Jackson. My breath hitches. I haven't seen Vito, but I'm sure he's been hurt too.

Buddy pushes me toward a black van. There's no fuckin' way I'm getting into that van without a fight.

"Ethan didn't send you here to get me! I'm not going with you!" I scream, dragging my feet, and try to drop all of my weight to the ground like Jerry taught me. Dammit! I dropped my phone.

A man in a black hoodie jumps out of the driver's side door and picks up my feet. They are trying to carry me toward the van, but I'm kicking and twisting trying to get free. I can't let them take me to a secondary location. I free one of my legs from the man's grip and connect with his knee. He falls to the ground and drops my legs.

"Son of a bitch!" Hoodie guy yells.

"Come on, man! Grab her!" Buddy yells at him. I push up with my legs, and my head connects with Buddy's chin, and I hear the crunch of teeth. He screams out in pain and drops me to the ground, and I run like hell. Ducking down behind cars, I make my way to the other side of the parking garage. I pull out my gun and take the safety off.

I'm panting, but I need to get control of myself. I have to figure out a way out of here. I see the stairwell off to the left and decide that's my best chance. Slowly weaving between the cars, I stay as close to the ground as I can. When I'm about a car's length away, I make a break for the stairwell. A large body comes out of nowhere and slams into me. On my way to the ground, I pull the trigger. My body screams in pain when I hit the concrete with Hoodie guy on top of me.

"You fuckin' bitch!" the man yells. I smile with satisfaction when I see blood seeping through his shirt at his shoulder. He stands and yanks me to my feet with his good arm, and Buddy comes back into view.

"What else are you hiding under these clothes, you little bitch?" He starts to search my pockets, fondling my breasts as he goes.

"I told you the next time I had you alone, I would take what I wanted from you, didn't I?" he snarls. He reaches into the pocket of my hoodie and finds the knife. He slaps me across the face, and a warm trickle of blood runs from my lip.

"I'm never going to stop fighting you. You can't do this!" I scream as I push and pull and jerk with all my might to get free.

"I can and I will, you *bitch*!" I feel a pinch on the side of my neck, and everything goes black.

When I wake up on a bed in a strange room, I'm only wearing my bra and panties. My wrists and ankles are spread wide and attached to the bed by black cuffs. I'm so cold. I shake my head to try to pull myself out of the fog from the sedative.

My eyes search the empty room, and I realize I'm alone. What the fuck am I waiting for? I begin to scream.

"HELP ME! PLEASE! SOMEBODY HELP ME!" Buddy comes busting in the door.

"Shut up, you stupid slut. No one can hear you screaming."

"Please let me go, Buddy. I won't tell anybody. Just let me go," I beg.

"No fucking way!"

"What does Antonio want with me now?"

"Antonio didn't send me to take you."

"Who did then?"

"DeLuca."

"DeLuca? I thought you work for Antonio?"

"DeLuca has been after you since he saw you at the restaurant that night. As soon as he connected you to Rocco, you had a target on your back."

"I don't understand."

"I've been working for DeLuca this whole time. Feeding him information to help take Antonio down. He's going to you use and Rocco to do it."

"Why does he want to kill Antonio?"

"The man has is reasons. I don't ask questions. DeLuca had me kidnap you to lead Rocco here. Then he's going to take him out. While Antonio is weak and grieving the death of his only beloved son, he'll kill him. And I get to see how good you look on my dick like I promised."

"Ethan won't fall for your plan."

"Oh really? Let's find out, shall we?" He walks over to the side table and picks up a piece of black material. He winds it around his fists and stalks toward me.

"Open your mouth," he barks.

I shake my head, but he grabs my cheeks and forces me to open wide. He puts the gag in my mouth and pulls it tight to the back of my head. He powers up my cell phone, which I thought I lost in the parking lot, and calls Ethan on FaceTime.

"Lola! Oh my God. Where are you, baby?" Buddy's dark, menacing laugh fills the room.

"Who the hell is this? Where's Lola?" Ethan snarls.

"It's me, Buddy. Don't you recognize me, Boss?" he says, turning the camera to his face.

"Buddy? What the fuck! Where's Lola?"

"Oh, she's here. But she can't talk to you right now. She's kinda… tied up."

"Let me talk to Lola!" his voice roars through the phone.

"If you insist." Buddy turns the camera around and points it at me, panning it across my body. He shows Ethan my bound hands and ankles, lingering on my almost naked body. I struggle under the restraints and try to scream, but the gag is too tight.

"You motherfucker! I'm gonna fucking kill you!"

"Now, now, now, Rocco. Mr. DeLuca wouldn't like it if I lost his bargaining chip."

"DeLuca? What the hell's going on, Buddy?"

"Mr. DeLuca will explain it all to you when you get here. I'll send you the address. Be here in thirty minutes." He hangs up on Ethan, types into the phone, and sets it back on the table. He leans his face close to mine. I can feel his hot whiskey breath on my cheek.

"Take a little nap before the festivities begin. You're going to need it. Because I'm going to see how you look on my cock before this is over with." He licks the side of my face before leaving me alone in the room.

Chapter 46
Ethan

finish the strategy meeting with all the captains and check my phone before leaving for the penthouse. There's a voicemail from Lola.

Ethan, Buddy says there's a threat, and he's bringing me to you. I'll see you soon. Until then.

I didn't tell Buddy to bring her here. What the fuck is going on? I try to call Jackson and Vito, but there's no answer. Fuck! Running to the control room, I find Daniel at his computer.

"Daniel, bring up the penthouse cameras," I demand. He works his magic, and the camera by the front door comes up on the screen, along with the parking garage and elevator cameras. No one is standing at their posts.

"Roll it back and see if you can see where everyone went." He hits some keys, and the video shows Jackson and Vito standing at their posts by the elevator. Shots are fired, blood splatters, and they both go down.

"What the fuck!" I slam my fist on the desk.

A tall man in a black hoodie grabs them one at a time and drags them out of the picture. On another camera, Buddy is escorting Lola into the elevator. She looks nervous. Daniel changes the camera view to inside the elevator. Lola is staring into the camera. She puts her hand in her hoodie pocket, and I can see the switchblade push at the material, and then she pats her leg. Or is that her pocket?

"She has a weapon. Good girl."

The elevator doors open, and they exit. She's looking all around and tries to turn and get back into the elevator, but Buddy grabs her by the arm. He's pulling her toward a black van. She's struggling and dragging her feet.

"Fight, baby, fight!" I yell at the screen.

The guy in the hoodie jumps out of the van and grabs her feet. She's bucking and twisting her body to get free. She wiggles out of his grasp, and one of her legs gets free. She wastes no time kicking the hoodie guy in the knee and pushing herself to her feet. She comes up right under Buddy's chin with her head. He drops her to the ground, and she breaks off running.

"Find her. Where did she go?" I yell at Daniel. He types, switching cameras until he finds her hiding behind a car near the stairwell. She waits and looks around, then takes off running toward the stairs. Hoodie guy comes into the frame and body-slams her to the ground.

"Son of a bitch!" I yell and turn away from the screen, punching the wall.

"Wait! She got off a shot," Daniel says. "He's bleeding."

"That's my girl!"

I'm so fucking proud of her. Hoodie guy pulls her back to her feet and holds her while Buddy puts his goddamn hands all over her. He finds the knife and pockets it. He slaps her across the face and yells something at her. Hoodie guy puts a needle in her neck, and she goes limp. They drag her body to the van and toss her into the back.

"Find out where this van goes and call me when you have a location."

"Yes, Boss." I storm out of the building and get into my car, headed for the location Buddy texted me. Calling my father, I put him on speakerphone.

"DeLuca has Lola."

"Goddammit, Rocco, I told you this would happen."

"Shut the fuck up! I need you to mobilize the men. Send half of them to meet me at the address I'm texting you now and have the other half hold for further instructions."

"Fine, b…" I hang up on him and drive like a bat out of hell. As I get closer to the address Buddy gave me, I realize it's the bridal shop where Freddy first saw DeLuca. I park around the corner and wait for the team.

Freddy meets me in the alley.

"What the fuck are we doing here?" he asks.

"This is the address Buddy sent me."

"Buddy?"

"Yeah, long story."

"I'll take Beckett and Rosco, and we'll go check it out." I watch the three of them approach the building. When I lose sight of them, Freddy keeps me posted on the earpiece. Beckett picks the lock on the back door, and they enter. In just a few seconds, there are screams, and women come running out of the front of the building. One is in a wedding dress.

"What the fuck is happening?" I yell.

"Boss, there's no one here. Just a bunch of women trying on dresses," Freddy says,

"Did you check the whole place?"

"Yes, Boss. Nothin'."

"Dammit!"

My phone rings, and it's Daniel.

"Please tell me you've got something."

"I followed the black van on the cameras. I know where it went."

"Send me the address and send it to Antonio too. Tell him to send the team to meet us there instead. We're on our way."

Lola

Buddy is laughing hysterically when he comes back into the room. My eyes spring open, and my breathing increases as he moves toward me like a lion stalking its prey.

"Well, Lola, your boyfriend fell for the bait and went to the wrong location. There'll be no one coming to save you. I get to have my fun with you after all." I'm pulling on my restraints and screaming into the gag.

Coming to a stop with his face directly above mine, he looks into my eyes and growls, "You might as well just give in, bitch, because this is going to happen. Just relax and enjoy the ride." His slimy tongue glides up my cheek once again, and I cringe at the touch. He takes my switchblade out of his pocket. I hear the swish of the blade as it snaps to attention.

"Let's get rid of these clothes, shall we?" He climbs on top of me and licks his lips while he pulls one bra strap away from my shoulder and cuts it free and then the other. I try to buck him off me with my hips, but he's up too high on my stomach, and the maneuver doesn't work. He pulls at the center of my bra and cuts it in half. Smiling like a psychopath, he stills above me as he focuses on my breasts. I'm surprised I don't see drool coming out of the sides of his mouth.

He runs his fingers across my breast and outlines my nipples. He takes one breast in each hand and squeezes so hard it causes me to whimper. He moves his fingers to my nipples and pinches hard, and I scream out in pain through my gag.

"I knew you liked it rough," he says as that loud menacing laugh escapes his lips once more. He moves down my body to sit on my thighs and takes in my panties, then runs his finger across the lace. Tears run out of my eyes and into my hair as I shake my head and cry into the gag.

He uses the knife to cut my panties free. After pulling them from my body, he pockets them in his black jeans.

"Now. This is what I'm talking about. Look at that sweet pussy just waiting for me to fuck it." I try to clutch my thighs together to keep him out, but my legs can only move so far in the restraints. He stands and removes the gag from my mouth.

"I want to hear you beg, bitch."

"I'll never beg for you!" He slaps me across the face.

"Shut up and take it like the little whore you are."

"Ethan is going to kill you! You son of a bitch!" He moves to the side of the bed, pulls his belt from the loops, and drops it on the bed beside me. He removes his pants and boxers, leaving him just in his black T-shirt when he climbs between my legs.

"No… Please… Stop…" I buck and struggle. He takes his cock in his hand and strokes it once, twice, three times. My eyes are on his every move. I won't give up. I'll fight until the very end. I pull on my restraints and scream as loud as I can.

"HELP ME! PLEASE! SOMEBODY HELP ME!" My throat is burning, scratchy, and raw, but I keep screaming.

"No one can hear you, bitch!"

There's a loud crash as the door bursts open with such force it slams against the interior wall. Freddy comes in first, gun drawn, followed by Nico, Beckett, and Roscoe.

"What the fuck!" Buddy yells. Before he can move a muscle, Freddy's muscular arm is around his neck and throwing him to the floor. He pins Buddy's half-naked body face down with his knee in his back.

"Clear!" Freddy yells.

Nico, Beckett, and Roscoe secure the area and take places around the bed to protect me. They turn their backs to me out of respect. Ethan comes in the door. There's shock on his face as he sees me lying naked, tied to the bed, but he moves in calm strides toward me. He rips off his shirt and covers my body with it.

He wastes no time removing the restraints that hold my wrists and ankles. I'm still shaking my head. My breathing is erratic, and I can't get control. I'm gasping for air as he takes my face in his hands and makes me look at him.

"Lola baby, breathe… breathe… breathe," he chants, staring into my wide eyes. I try to do as he says. "I'm going to move you." My eyes are trained on him as I shake my head frantically. He gathers me in his arms and places me in his lap, and I melt into his chest. My safe place, my home.

My arms and legs are numb from being tied up for so long, and I'm shivering with fear. He moves his shirt to my back, puts my arms in the sleeves, and buttons it up.

"Freddy, come take Lola to the other room. I don't want her to see this."

"No! No! Don't leave me!" I scream and cling to him like a child. "DeLuca is going to kill you. No! Please don't make me go." Tears stream down my face as panic takes over my body once again.

"Shh... Shh... Shh. It's okay." He runs his hand over my hair like he's petting me. Trying his best to calm me, he says, "I got you, baby. Shh, you're okay."

More men secure other areas of the building, and we hear shots fired. With each gunshot, I cower more into his chest. A guy I've never seen before comes into the room.

"Boss. The building is secure. We found a man with a bullet wound in his shoulder bleeding out in the outer room and five more guys outside. We took care of them."

"Good work, Holden. Call the cleaners," Ethan orders as he sets me gently on the bed, and I grab his arm. Before I can speak, he says, "I'm not leaving you, baby. I just need a few words with Buddy over there." I nod my head and pull his shirt tighter around my body. Freddy removes his knee from Buddy's back while Ethan grabs a fistful of his hair and pulls him to his knees.

"Where the fuck is DeLuca?"

"He's not here?" he asks sarcastically. Ethan punches him in the face, and his head snaps to the side. He lets out a groan.

"Where the fuck is he?" Ethan holds him by the neck of his shirt, shakes him, and punches him again.

"The... The... The bridal shop," he spits out.

"Bullshit! That's where your wild-goose chase sent us." *Smack. Smack. Smack.* "Stop protecting him and tell me where the fuck he is, and maybe I won't blow your fucking head off." Ethan takes out his gun and points it between his eyes.

"H-H-He's at the docks," Buddy finally stutters out.

"Why the docks?"

"While I was distracting you, he and another team were going to raid your Conex containers."

"Fuck! Nico, call the guys at the warehouse and tell them DeLuca is coming and to get ready, and we're on the way." Nico pulls out his phone and motions in the air to some guys, and they take off.

Before Ethan lets go of Buddy, he rears back his fist and hits him repeatedly in the face. When he releases the grip on his hair, he falls to the floor unconscious. I wince when I see his bloody, mangled face.

"Freddy, do you have this piece of shit handled so I can get Lola out of here?"

"Yes, Boss. I would be happy to take care of this *little* problem." He smiles, and I know he's talking about Buddy's shriveled-up little dick that's exposed to the room. Ethan looks down and sees Buddy's pants on the floor with my panties sticking out of the pocket.

"I believe these are mine," he grits as he pulls them from the pocket, and places them in his own. Ethan picks me up and holds me tightly to his chest, and we leave the room. As he walks down the hall toward the front door, he presses my head to his chest and covers my ear with his hand.

BANG.

The sound makes me jump, but Ethan doesn't stop walking until I feel him setting me in the back seat of the Escalade. He climbs in beside me and pulls me onto his lap. I know we are in the car and Ethan is holding me, but I'm still shaking uncontrollably. After Beckett gets in the driver's seat and Roscoe slides into the passenger seat, we speed toward the docks.

"I think she's in shock. Roscoe, give me your jacket, and turn up the heat back here."

"Yes, Boss." He takes off his jacket and reaches it over the seat. Ethan covers my legs with it and pulls me closer to him, kissing my temple and running his hand down my cheek.

"Lola, baby, I love you so much. Please don't hate me."

"What?"

"This is all my fault. I never should have let Buddy anywhere near you. I should've taken care of him the first time he tried to touch you. I'll never make that mistake again."

"Eth—" He cuts me off. This time, he's the one talking a mile a minute.

"I'm sorry. I never wanted you to get hurt. I'm so sorry."

"E—"

"I'm so fuckin' proud of you. I saw you on the cameras from the penthouse. You fought like hell."

"Ethan!" I chirp. His mouth snaps shut, and his body stills. "You didn't do this."

"Oh, Lola." He pulls me in close to his chest again. "I don't know what I would do if I lost you." He peppers me with kisses.

"I tried to remember the things Jerry taught me. But they still took me." My voice is shaky and defeated.

"You were amazing. There wasn't much you could do about a needle in your neck."

Chapter 47
Ethan

We arrive at the dock in record time. The crane is uploading our containers to the cargo ship as we pull in. The process is slow and methodical. The containers are filled with expensive stolen cars, and each one is filled with weapons. Lola has stopped shivering and has relaxed into my chest. I turn to move her to the seat, and her body tenses.

"Lola, I have to go. Just for a little while."

"No, you can't leave me." Her hands cling to my neck, and her eyes widen with fear.

"I don't want you to get upset again, but you need to stay here with Beckett. He won't leave you alone." Her fingernails sink deep into my arm as she frantically shakes her head. I take her face in my hands and hold it still, forcing her eyes to focus on mine. I calmly say, "He'll keep you safe while I check on my men." She looks from Beckett to me.

"He's not like Buddy. I promise. We can trust him." She nods and sits back on the seat, smashing herself into the corner by the door. Curling her knees into herself, she covers up with the jacket. I snarl, pointing my finger in his face.

"If you let anyone near her, I'll kill you."

"Yes, Boss." His back snaps to attention. I wait for him to lock them both inside the Escalade before Rosco and I head for the warehouse.

We meet up with the team Antonio sent. The sound of gunfire fills the air, and we run toward it. Stopping at the side of the building, I peek around the wall to see two of my guards lying on the ground.

"Dammit! Half of you go with Roscoe, and the rest of you come with me. If they're not with The Organization, shoot them. Let's go!" Guns drawn, we cautiously enter the warehouse and find DeLuca sitting in a chair off to the side of the room, waiting for us. He leans back, his left ankle perched on his right knee, cigar to his lips.

Blowing out the smoke, he says, "I knew you would figure out where I was. Buddy's such an idiot, but he made a good distraction for a little while." He speaks in his thick Italian accent.

"Yeah, well, he's dead," I snap.

"I figured he would be. We're almost done here. Have a seat," he says, motioning for me to sit in the metal chair off to his left.

"What the fuck do you think you're doing, DeLuca? Why did you take Lola?" I bark.

"That was Buddy's idea. Something about she owed him a good fuck or something," he says, waving his hand. "It was supposed to be a distraction to keep you away from the docks so I could take your inventory."

"You know I can't just let you *take* our inventory."

"I'm tired of you telling me what I can and cannot do. I came to this country for revenge, and that's exactly what I'm going to get."

"You want revenge on who?" I ask.

"I've come for your father."

"My father. Why?"

"Oh, Rocky, my boy. You don't know who I am, do you?

"Am I supposed to know who the fuck you are?"

"I'm your big brother."

"Bullshit!"

"Here, let's bring *our* father out, and you can ask him." He turns to a tall woman with tons of curly red hair standing off to the side. With a nod of his head, she leaves. Shortly, two guards bring in a tied-up Antonio. He fights them with every step. The guards throw him down in the other chair and pull the duct tape from his mouth.

"You motherfucker!" he barks out as he thrashes around.

"Now, now, *Father*. Tell Rocco here who I am." My eyes shift between my father and DeLuca. Someone better start talking.

"He's your older brother," he says hesitantly.

"What the fuck! How?"

"Yes, tell him *how* we are brothers, *Father*," DeLuca says teasingly.

Antonio clears his throat and begins.

"My father arranged a marriage for me in Italy when I turned eighteen. Her name was Angelica. I had already fallen madly in love with your mother and refused to marry the girl, but my father wouldn't hear of it.

On your mother's eighteenth birthday, we were all set to sneak away to France. Somehow they found about our plans and stopped us.

Angelica's father and brother drug me from your mother's home. The priest and Angelica were waiting in the living room at the farm when we arrived. Our fathers forced us to marry. Then they made us consummate the marriage on the desk in his office, while they watched. Your mother was heartbroken."

"My father assumed I had given up. I let him think I had let your mother go and accepted the life he arranged for me. All the while, Lucia and I secretly planned our escape. The night finally came to leave. I said goodbye to Angelica like every evening when I went to work in town. I walked out the door, and I never saw her again. Your mother and I ran for our lives under the cover of darkness. We left with the clothes on our backs and what little money we had in our pockets, intending to never look back."

"How did you find out about DeLuca?" I ask.

DeLuca continues the story. "Her father, my grandfather, applied to the church for an annulment because you deserted her. She was married off to a cruel man by the name of Alessandro DeLuca. That son of a bitch would beat my mother to a pulp when he drank. I would hide in the closet and cover my ears to block out her screams. He went too far when I was eight.

"My mother was begging him to stop hitting her. She told him she couldn't take anymore but he kept punching and kicking her, all the while calling her names. He told her when he was done beating her, he was going to beat me next. She pleaded with him to leave me alone. All she ever wanted to do was keep me safe. When I heard the front door slam, I came to the kitchen and found my mother lying on the kitchen floor. One eye was swollen and the other was black and blue. There were cuts on her arms and legs and blood ran from her nose. I wanted to run for the doctor, but she grabbed my hand and begged me to stay. With her dying breath, she told me that beast was not my father, but you were." He points at Antonio.

"That your fathers forced you to marry, but you ran like a coward to America with another woman. She died in my arms that day, and I was left to be raised by that monster. He raised me as his only heir, and he punished me every day for it. I took my share of beatings until I was old enough to beat the shit out of him instead. When the time was right, I killed the motherfucker and took over everything, vowing I would come to America and find Antonio Martinelli and kill him for what he did to my mother and for ruining our lives."

"How could you marry my mother if you were married to Angelica?" I ask, turning to face my father.

"We thought we could never marry, but we didn't care as long as we were together. When I got word from Italy that Angelica had died, we knew we were finally free and could be man and wife. By then, we were twenty-five years old, and our empire was beginning to grow."

"Why don't you tell him about his mother?" DeLuca says as his lips turn into an evil grin.

"What are you talking about?" I ask.

"Go on, tell him, *Father*. Tell him how your beloved Lucia died."

"She had cancer, and she died at the hospital," Antonio says somberly, looking down at his tied wrists.

"Now, you and I both know that's not the whole story," he says, shaking his head.

"I don't know what you're talking about," Antonio barks.

"Sure, you do. You know there are cameras in hospital rooms for monitoring purposes, right?" My father's face goes as white as snow.

"Father, what's he talking about?" I ask.

"I didn't have a choice. She made me do it."

"Made you do what?" I growl.

"She was in so much pain. She said she couldn't go on. She told me to give her the shot and end her pain," he says, tears filling his eyes.

"You what?"

"He killed her," DeLuca says, his lips returning to his sadistic smile. My eyes snap to my father.

"No! It wasn't like that," Antonio defends.

"Please, tell us what it was like then, Father." My voice is haunting.

"I loved your mother with every ounce of my soul, Rocco. You know that. We were destined to be together forever, and I haven't been with another woman since. When she got sick, I took her to every doctor for every treatment I could find. I couldn't lose her." He's wringing his tied hands, and tears are running down his face. "The day she left us... she begged me to do it."

"She begged you to do what?" I lunge at him, but DeLuca's men hold me back from him.

"I didn't want to do it. I begged her not to make me, but she said she couldn't go on. She didn't want her children and grandchildren to see her suffer." Emotions pouring from his soul, he says, "I loved her." I can almost see his heart breaking in his chest.

"What did you do to her?" I grit out, clenching my teeth.

"She had a vial of medicine on the counter."

"Where did she get it?"

"I don't know. She told me to fill the syringe and inject her with it. I said no, but she pleaded with me to do it. To let her go. She begged me...I filled the syringe, climbed into her bed, took her into my arms, and held her while the medicine took her from me." Leaning over like he was just punched in the gut, he cries uncontrollably. "I didn't want to do it! I loved her!"

"Oh my God. That's why you became so heartless. Because *you* killed her," I say, shaking the goons off me. "I should kill you myself!"

"Now, now. Can't you see the man is in pain?" DeLuca says condescendingly. "I have a deal for you, Rocco."

"What kind of deal?"

"I know you have this dream about being *Le. Gi. Ti. Mate*," he says slowly, stabbing every syllable.

"So."

"You give me the guns and the cars that I want, and I will kill our father. I'll fly back to Italy where I belong. The laced drugs will be out of your city for good, and you will never hear from me again. We can all live out our lives in peace."

"Or?"

"You don't make a deal. I kill you both and your little girlfriend out in the parking lot in the black Escalade. Then I will take everything you have, *Brother*." I look from DeLuca to my father and back.

"Rocco, no, Son. You can't be thinking about it?"

"Why wouldn't I? *Father*. You killed my mother, you kidnapped Lola *twice*, and you forced me into a life I never wanted."

"It was for your own good. For the family."

"Well, this is for the family." I shake DeLuca's hand and say, "Let me get Lola out of here before you do it."

"Of course."

"No. Son. No. You can't do this!" Antonio is screaming as I walk away. Never looking back, I snap my fingers and *my* men follow me. Making my way to the car, I slide into the back seat and pull Lola back onto my lap.

"Get the fuck out of here," I instruct Beckett.

"Where to?"

"Home."

BANG.

Lola is asleep in my arms when we reach the penthouse. She's physically and emotionally drained from this ordeal. Carrying her inside, I lay her on the bed and cover her with the duvet. I take the burner phone out of the dresser drawer and step into the hallway. I bring it up to my ear, and it's answered after two rings.

"Yeah," Sasha answers.

"Antonio's dead. DeLuca killed him."

"Dammit. I wanted to do it."

"I have a new assignment for you."

"Who?"

"DeLuca."

Chapter 48
Sasha

Dressed in a dark-blue flight attendant uniform, black patent leather flats, with my black hair pulled back into a tight bun, I'm in the galley of Eliseo DeLuca's private jet preparing the cabin for departure.

I walk to the front of the plane and address the pilot.

"Are we all set?" Rosco turns and gives me a thumbs-up, and I lock him in the cockpit. I stand by the entrance to the plane and greet DeLuca and his five flunkies with a friendly smile. The men take their seats, and I ask for DeLuca's drink order.

"Would you like something to drink, sir?"

"Scotch."

"Yes, sir." I turn and go to the galley and come back with his drink. I take drink orders for the other five men. I prepare their drinks with an added ingredient and pass them out with a big smile. Taking my empty tray, I return to the galley and prepare for takeoff.

By the time we're cruising at 30,000 feet, the five men are fast asleep. DeLuca's nose is buried deep in his phone. He doesn't notice me as I walk by each of his men and bump them with my leg to be sure they're out cold. Moving to the back of the plane, I retrieve my gun, place the suppressor on it, and slide into the seat behind DeLuca.

Readying myself for what I'm about to do, I take a cleansing breath and stand, pointing the gun to the side of his head.

"What the fuck is this?" he yells. I glance at the other men, and none of them stir, so I move forward and speak in my sweet flight attendant voice.

"Good afternoon, Mr. DeLuca. I will be your entertainment for this flight."

He turns to look at the guards, then turns his head back to me.

"Look. I don't know who you think you are, but you can't do this."

"Oh, but I can. I was sent here to do a job. And that's exactly what I'm going to do."

"Who sent you?"

"Your brother."

"My brother? How the hell—" I cut him off before he can continue.

"You shouldn't have underestimated the younger Mr. Martinelli. He's very resourceful and was eager to take over for his father all along. You just made it easier for him."

"What are you going to do? Turn the plane around and take me back to Rocco?"

"Oh no, that would be inconvenient. I'm going to shoot you all in the head right here."

"What the fuck?"

"But first, I need you to sign these papers Rocco sent for you."

When I reach for the papers, he moves to stand.

"Tsk... tsk... tsk... that's not a good idea," I say, pointing the gun between his eyes. His eyes grow wide, and he slowly sits back down.

"I can tie you up if I have to, but I thought we could be civil about this." Knowing I only have a little more time before his thugs begin to wake, I hand him the pen.

"Sign on the dotted lines, please."

"What the hell am I signing?"

"You're signing all of your business interests, homes, cars... everything you own over to Rocco Ethan Martinelli."

"Like hell, I will!"

"You can, and you will," I grit out as I point the gun at his forehead and cock it. Just then, one man begins to stir. Without hesitation, I turn my gun, shoot him in the head, and immediately turn back to DeLuca. His eyes are bulging from their sockets, and he begins to shake.

"Okay. Okay. Whatever you want, just don't kill me." He takes the papers I'm holding and begins to sign.

"Make sure you sign all six places." He signs them all and hands the papers back to me.

"Thank you for your cooperation today."

BANG.

I walk over to the four other sleeping men and shoot them.

BANG.

BANG.

BANG.

BANG.

Heading to the front of the airplane, I knock on the cabin door three times, and Roscoe opens it.

"Everything good?"

"Yep, all dead. I'll get them ready for disposal. You can turn the plane around." Roscoe gets on the radio and tells the air traffic controller we need to turn the plane around for medical reasons. They give him the clearances he needs, and we bank to the left.

Upon landing, an ambulance waits on the tarmac to take away our "sick" patients. It's really our cleaning crew. They load the bodies into the ambulance and board the plane to clean up the mess. Roscoe and I exit and head in separate directions to meet up with the team at the mansion.

When we enter the room, Rocco, Jackson, Vito, Freddy, Nico, and Beckett are there. Rocco raises his glass to us.

"Here they are! How did it go?"

"Just like you planned, Boss," I say, handing him the papers.

"Good, and the cleaning crew took over before you left?"

"Yes, Boss," Roscoe answers.

"You now own all of DeLuca's interests in Italy and Antonio's here."

He stands and raises his glass of scotch for a toast.

"To the new era of The Martinelli Organization."

Chapter 49
Ethan

Upon entering the penthouse, I see Lola asleep on the couch by the windows. It's been a week since everything went down at the warehouse. She took off work with a warning from Mr. Kingsley that if she missed any more work, he'd let her go. She doesn't need to work, but I know my Lola wants to work. She's so passionate and creative that she needs an outlet for it. I get on my knees beside the couch and rub my knuckles over her soft cheek until her eyes flutter open.

"Hey," she whispers. Taking in a deep, cleansing breath, she stretches.

"Hey, you. How are you feeling?"

"Good," she says. I place a kiss on her sweet lips.

"I have a surprise for you." She sits up on the couch.

"A surprise? What kind of surprise?" She leans forward, looking for something behind my back.

"It's not that kind of surprise. It's more of a… place."

"A place? I'm confused."

"I need to go to Italy to take care of some business. I thought maybe you would like to come along. We can go shopping and take in some museums and restaurants. What do you say?"

"Mr. Kingsley will fire me." She frowns.

"Would that be so bad?" She opens her mouth to argue, and I put up my hands for a time-out.

"Hear me out first." She closes her mouth and gestures for me to continue.

"I know you love working there, but if you think about it, you've already gone as far up the ladder as you can go. Unless you want Kingsley's job? Why not leave and build something of your own? It can be advertising or anything else you want it to be. We have plenty of money. You can do whatever you want." I motion for her to say that it's her turn to speak.

"I would love to build something of my own, but the money is yours, Ethan. It's not mine."

"Marry me then, and it'll all be *ours*." I'm already on my knees, so I reach into my pocket and pull out a ring box. I open it and hold it out to her.

"Lola Marie Patterson, I love you with all of my heart. I think I knew you were the one for me the moment we met. Will you marry me?" Her hands fly to her mouth, and tears fill her eyes. "I told you when everything with my father was over, I would propose to you with the biggest ring I could find. It's not the biggest, but it was my mother's." She doesn't move. A soft glow comes over her face as the sun sets over our city. "Well… will you be Mrs. Rocco Ethan Martinelli?"

"Yes!" she squeals and jumps toward me. After pushing me over onto the floor, she climbs on top of me. Taking my cheeks in her hands, she kisses me over and over. When she pulls back, we laugh, and I flip her over on her back.

"I love you so much," I croon into her neck, and she raises her hips to me. "What does my baby girl want?"

"You. Only you, Ethan. It's only ever been you," she says, kissing me back. Her eyes spring open, and she says excitedly, "Can we take Amelia and Freddy too? She can help me pick out a wedding dress." She has the biggest smile while she holds her breath for my response.

"Yes, of course." I chuckle at her excitement. "You girls can do that while I meet with the Mafioso."

"Mafioso? What are you talking about?" She pushes me back.

"I can't run DeLuca's interests effectively from here. Why would his men listen to me from thousands of miles away? If I can sell his interests to them, we can finally be free of this nightmare."

"Do you think the Mafioso will go for that?"

"I don't know, but it's worth a try. I've already called and spoken to their leader, Enzo Troponi, and he's willing to meet with me."

"I have a lot to do before I can go. I have to tell Amelia. I have to clean out my office. Oh, and I'll have to quit my job first, of course." She's smiling and talking fast while her hands are gesturing all around. I grab them in mine and pull them above her head.

"But first, Miss Patterson, can I make love to my future wife?" I place a soft kiss on her lips.

"Yes, please, Mr. Martinelli."

Chapter 50
Lola

Things are happening so quickly that I can barely keep up. I went into the office this morning and resigned from Kingsley and Masters. As part of my NDA, I requested Amelia receive one week of paid time off without retribution so she can travel to Italy with us.

"Amelia, I need you to come in here, please," I say over the intercom. She comes into my office with her notepad and sits down.

"You won't be needing that."

"Why? What's going on?"

"I resigned this morning."

"You did *what*?" She jumps to her feet.

"I had to. Everything is changing so fast after Antonio's death. Ethan found out he had a brother in Italy. Then he mysteriously died, leaving everything to him. And then yesterday... Ethan proposed." I hold out my hand, showing her the beautiful two-carat oval-cut diamond ring. "It was his mother's."

Inspecting my finger. "It's gorgeous." She sighs, sitting back in her chair.

"Thank you. When he told his sisters he was proposing, they insisted he give it to me."

"What else is changing?" Amelia asks.

"I'm thinking about starting a battered women's shelter. I've been throwing around some ideas, and Ethan said he would support me." The expression slides off her face again.

"When I decide what I'm doing, I want to know if you would come to work with me?"

"Oh my gosh, yes, of course!" She pulls me in for a hug, and there's that smile again.

"And one more thing. Will you be my maid of honor?" Now she is jumping up and down and hugging me.

"Yes, I would love to."

"I worked out a deal with Kingsley for you to get a week off with pay starting Wednesday… to come with me to Milan to look at gowns."

"What do you mean by worked a deal?" she asks.

"Well, I had to sign an NDA when I resigned. I insisted he give you a week of paid vacation with no retribution."

"Wow! I bet he hated the shit out of that." She laughs. "Thank you. I would love to go with you."

"Well, it won't just be me. There will be the security teams, Ethan, Freddy, and… we are flying on a private jet."

"Are you *trying* to kill me? Are there any other surprises you haven't told me about? Like, are you pregnant too?"

"No… not pregnant." I laugh. "I told you everything has been moving fast lately. So get your shit together and be ready for Bennie to pick you up at eight o'clock on Wednesday morning."

"I'll be waiting on the curb if you want me to be." She laughs.

DeLuca's jet is part of the deal Ethan has been negotiating with the Mafioso. Roscoe is flying that jet, along with four guards, to an undisclosed location, and they will wait for Ethan. Vito is flying Ethan, Freddy, Amelia, four guards, and me on the Martinelli jet.

We land in Milan and go straight to our hotel, Radiante Paradiso. It's near shopping and restaurants and has extensive security. The elevator has direct access to our suite for safety.

Amelia and I can't speak when we're ushered into the four-bedroom, five-bathroom suite. It's stunning. There's a large living room, a kitchen, and an elegant dining room. I let Amelia have the princess room because her eyes bugged out of her head when she saw the lavender accents and shell-shaped headboard. I'm sure Freddy will be sharing it with her—for her safety, of course. Ethan and I will be in the primary bedroom with the crystal chandelier, private sitting area, walk-in closet, and king-sized bed. It has a large oval tub and a steam shower, and the views are incredible.

Beckett and Holden will be our guards while we're here. I knew Holden looked familiar. He was the guy who was there to give Ethan a report when they found me after the kidnapping. Ethan has arranged a butler service to provide meals and anything else we might need.

"This is incredible, Ethan, but it's so expensive."

"Only the best for my fiancée." He cuddles me into a big hug. "I want you two to have fun, but you need to remember to be safe. Even though no one knows who you are here, you still need to be aware of your surroundings and always have a guard with you."

"We promise," we say in unison.

"I'm taking two of the guards back to the airport with me, and I should be back sometime tomorrow. I'm leaving Beckett and Holden here with you. Freddy will be up in a few minutes."

"Where are you going?" Amelia asks.

"To an undisclosed location. They want to keep it as private as possible. This is their territory, so we follow their rules."

"Please be careful."

Taking my face in his hands, Ethan kisses me long and hard. "You know I will. Because I want to come home to these lips." He kisses me again, then walks to the elevator, and the three of them get inside.

"See you tomorrow," I say. He leans out of the elevator for one more quick kiss.

"Until then," he says, and the doors close.

Beckett takes our luggage to our rooms, and Holden plants himself in a chair next to the elevator. Freddy comes up shortly after with the butler.

"This is Jeffrey. He'll be our butler," Freddy says. He takes Amelia in his arms, and I look away to give them a little privacy as they say hello.

"Signora… Signora…" he says as he nods to each of us and speaks in a thick Italian accent.

"We're all exhausted. Do you think we could get something to eat before we go to sleep?" I ask Jeffrey.

"But of course, Signora. I will get something ready while you relax."

"Thank you."

We go to our rooms and unpack. I take a long bath in the enormous tub, and the food is on the table by the time I'm done. Jeffrey leads us to the dining room, and there's pizza waiting for us. The most delicious-looking pizza I have ever seen.

"Americans like pizza, yes?" Jeffrey asks.

"Yes," we all say. There was Neapolitan style with a thick, fluffy crust and Roman style with a thin crust. He brings wine to wash it down with. When we are all stuffed to the gills, I find my bed and collapse.

Amelia and I are up early the next day and ready to shop. Jeffrey has a gourmet breakfast of crepes, fruit, assorted pastries, and coffee waiting for us.

"This is amazing, Jeffrey. Thank you so much," I say. Holden was up all night, standing guard. He eats and goes to bed. Beckett takes over guard/shopping duty.

After breakfast, Amelia and I get ready for a long day of dress shopping. I'm sure I'll hear *it has to be the perfect dress* a thousand times today, but I still can't wait. Freddy and Beckett escort us to the city center to see the architecture and statues before we venture into a nearby bridal salon.

Amelia finds a gorgeous, off-the-shoulder lavender chiffon gown for her maid of honor duties. They have lavender shoes and a bag to match. She looks like an angel.

Feet hurting and arms full of bags, we return to the hotel. No word yet from Ethan or Roscoe, but I try to push down the worry and take a nap.

Chapter 51
Ethan

I leave Lola at the hotel with Amelia, Freddy, Beckett, and Holden while the rest of us make our way back to the airport. Vito had the plane refueled and was ready for departure. A messenger arrives with an envelope that holds the coordinates to the designated location. They already had a flight plan filed, so we took off immediately.

We land at our top secret destination. Roscoe and two guards stay behind to prepare the plane for takeoff, and the rest of us exit onto the runway. Three black Mercedes Benz G-class vehicles are waiting for us. We climb in and are driven about ten minutes to a large mansion built into the side of a mountain. I don't think I would have noticed it if I hadn't been looking for it. On the porch is a short, gray-haired man with a thin mustache standing with his arms outstretched.

"Ciao a tutti," (hello everybody) he bellows. This man is way too friendly to be the Enzo Troponi I have heard stories about. The cold-hearted killer who takes what he wants and leaves no survivors in his wake. I walk up the stairs and shake his hand with a friendly smile.

"Grazie Bello" (thank you), I say.

"Ah, do you speak Italian?" he asks in broken English.

"Not really." I smile.

"But at least you try." He chuckles. "Come in, come in."

We are all led into an ornate dining room. It has a large, intricately carved mahogany table in the center of the space that can easily seat twenty or more people.

"Sit. Sit." He gestures to me. My men spread out around the room and keep watch.

"Thank you for agreeing to meet with me," I say.

"But of course. I think this arrangement will be beneficial to both of us," he says.

"You had a chance to look over my proposal, then?"

"Yes, and I'm very interested. Please, tell me what happened to DeLuca?" He gestures to the butler to fill our glasses with wine.

"Let's just say, he killed my father, and I killed him," I say matter-of-factly.

"He always was an idiota."

"Before he died, he signed everything over to me."

"That was very kind of him." He smirks.

"Yes, it was." I chuckle. "I love your beautiful country, but I have no desire to run his interests from such a great distance. I was hoping you would take them off my hands... for a reasonable price. I want to wash my hands of Eliseo DeLuca forever."

"Everything, you say?"

"Yes, all of his interests. His home, cars, plane...everything."

Enzo spins the end of his mustache between his index finger and thumb while he thinks. He pulls a folded piece of paper from his pocket and lays it flat on the table. Holding it down with his fingers, he slides it across the table to me.

"This is what I can offer you."

I pick up the piece of paper and discreetly look at it. "House, plane, cars... everything?"

"Yes," he says, nodding in agreement.

I take a pen from my jacket pocket and write a larger amount underneath his. I place the paper back on the table. Using my finger, I slide it back across the table to him.

"I was thinking more like this."

Enzo is quiet for a few moments. A wide smile crosses his face, and he stretches his hand out to me.

"Deal. My lawyer is in the office down the hall. While he draws up the *official* papers, let us eat! Tell your men to sit."

I gesture for the men to sit at the table. A flurry of people entered the room carrying dishes, silverware, wine, and trays full of food.

When our meal is over, Enzo and I retreat to his office to sign the final papers. The money is electronically transferred into my account. When I get confirmation from Sheila it has been received, it's time for us to leave.

"It was nice to meet you, my friend," I say, holding my hand out to shake. He pulls me in for a hug and kisses me on both cheeks.

"If I am ever in America, I will look you up, as they say." He waves his hands around.

"Of course." I chuckle.

"We are friends now. If you ever need anything, you can count on me," he says.

"I feel the same way...my friend."

The men and I are taken back to the plane. Our takeoff is smooth, and we are on our way back to Milan and my Lola.

When we arrive back at the hotel, it's after midnight, and we're all exhausted.

"Get some sleep. You all deserve it. I'll text you with plans for tomorrow," I tell the men before they set off to locate their rooms on various floors.

Exiting the elevator into our room, Holden stands at the ready.

"It's just me, Holden. Is everyone asleep?" I ask quietly.

"Yes, sir. But Miss Lola is asleep on the patio. She was looking at the stars or something and fell asleep. I didn't want to wake her."

"Thank you." I head for the patio. Sure enough, I find Lola sound asleep on the couch. She's lying on her side, surrounded by brightly colored pillows and covered in a cream-colored throw. I stand above her, stroking her cheek, watching her sleep. Her eyes flutter open, and they focus on me.

"Are you watching me sleep... stalker?" She giggles.

"I can't help it. You're so beautiful." She sits up and pulls me down to her for a hug.

"Did everything go the way you wanted it?" Sitting down beside her, I put my arm around her. She lays her head on my shoulder and cuddles into me.

"Yes, he bought it all."

"Everything?"

"Yes, the house, plane, cars, and businesses. All of it."

"Ethan, that's amazing!"

"How was your day shopping with Amelia? Did you find a wedding dress?"

"No, but Amelia found a dress for the wedding."

"You didn't find anything you liked at all?"

"I tried on some beautiful dresses. But none of them felt like *the one*."

I hear the sadness in her voice. Turning her face to look at me, I ask, "What's the matter?"

"I don't know."

"Are you having second thoughts about the wedding?"

"God, no, I love you so much. I want to marry you. It's just..." Tears start to well up in her eyes.

"It's what, baby? Tell me."

"I miss my mom. I wish she would've been there with me today." She bursts into tears.

"Oh, honey, I'm so sorry."

"I'm being silly," she says, wiping the tears out of her eyes. She's trying to shove her emotions down, but I know this is killing her.

"You most certainly are not. You miss your mom. I miss mine too, but I think it's different for a woman."

"It's every girl's dream to have their mother with them when they pick out their wedding dress. To know it's the perfect one when she bursts into tears when she sees you in it. I will never have that, Ethan. I'm afraid I'll never have that feeling." I pull her onto my lap and cuddle her.

"You know. I have three sisters at home who would love to go dress shopping with you. You all need to get to know each other, anyway. Why not do it while wedding dress shopping in Italy?" I bring up the group chat with my sisters.

Hey, anyone still awake?

LIL

I have three children, Rocky. You know I'm awake.

MEME

I'm here. The baby kept me up all night too.

GILLY

I'm here. I haven't been to bed yet.

Would any of you be interested in wedding dress shopping with Lola?

LIL

YES!

MEME

Yes!

GILLY

You're paying, right?

Of course.

GILLY

I'm in.

LIL

Where are you?

Italy. I can send the jet for you.

MEME

Dress shopping in Italy. OMG!

GILLY

Where are we staying?

Radiante Paradiso.

GILLY

Little brother, you splurged!

> Only the best for my bride-to-be.

LIL

I'll be ready.

MEME

Me too.

GILLY

Me too.

> Let me get the flight plans going, and I'll text you the details.

MEME

Can't wait to meet Lola.

LIL

Me too, a few days with no children. Woo Hoo!

GILLY

See you soon, little brother.

"See, I told you. I know it's not *your mom*, but now you have three sisters."

Lola straddles my lap and kisses me deeply.

"Can we go to bed now?"

"Your wish is my command."

Chapter 52
Lola

While we wait for the sisters to arrive, Ethan, Freddy, Amelia, Beckett, Holden, and I board the high-speed train to Rome. It takes three and a half hours to get there from Milan.

Amelia's organizational skills kick into high gear. She planned a bus trip for us to get the most out of our few hours there. We saw San Pietro and the Colosseo, Villa Borghese, and the Pantheon, and had a magnificent meal in Testaccio. We walked back to the hotel at dusk and enjoyed the scenery.

Amelia and I were up early for a quick shopping trip before we boarded the train back to Milan. We have been in Italy for four days, and it's been a whirlwind.

His sisters arrive late Sunday morning in a flurry of sound and excitement. I looked them all over quickly as they came into the suite. Trying to see who looks the most like Ethan. I think it's Guilia. She has his eyes and nose.

"This place is amazing," Guilia says, walking into the suite and right past us.

"Everybody, I want you to meet Lola, my fiancée," Ethan says. His arms circle my body from behind. I awkwardly wave.

"Hi. It's nice to meet you." I'm nervous as hell. What if they don't like me?

"Hi. I'm Lilliana, but they call me Lil." She pulls me into her for a big hug. "Welcome to the family."

"Thank you," I say shyly.

The next to step forward is Maria.

"I'm so glad my little brother got his shit together and proposed. We've never seen him this happy before." She plants kisses on both of my cheeks. "Oh, and they call me MeMe."

"Thank you, MeMe."

Ethan points at the last sister.

"And this ball of energy is my sister, Guilia, but we call her Gilly. It sounds like Jilly, but we spell it with a G."

"Nice to meet you," I say, not knowing what to expect from her: a hug or kisses on the cheek. Instead, what I get is annoyance.

"Yeah, good to meet you. Where do I put my stuff?" she says abruptly.

"We changed rooms around so we all could stay in this suite together. I thought it would be fun. Like a giant slumber party," I say. Freddy has already been staying in the room with Amelia. We moved Beckett and Holden down the hall to a suite. Bags in hand, we start down the hall.

"This one's mine," Lilliana says quickly, like picking shotgun. Her smile is wide as she claims the largest bedroom.

"Oh, shit. Here we go," Ethan whispers under his breath.

"Why do you get the biggest room?" Gilly snarks.

"Because I'm the oldest, and I have three kids. I'm exhausted and need my rest." Sticking out her tongue, Gilly moves down the hall to the last room. It has two big beds and a sitting area.

"This is some fancy shit, little brother," MeMe whistles.

"Yeah, I guess this room will do as long as MeMe doesn't snore," Gilly says with a wink.

She spins around with her hands on her hips.

"I. Do. Not. Snore."

"I guess I'll be the one to find out, now, won't I?" Gilly says, tossing her luggage on the rack and starting to put away her things.

"We'll let you guys get settled. Freshen up or whatever you women do, and lunch will be at one," he says. I pull him by the arm, and we sit on the patio and enjoy some sunshine.

The girls are tired from their travels, but when Monday morning rolls around, they're up and ready to go dress shopping. I kiss Ethan quickly, and we're out the door with Holden and Beckett hot on our heels.

"What kind of dress are you looking for, Lola?" Lil asks.

"I'm not sure."

Amelia chimes in. "It has to be the perfect one." *Yeah, yeah, I get it.*

"What styles have you tried on so far?" MeMe asks.

"I tried a mermaid and a trumpet at the first store and an off-the-shoulder and a backless one at the second. They were nice, but just not right for me."

"You looked knockout gorgeous in all of them. But you weren't *feeling it*," Amelia says, making air quotes with her fingers.

"The three of us love to shop, and with Rocky's black AmEx card, this will be a blast," Gilly says, twirling the card in her hot little fingers.

"Oh, I don't want to spend too much," I say.

"Don't want to spend too much? That's what a black AmEx card is for, honey," she says. We all follow her into a bridal salon. We are met by a somber older woman who looks bored and a younger lady dressed in all black.

"Please come in. How can we help you today?" the older lady asks.

"I'm looking for my wedding dress."

"Ah, American. Welcome to Italia. Do you have anything in mind?" she says in broken English.

"No, not really," I say.

Amelia replies, "Something sparkly."

MeMe answers, "Something romantic."

Lil gushes, "Something she can dance in."

Gilly blurts, "Something sexy."

"Well, that's a start." The younger lady in black chuckles. "Ladies, have a look around while I get you something to drink."

We pull gorgeous gown after gorgeous gown off the racks and critique them. When the lady in black returns, she's holding a silver tray with five champagne flutes on it.

"My name is Sienna, and I will help you make your dreams come true today." She takes over the appointment, and the older lady disappears, bored with Americans, I'm sure.

"Now, if I may steal your bride away for a few minutes." She takes me by the hand and leads me into a dressing room in the back of the salon.

"So tell me, my dear, what is your name?"

"Lola."

"And Lola, what do *you* want your dress to look like?"

I think about it for a few seconds and say, "I like sleek and stylish. Not over the top, but elegant."

"Are you feeling okay today? You don't seem excited to be here."

"I'm okay. It's just that my mom passed away last year." I wring my hands. "I really wish she was here." Tears fall from my stupid eyes again.

"I'm so sorry, my dear. I'm sure your mama is looking down on you today, and is full of pride to see her daughter about to be married."

"I guess so."

"Do you love your man?"

"Oh yes, with all of my heart."

"Then I know she's smiling down on you. What do you think your mama would like to see you in?"

"Something vintage looking, with lots of lace."

"Please change into this robe, and I will go pull some dresses and be right back." She's gone about fifteen minutes and comes back in with an armload of dresses. "I thought we could try some of these."

"Okay," I say hesitantly.

"Let's start with this one that your sisters-in-law picked for you." It's a trumpet style with a sweetheart neckline."

She helps me get into the dress. "How do you feel?"

"Heavy." I giggle. I walk out of the room to oohs and aahs.

"I like it," Gilly speaks up first.

"It's pretty," I say, turning around to look at myself in the mirror. I'm hesitant to give my honest opinion because I don't know who chose this one. "But it's not the one."

"Boo," Gilly says under her breath and flops back on the sofa. I guess it was her pick. Sienna ushers me back to the room, and I put on the dress Amelia chose for me. I know it's her pick without asking because it is a *huge* princess ball gown with an overlay of sparkles. I can barely walk in it, let alone dance.

When I step onto the pedestal, the room fills with oohs and aahs again. I do a little twirl for Amelia, and the whole skirt poofs out. Her smile is so wide.

"It's so heavy. I can hardly move."

"Next!" Maria says, throwing her hand in the air. And with that, Sienna escorts me back to the dressing area.

"This dress is a vintage style in honor of your mama. Let's try it next."

"Okay."

This dress is delicate and sweet. It has an illusion lace neckline with short flowing cap sleeves. There are lace appliqués and beading all over the tulle skirt. It's light and flowing with an innocent feel to it.

"My mom would've liked this one," I say with a smile.

"Let's go show the crowd," she says, patting me on the arm. Sienna ushers me to the round pedestal and faces me toward the mirror this time. There's not much talking going on behind me. When I turn around to look at them, their mouths are all gaping open, but still, no one says anything.

"Well?" I say, with my hands out. "What do you think of this one?"

Lil sighs. "It's so pretty."

Maria replies, "It's romantic."

Gilly says, "It's so… sweet. But, don't you want a little *boom pow*?" I like Gilly's honesty.

I look back at myself in the mirror.

"Yeah, I guess you're right. It *is* pretty. But maybe I need something a little sexier for Ethan."

"I have one more to try," Sienna says, reaching her hand to help me down from the platform. She puts me in a trumpet/mermaid ivory-nude gown. It's a mermaid in the front and a trumpet in the back. It's lined and has sheer long sleeves with dainty appliqués of falling leaves, a plunging neckline, and a sheer keyhole back. There are covered buttons from the middle of my back down my backside, and then they flare into the skirt. It's all covered with sheer fabric and hundreds and hundreds of appliqués of leaves and flowers. It's stunning.

When Sienna turns me around to look at myself in the mirror in the changing room, all I can say is, "Wow."

She leads me to the platform once again, and I can't take my eyes off the mirror. I realize everyone is silent. When I turn around, they're all crying.

"It fits you perfectly," Amelia sniffles.

"You look gorgeous." Lil blows her nose.

"Rocky is going to lose his mind," Gilly says.

"How do you feel?" MeMe asks.

"Incredible. Like I never want to take it off."

Sienna clips a long, sheer veil to the back of my head, and I begin to cry.

"It's a little bit of what everyone suggested, even my mom." They all stand and circle me. "Thank you for today."

"That's what family's for," Lil says.

Gilly uses the black AmEx card to purchase the dress, veil, and shoes. Gotta have shoes. She has the shop courier everything to the hotel. With Beckett and Holden flanking us, we exit the little shop and head off to find someplace to eat.

We are seated at a quaint bistro. The guards are at a table across the aisle from ours.

"This reminds me of a place I waited tables at while I lived in Paris," Gilly says.

"You never waited on a table in your life," Lil spits.

"That's a story for another day," Gilly says, waving her hand for Lil to continue.

"Tell us about yourself, Lola. We don't know anything about you." Lil gives Gilly the side-eye.

"I am. I mean, I *was* an executive at Kingsley and Masters until last week."

"What's that supposed to mean?" Gilly asks.

"I quit on Monday."

"Why?"

"I took off a week when I was kidnapped."

"Kidnapped!" they all shout at the same time.

"Shh… I guess we *do* have a lot to catch up on." I giggle. "Anyway, when Ethan asked me to take this trip, I knew they would fire me if I asked for more time off, so I turned him down. But then he proposed, so I decided to quit."

"How romantic," Maria swoons. She's definitely the ooey gooey one of the bunch.

"The kidnapping, go on…" Gilly gives a rolling motion with her hands.

I tell them about everything their father did to me. Ethan had already told them about the warehouse, how DeLuca was their brother, and how Sasha killed him and his men.

"Sasha's such a badass!" Gilly says, digging into her pasta.

"What are your plans when we get back home? Are you job hunting?" Lil asks, taking a drink of her wine.

"I don't think so. Ethan has offered to help me set up a nonprofit, and I think I'm going to go for it."

"What kind?" MeMe asks.

"I would love to see a battered women's shelter, but I'm not quite sure yet."

"You know the story of Sasha, right?" she chimes.

"I met her at the gun range," I say, tearing off pieces of my bread and soaking up my pesto sauce with them.

"You know who she really is though, right?"

"Would you please just tell her and get it over with, MeMe?" Gilly barks.

"She's Sheila."

"No," I say. "The homely girl who was Antonio's secretary? How?" I met her at the office when Ethan took me there after Antonio was killed. He wasn't comfortable leaving me alone in the penthouse so soon after being taken, so he took me along.

Gilly explains, "Rocky, I mean… *Ethan* saved her when he was in college. She had overdosed on the street. He paid for her to go to rehab, and she trained exclusively with Jerry for a year. They turned her into the badass assassin she is today. She takes on contracts from abused women who want to *take care of* their perpetrators. She's a ruthless bad bitch."

"Why was she working at the office?"

"Ethan planted her there to watch our father, and when the moment was right, *she* was supposed to take him out. But DeLuca beat her to it."

"Oh my," I say.

"Enough about Sasha. How did you and Rocky meet?" MeMe asks.

"I literally ran into him at Anthony's one afternoon, and we shared a table." I fill them in on that day, our evening at Mariah's, and when I threw up all over him. But I left out the masked ball and the one-night-only sex-with-a-stranger story. It's amazing having other women to talk to and share with.

After a few glasses of wine and lots of conversation later, we roll into the suite. Ethan is waiting when we arrive.

"A big box arrived for you," he says, pulling me into his arms and placing a quick kiss on my lips.

"You didn't open it, did you?" I whine.

"Of course not. I know all about that superstitious stuff you women believe in. Three sisters, remember?" He points at all of them. "Did you have a good time today?"

"Yes, it was so much fun talking to your sisters... *Rocky,"* I say teasingly.

"Oh God." Turning to the three of them, he finds shit-eating grins covering their faces. "What did you tell her?"

Gilly pipes up first, "Just how we used to dress you up like a girl, complete with makeup and high heels."

"Oh my God! High... heels... I understand now!" I squeal, turning to look at Ethan. He has his finger up to his lips as if to say shh.

Lil is next. "How we took you shopping at the mall and lost you, and how Momma about killed us all when we found you swimming in the fountain."

MeMe brings it home. "Or the time you got naked at Lil's Sweet Sixteen party."

Before she can continue, Ethan puts up his hand.

"Okay, that's enough." He pulls me away from them and out onto the patio. They are all laughing hysterically. "I'm glad you had fun with my sisters, even if it was at my expense."

"I did. And they cried when I put on *the* dress."

"You got your moment." Happiness fills his voice. He kisses the top of my head as he pulls me in for a hug.

"Yes, it was amazing. Thank you for all of this. I can't wait to be your wife."

"And I can't wait to be your husband."

"Hey," Ethan says.

"What?" I say, rummaging through my shopping bags.

"Let's get married."

"We are, silly." I giggle, waving him off.

"No." He turns me around by my shoulders. "Let's. Get. Married. *Here*."

Chapter 53
Ethan

I think Lola is about to pass out.

"You're kidding me, right?" she gasps, lowering herself slowly to the couch.

"No, I'm not kidding. Think about it. My sisters and Amelia are here. Freddy can be my best man. We are in this beautiful place. It would be amazing."

"I... Uh... I... Okay," she stutters out.

"Really?"

"Yes!" She leaps into my arms and wraps her legs around me, smothering me with kisses.

We walk into the dining room, where the girls are playing euchre.

"What's going on with you two? You look like the cat that ate the canary or some shit," Gilly says.

"How would you like to go to a wedding?"

"Whose wedding?" Lil says, taking a card from her hand and laying it on the table.

"Ours." I pause for a reaction. They all turn and stare at us.

"Here in Italy? Now?" MeMe asks.

"Yes. What do you say? We're all here, so why not?" Everyone jumps from the table, congratulating us, and Lil goes into full-on party-planning mode.

"We have a lot to do, girls. Let's get on it. I'll go speak with the concierge. You three start making lists. Gilly, I'm gonna need that AmEx card." And with that, she's gone.

In twenty-four hours, my sisters have thrown together a gorgeous impromptu wedding. We hold it at the Church of St. Augustine, around the block from the hotel, on Tuesday afternoon. Since it was in the middle of the week, we had no problem booking it and the priest. White lilies fill the alter and tall candelabras line the aisle on both sides.

Freddy and I are posted at the base of the marble stairs that lead to the altar. Amelia walks down the aisle first. Freddy watches her float down the aisle in the flowing lavender dress. I know he likes her, but Freddy doesn't say much.

MeMe is already blubbering when I see my bride at the end of the long aisle. My breath hitches in my throat as she comes into view. Tears sting my eyes. She's the most beautiful woman I've ever seen, and she's about to be mine forever. Her smile is wide, and mine mirrors hers. She glides down the aisle in her stunning dress, and all I can think of is sliding it down her body tonight.

She hands her flowers to Amelia. Holding out my hand, she places hers in mine, and we turn toward the stairs.

When we're standing before the priest, I lean close to her ear and whisper, "You look beautiful."

A blush falls over her cheeks as she mouths a sweet, "Thank you."

The priest's loud Italian/English accent is thick and melodious as it echoes through the church.

"Dearly beloved, we are gathered here today in the sight of our Lord God to join Rocco Ethan Martinelli and Lola Marie Patterson. Is there anyone here who objects to this union?" Turning around, I look at all three of my sisters. Gilly puts up her hands as if she's surrendering. I smile and turn back to the priest.

"Fine, then, let's continue." We turn to face one another and hold hands. "Ethan, do you take Lola to be your wife? To be faithful to her always, in joy and in pain, sickness and in health, to love and to honor all the days of your life?"

"I do."

"Lola, do you take Ethan to be your husband? To be faithful to him always, in joy and in pain, sickness and in health, to love and to honor all the days of your life?"

"I do."

"May I have the rings, please," he says, holding his hand out. I turn to Freddy, who pulls two bands out of his breast pocket and places them in the priest's hand. He says a blessing over them and holds Lola's ring out for me to take.

"When did you...?" Lola asks.

"You don't think we could get married without rings, do you?" Smiling wide, I place the gold band at the tip of her finger and hold it there. Tiny vines wrap around it, and diamonds are embedded in the vines. I repeat the priest's words, "With this ring, I thee wed," and push the ring onto her finger. She gasps and holds out her hand for my ring.

The priest places it in her hand. It's black tungsten with a strip of 18k gold running through it. Placing it on the tip of my finger, she says, "With this ring, I thee wed." She slides the ring onto my finger.

The priest continues, "Please kiss each other's ring, symbolizing your bond and that you shall never remove them." We do as he instructs and kiss the rings on each other's fingers.

"With the power vested in me by God and Italia, I now pronounce you husband and wife. You may kiss your bride." I take Lola into my arms, dip her, and place a sweet kiss on her lips.

We turn around to walk back down the stairs.

"Ladies and gentlemen, Mr. and Mrs. Rocco Ethan Martinelli," the priest says, and everyone claps and meets us at the bottom of the stairs to congratulate us. I think Rocco might be growing on me now. At least when it's said in that sentence.

We take the customary photographs in the church and emerge into the streets of Milan. It's a six-minute walk from the church back to the hotel. Gowns are floating, motorists are honking, and my new wife is smiling wider than I have ever seen before.

We rented a banquet room in the hotel, and the girls brought in a DJ to play music all evening. Champagne is flowing, and there is a small cake we share the first piece of. After I feed her, I boop her on the nose with icing and lick it off. She laughs, dipping her finger into the cake and wiping it across my mouth. I kiss her, and everybody says, "Aw."

We share our first dance as husband and wife to the John Legend song "All of Me" and spend the evening dancing in each other's arms.

At almost ten o'clock, I pull Lola close.

"Can we go now? This is our last night in Italy, and I want to spend it between my *wife's* legs." She nods. "Come with me." I lead her to the DJ, and he stops the music. I take the microphone.

"Thank you all so much for putting together and sharing this amazing day with us. Shit, thank you Lillianna, Maria, and Guilia for planning it." Everyone laughs. "We are going to retire. My new bride and I have some *business* to attend to."

"You mean you want to have sex?" a half-drunk Gilly rings out. "We're all grown-ups here, Rocky."

"Please feel free to dance the night away. But don't forget the cars will be here at eleven in the morning to pick us up to go to the airport." We give quick hugs to my sisters and Amelia. Grabbing a bottle of champagne from an ice bucket, I lead Lola to the elevator.

Lola

Ethan pins me against the wall of the elevator and kisses me passionately.

"I can't wait to get you to our room," he croons into my neck. When the doors open, we're not on our usual floor.

"Where are we going?"

"You'll see." We exit, walk a short distance down the hall, and stop in front of the bridal suite. He unlocks the door, holds it open with his foot, lifts me into his arms, and carries me over the threshold. The door slams closed as he stands me on my feet in the middle of the room. I take a moment to look around the room. There are appetizers on trays and candles flickering softly around the room.

"I wish we had a few more days to watch the sunset from the balcony," I say.

"How about we watch the sunrise after I make love to you all night?"

"Ethan, this day has been a dream come true. Thank you."

"You know I would do anything for you, my love." He places a soft kiss on my lips. "How do I get you out of *this* dress? I should be a pro at dress removal by now." I lift the front of the dress like I did that night at the masked ball and wink at him.

"Nope, not tonight," he says sharply and I laugh. Turning me around, he carefully unfastens the pearl buttons that follow the shape of my ass.

"That wasn't too bad," I say as he lowers the dress down my shoulders to find me wearing a white bustier and garter set complete with stockings, Jimmy Choo satin shoes with little pearls on them, and no panties. A deep, lust-filled growl comes from his chest, and he looks like he could eat me alive. He whisks me into his arms and carries me to the bedroom.

"I want our first night as man and wife to be special," he says. I hum in agreement, lost in the passion of his kisses. He runs his fingers down my forearms, and goose bumps play across my skin, giving me a chill.

"Make love to me, Ethan."

"Lie down in the middle of the bed." I lean down to take off my shoes. "Leave the shoes on," he growls, and I giggle. My stomach flutters with excitement. Doing as I'm told; I climb into the center of the bed. He lowers himself between my legs.

"First, I need to feast on this glorious pussy." Resting one hand on either thigh, he spreads me wider and blows a gentle stream of air across my clit, sending chills up my spine and making my nipples harden. He places tiny little flits on my nub, and my hips buck up into him for more.

He rests his hand across my stomach. "Now, now, now, Mrs. Martinelli, I'm going to take my time. I want this to be a night you'll remember when we're old and gray, rocking on the front porch." He continues to lick me like a kitten drinking cream from a saucer until I'm close to my release.

"Ethan. Please, let me come," I pant. He plunges his tongue deep inside me and uses his thumb on my clit.

"Come for me, baby. Come all over my tongue." Those words throw me over the edge, and I come hard all over his face. Not allowing me time to recover, he continues to bombard my core with long, languid licks. I can almost come again just from that feeling alone.

I rock my pussy into his face, trying to get every last sensation. He moves his attention back to my clit, licking and sucking it. When he nibbles on it with his front teeth, I lose all self-control. He pushes one finger in and then another, and I explode around them. I love what his sinful mouth does to my body, but I need his cock. I want to feel him filling me and making me his.

"Ethan, I need *you*." I reach for his belt.

"Tonight is all about you, my love."

"Then please, I need you inside me."

"Soon, baby girl, soon." He leans back on his knees and takes my leg in his hands. His eyes fix on mine while he places soft kisses down to my shoe. He slides it from my foot and drops it to the floor. Taking my bare foot in his hand, he rubs it, releasing a groan from my throat. The feeling is sensuous and electrifying. He lowers his mouth to my foot, kisses each of my toes, and then places it back on the mattress. He smiles and moves to the left leg, giving it the same love and attention as he did the right. By the time he's finished, I'm rubbing my legs together.

"Does my girl need some relief?"

"Yes," I beg.

He kisses his way up my stomach, taking my breasts in his hand and rolling my nipples between his fingers and thumbs. The sensation sends shock waves to my pussy. His mouth envelops mine. His kisses are possessive and hot.

"Ethan, please." The need I have for him almost brings me to tears. I think he's trying to kill me with pleasure.

"Shh…" He stands from the bed, finally removing his dress shirt, tie, tuxedo pants, and black boxer briefs. I sit up, licking my lips, and scoot to the edge of the bed. Reaching for him, I grip his stiff cock in my hand and lick the precum from his tip. I open my mouth wider to take him inside, but he cuts me off with a grin.

"Lie back, baby girl."

"Ethan, I don't know if I can take any more of your teasing. I need you inside me."

"Patience, my love."

I let out a loud growl but do as I'm told. I spread myself wide for him as he takes his cock in his hand and strokes it once, twice, then notches it at my entrance. Finally. Finally, I will get what I've been craving all night.

Knowing my relief is coming soon, I try to control my breathing and be patient. Leaning his body down on mine, he presses his elbows into the mattress on either side of my head while his hands cup my face. Peppering me with soft kisses, he slowly presses into me. The groan that leaves my body is needy and desperate. I need more, so much more. I raise my legs around him, trying to get him deeper inside me. He rocks into me slowly, giving me only what he allows me to have until I'm writhing beneath him. He's trying to hold himself back to make this experience romantic for me. That's sweet, but I know what I need, and I'm going to make him give it to me now.

"More," I rasp, and he increases his pace.

"Deeper," I plead, and he moves one of my legs to rest on his shoulder and hits that spot deep inside my core that I love.

"Harder," I pant. He releases the beast, and I finally get what I want. *My Ethan*. My take-no-prisoners, hard-fucking *husband*.

He pulls his hips back until his tip is just inside me, looking into my eyes and straight into my soul as he thrusts into me hard and deep.

"Yes! Fuck... Yes... Ethan!" His strokes are rough, just the way I like them.

"I love this tight pussy, and it's all mine. Say it, baby. Say you're all mine."

"I'm all yours, and you're all *mine*."

"You're fucking right. I'm all yours."

Once he finally gives me what I've been begging for, it doesn't take long for us to fall over the edge together.

Our breathing quells, and we're glazed in sweat. He dusts his lips over mine and starts to pull out.

"Please don't leave me yet," I say, holding him to my body tightly.

"I'll stay inside you all night if that's what you want."

My pussy spasms around his dick, like little shocks of electricity pulsing through us. His cock jerks inside me, and I jump, causing us both to laugh. When our bodies finally relax, he slides out of me and wraps me in his warm embrace.

In the darkness before the dawn, Ethan opens the French doors to the balcony. We lie entangled in each other's bodies and watch as the sun rises from our king-sized bed. Beginning our lives together as husband and wife.

Chapter 54
Ethan

The jet landed a few hours ago. Lola went back to the penthouse to rest. I got some sleep on the plane, and I'm anxious to get to work. It's time I take control of The Organization and implement some changes. When I walk into the office, the first change I see is Sheila is no longer at her desk. Instead, Sasha is seated there.

"What are you doing here?"

"Working." She chuckles.

"No, I mean, why are you still working *here*?"

"I kinda like it here. Besides, you need me."

"I do. Thank you."

"Do you want me to rally the troops?"

"That would be great, thanks." She's always one step ahead of me.

All of my captains stand around the conference room table. I motion for them to have a seat. No one moves except to look back and forth at each other.

"Have. A. Seat," I say, louder this time. They do as they're told with confusion in their eyes. Antonio would stand everyone at attention and bark orders at them. I'm not that kind of *boss*.

"I've brought you all here today to get our house in order. We have a hundred and twenty-four men and twenty captains. I want you to split them up into teams." When a few mouths fly open, I hold out my hand. "Before you ask, I don't *care* how you decide who gets who." All the mouths snap shut.

"I want your groups divided into sergeants and soldiers. Sergeants are those you deem able to handle a job on their own or in a team of two with *zero* guidance. Soldiers are new to The Organization and need to learn and have constant guidance. They'll keep that title until *you* are confident they can move up. If you don't trust them to have your back, don't promote them. That means I will *never* see a soldier used to protect Lola. She will always have a sergeant or above keeping her safe. Do you understand?"

I look around the table, and everyone nods in agreement.

"Good. Now, there's going to be some major changes coming. I plan to get out of the illegal activity altogether, or at the very least divide our house into two different sections. Does anyone have a problem with that?"

"If you're going legit, what do you need us for?" Luke speaks up.

"It all takes time, and we will always have people who think they can run things better than we can or want to take what we have. We must protect what's ours, so I will still need all of you. If anyone wants to leave, now is your chance. I will let you go, no questions asked." They all turn their heads and look at one another, but no one protests.

"Good. As of today, everyone will get a ten percent raise, Christmas bonus, and one-week paid vacation." This mumbling is good, and I even see a few smiles. "You will all have a seat at *this* table. If there's a concern in the ranks, I want to know about it. I don't lead like Antonio did. I expect total loyalty, and in return, you will have my respect."

"Give all suggestions, complaints, and concerns to Sheila, I mean Sasha. She will see what she can do to help before she brings them to me. Treat her with the respect she has earned, or you will answer to me." Sasha holds her head a little higher, and a small smile turns up the corners of her lips. "Freddy has earned the title of second-in-command. Beckett, Roscoe, and Nico will be majors. If they give you orders, treat them as if they were coming from me."

"I'm not sure if you all know this yet, but Lola and I were married in Italy. You will treat her with the utmost respect and protect her at all costs. You may address her as Mrs. Martinelli or Miss Lola. Bennie will be staying on as her driver and bodyguard, but he's only *one* person. She will need a full security team with her whenever she goes out. She doesn't go *anywhere* without eyes on her. Even if she *thinks* she's alone, she won't be. Got it? We will start with two more guards and see how that goes." They all nod.

"Questions?" When there are none, I say, "Good. You may go." Everyone slowly leaves the room, offering congratulations on my recent nuptials, and I gesture for Sasha to sit.

"What's up, Boss?"

"Do you really want to stay on as my personal assistant?"

"Yes. I really like running things around here." She smiles.

"Well, if you're serious, then I'll be asking a lot of you these next few months. But if you get a *job* you need to take care of, just let me know, okay?"

"Okay."

"This is what I need from you:
1. When the captains pick their groups, I would like those lists.
2. I need you to coordinate the security team to rotate and keep watch on Lola when she goes out.
3. Can you please send a big bouquet of white roses to Lola and have them put this note on it for delivery this afternoon?
4. I would like a meeting with Daniel today.
5. I would like you to come up with some ideas for a rotated time-off schedule for the guys. Everyone needs time off with their family. I know it will be hard to organize, but they are loyal to The Organization and should be rewarded. It's good for morale."

"Anything else, Boss?" she asks.

"No, I think that's a good start. Thank you for staying, Sasha. I know I can trust you."

That afternoon, Daniel enters my office.

"Daniel, I would like you to put together a team of IT guys. I want hackers who know the dark web and can access anything we need.

Antonio wasn't much for technology, as you know, so I need you to bring us up to date on what we need to make us work effectively in this digital world. Your workload will be increasing exponentially, so you'll need some help. I want you to hire and oversee a select few to work closely with you. I want state-of-the-art cell phones, bugs, cameras, James Bond shit, ya know. I want your team ready to access cameras, bank accounts, or anything else at a moment's notice twenty-four seven."

"Yes, Boss."

"Also, how hard would it be for you to move all the computer equipment out of that small room into a larger one?"

"Not hard at all. Where do you want us?"

"I think there should be a main IT headquarters in this building and maybe a smaller one on a floor near the penthouse. Maybe have some equipment so you can work remotely if necessary and update the surveillance van while you're at it too."

"Will do."

"I'm counting on you to do thorough background checks on every person in The Organization. Everyone is starting with a clean slate. I need to know if there's anyone we can't trust. Check bank accounts, driver's licenses, tax records, passports, anything and everything."

"Yes, Boss."

Leaning in closer to him, I need him to know how important his job is to us. Antonio never showed him any respect, and he needs to know I need him. "Listen, you have carte blanche to get whatever you need to make this work. I will spare no expense to keep Lola safe. Sasha will give you the credit card information to order whatever you want. Make it happen."

"I will, Boss. I won't let you down." We stand and shake. I clap him on the shoulder and say, "I know you won't."

I sit at my desk, poring over accounts and dividing our investments and businesses into two piles. I'm finding out it's not as cut-and-dried as I thought it would be. Some of these businesses have been working flawlessly for forty years. There has never been any police involvement even though Father seemed to have the entire police department in his back pocket. My cell phone rings.

"Good afternoon, wife."

"Good afternoon, husband." She giggles. "Thank you for the beautiful flowers."

"Beautiful flowers for my beautiful wife."

"The answer to your question on the card is yes, always yes."

"What have you done today?"

"I slept in, unpacked, had Bennie take my wedding dress to the cleaners, thought about my handsome husband all day and what I'm going to do to him tonight when he gets home."

"Mmm, Mrs. Martinelli, are you trying to seduce me into coming home early?"

"Maybe," she coos, and I can almost hear her grinning through the phone.

"I just need to finish up here, and I'll be on my way."

"Until then."

"Until then."

On my way home, I stop at the bridal shop DeLuca commandeered while he was in town. When I step inside, an older woman approaches me.

"Can I help you?"

"Yes, I would like to speak to the owner, please."

"I'm the owner. How can I help you?"

"My name is Ethan Martinelli. I'm here to talk to you about Eliseo DeLuca." Her body becomes rigid, and she immediately goes on the defensive.

"Look, I don't know anything about him, nor do I care to. I have no idea where he is…"

"No, you don't understand. DeLuca's dead."

"Dead?" There's a pause, then she starts to speak really fast. "I don't know what happened to him. I had nothing to do with it…"

I put my hands out for her to stop. "It's okay. I know you had nothing to do with it… I did." Her mouth snaps shut. "I'm just here to give you this." I hand her a manila envelope.

"What's this?"

"I know he hurt your business these past months. He was here to hurt my family." She opens the envelope and looks inside. Her eyes are as big as saucers when she sees it is full of money. "I hope this will supplement your losses."

"Mr. Martinelli, you don't have to—"

I cut her off. "Yes, I do. Please take it, and my apologies for what he put you through."

"Thank you so much," she says, hugging me tight around the neck.

After dinner, Lola and I are on the couch facing the windows, watching our sunset. She's cuddled up to my side.

"I think I know what I want to do with my life," she says softly.

"And what is that?"

"I think I would like to open a battered women's shelter on the outskirts of the city. I've looked at the demographics and think that would be the most beneficial place for it."

"That's a great idea." I hug her to my side. "What can I do to help?"

"We'll need to find a building big enough to have about twenty rooms for the women and children to stay in, a room for group meetings or classes, a full facility for medical, a playroom for the kids, a kitchen, a living area, a private place to park cars so no one can see, and private outdoor space that's not visible to the outside either."

"You have put a lot of thought into this."

"Yes, I have."

"Line up a few places you'd like to see, and I'll go with you."

"Thank you for this, Ethan."

"Don't you think you're going to need an assistant to help you with all the details?" he asks, waggling his eyebrows.

"That would be amazing... Can it be Amelia?"

"Baby, it can be whoever you want." She climbs onto my lap and hugs me tight.

"I love you so much."

"I love you more."

Chapter 55
Ethan

One Year Later

It's been harder than I thought to eliminate all the illegal businesses from The Organization. We have made progress, but I've had to concede to divide everything into two parts. Freddy runs all the illegal operations. Some have been running just fine for years, so I decided to keep them, at least for now.

I run all the legal businesses and investments. The city is home to other illegal operations, but as long as we stay out of their way and they stay out of ours, I hope we can continue business as usual. Our side of the city is safer than it has been in years, with the removal of prostitution on every street corner and drugs. My teams provide security wherever it is needed.

My sisters are coming into their own as well. They bought a little strip of shops downtown. Lilliana runs the dress shop. She sells clothes, bags, shoes, and jewelry. Next to her is Guilia's salon. It offers everything from hair and makeup services to manicures and pedicures. They are promoting the shops as "Everything a girl needs for a night on the town." Maria opened the third shop as a romance bookstore. There's one more store left on the strip. Hopefully, when the tenant leaves, they'll also take it over.

Lola opened the battered women's shelter four months ago. They've already begun helping women get away from their abusers and learn new skills to return to the workforce and get on with their lives.

Lola

I wake up in bed cuddled into Ethan's side.

"Good morning, husband."

"Good morning, wife. What are your plans for today?"

"I'm going to the shelter to do some paperwork. Then Amelia and I are driving into the city for a late lunch. How about you?"

"I have a few meetings this morning, then I'll be free. Do you want to meet me back here, say, around three? I could have my way with you."

"As much as I would love to spend the rest of the day in bed with you, Mr. Martinelli, I have work to do." I giggle. "I do have a favor to ask though."

"Name it."

"Could Sasha come by the shelter this afternoon?"

"Why? What's up?"

"One of our ladies is having trouble with her husband. She came to us because he's been beating her. The night she arrived on our doorstep; she was hurt pretty bad. Broken ribs, black eye, fat lip, and lots of bruises. Ruck said the X-rays showed extensive past injuries. This guy is a monster. He won't stop texting and trying to call her. Having Nico and some guys in the construction office out front makes us feel safe, but Sasha can be with us *inside* the facility. The ladies love her, and I would feel safer with her there."

"I understand," he says, kissing me on my temple. "I'll send her your way after our morning meetings."

"Great, thank you."

Bennie drives me to the shelter. He enters the passcode to the underground parking area. We've tried to think of creative ways to keep these women safe from their abusers. One thing is underground parking, so no one can find their vehicles. We'll continue to tweak things as we continue to learn.

This location was exactly what I was looking for. The bare bones of the building were here, and it came with some land when we bought it. Ethan's construction crew worked their magic and made it exactly how I pictured it in my head.

The main living space is accessed through a secret door from the parking garage. Entering into the kitchen, there are long cabinets that outline the room where buffet-style meals are set up and a custom table big enough for everyone to eat together if they would like. The living room is large with big, comfy furniture and a large-screen television. The playroom is off to the left, so moms can relax, and the children are still in view.

A second secret entrance can be accessed from the construction office next door. Nico is currently managing the construction office, which adds an extra layer of security to our residents. The shelter's side of the door looks like an ordinary bookcase filled with cookbooks and other reading materials. However, from the construction side, it looks like a metal shelf with tools and supplies on it. Men are not allowed inside the shelter unless it is Ethan, but just in case a male ever needs to enter, they would not be seen immediately by skittish female residents if they come in through the secret door.

The security room is directly to the left of the construction door, and the main living space is out of sight. It is operated twenty-four seven by an all-female former military staff. Continuing down the hall past the security office, my office is on the left, and Amelia's is on the right. My office has an added door to a bedroom built in the back, just in case I ever need to stay the night.

Ruck set up a medical facility that handles minor issues and takes X-rays. We will need to have medical transport to the hospital in life-threatening situations. We hired a full staff with Marissa, our house manager, leading the way, and everything has been running smoothly so far.

The second floor houses our guests. Each room has its own bathroom, complete with a shower/bathtub combo, and kitchenette with fridge, microwave, and sink. There are beds for kids and moms. We have twenty rooms for residents. So far, the most residents we have had at one time have been six families.

The third floor is filled with meeting rooms. We wanted confidential spaces for counseling sessions, therapy, as well as classrooms. There's a computer room for résumés, job searches, and schoolwork. If need be, there's a safe room in the basement where we can lock ourselves in from intruders until the police arrive. I am so proud of how far we have come in the past four months.

Amelia and I spent the morning arranging some job interviews for a few of the residents. The therapist is here today conducting a group session. I wanted to connect with our newest resident, Donna. She has kept herself closed off from the rest of us and doesn't come out of her room. I knock on her door. "Donna, it's me, Lola. Can I come in?"

"Yes," she says quietly from the room. Turning the knob, I walk inside.

"Hi, honey. How are you doing?" I walk tentatively toward her as if she's a scared kitten.

"I'm okay." She's sitting on her bed, curled up by the headboard.

"May I sit?" I ask, pointing at the foot of the bed.

"Yes."

"How's your pain level today?"

"Better, I guess. I can move my arm around more." She lifts her arm and rotates it.

"Well, that's a start. Would you like to come down for some breakfast? I'll stay with you."

"I don't think so." She lowers her eyes and pulls her body in tight on itself.

"You need to keep your strength up." I put my hand on hers. "No one here is going to hurt you. We only want to help."

"I'm scared."

"I know you are, Donna." I pause a moment before I ask, "Has he tried to contact you anymore?"

"Yes," she whispers.

"May I see?" She hands me the phone.

TOMMY
Where are you, bitch?

DONNA
Somewhere you will never find me.

Oh, I will find you, and when I do, I am going to kill you!

> Leave me alone.

You are mine.

> Not anymore. I'm never coming back to you.

You'll always be mine.

I will find you, and you will regret ever leaving me.

> I want a divorce.

NEVER!!!

> Please just let me go.

When I get you back, you will never leave me again.

There's more, but I stop right there.

"You need to stop engaging with him."

"I know... but he's all I have," she says, tears brimming in her eyes.

"That's not true. You have all of us. We're all here to help and support you."

"He'll just find me. I'm afraid he'll kill me next time."

"I know you're scared, but he can't get to you here."

"I can't stay here forever."

"You can stay here as long as you need to." I take a deep breath and try to remain calm. "My husband is sending someone over to help us with your husband. She'll be here this afternoon."

"*She'll* be here?" Donna asks, confused.

"Yes, her name is Sasha, and I believe she can help you. Would you like to come down and eat something while you wait on her?"

"I-I guess so," she concedes and stands from the bed and puts on her slippers. Like a timid little child approaching the slide for the first time, she follows me down the stairs to the kitchen. Arms surround her body, and her head hangs low.

"Everyone, this is Donna. Donna, this is Kara, Jen, April, and Lisa." They all smile and say their respective *hellos,* but no one moves. They've all been in her shoes and don't want to push her for fear she'll bolt. Thankfully, she pulls out a chair and sits at the end of the table, away from the group. The ladies talk quietly about things they learned in the budgeting class this morning and discuss what classes they want to take next. Donna listens but doesn't speak. She pushes her eggs around her plate, and when she's done, she goes back to her room. It was a start.

Amelia and I go to lunch in the city. We have time to discuss Donna.

"I think Sasha's presence will help her, don't you?" I ask.

"Maybe she can teach her some things to do to protect herself when she is feeling stronger," Amelia adds.

"That would be a great class for everyone," I agree. "Donna is frightened. She thinks he's going to kill her next time."

We do a little window-shopping, and Bennie drives us back to the shelter. When we approach the door to the underground parking area, we see the beat-up black pickup truck sitting in front of the construction office. Amelia and I crane our necks to look at it, but Bennie doesn't stop. He punches in the code for the door, and we enter. I exit the Escalade and head for the security office. Amelia is hot on my heels. There on the screen is a dirty, unshaven sight of a man. He looks like he hasn't showered in a week and probably smells just as bad. He's arguing with Nico.

"Can you turn up the sound?" I ask, pointing my finger at the screen.

"I know she's here!" the man yells.

"Look, man, there are no women here," Nico says, throwing out his arms to show him.

"Her phone says otherwise." He puts his phone in Nico's face and points at the little dot on the screen. "Now, where is she?"

"Listen, I'm not going to tell you again. She's not here."

"I know she's here! She's mine!"

"Look, man, you need to leave," Nico shouts.

"I'll leave for now, but I'll be back, and you'll be sorry for keeping her from me." He turns and staggers out of the building. Nico follows him to the door and engages the deadbolt. He heads through the hallway to the secret entrance that connects with the shelter. He releases the switch, the shelf/door pops open, and he enters the shelter. He leans into the security office.

He's surprised to see me standing in the office, and his eyes are wide.

"Hey, did you get that?" he asks.

"Yes, we saw him, Nico. Was he here for Donna?" I ask.

"Yeah, said she *belongs* to him and made a bunch of threats."

"You handled him great, thanks." Picking up my cell, I call Ethan.

"Hey, beautiful, what's up?"

"Do you know if Sasha is on her way over here yet?"

"She left about ten minutes ago. Why? What's wrong?"

"Donna's husband just showed up. He threatened Nico and said he'd be back for Donna."

"Boy, he's not giving up, is he?"

"Not at all. I just got Donna to come out of her room this morning. If she finds out he tracked her here, I don't know what she'll do."

"I'm coming over there."

"You don't have to do that."

"Yes, I do. You are there, and I can't be across town from you when there's a crazy man on the loose, threatening people."

Sasha comes into my office about twenty minutes later. I fill her in on Donna's husband.

"I can take care of him. Just give me the word, Lola," she says, removing her gun from the back of her pants.

"Put that away. I don't want to terrify the little ones."

"I forgot, sorry." She puts the gun back and pulls down her jacket. "Can I talk to her?"

"Yeah, I told her you were coming. I'll take you upstairs." She follows me to the second-floor rooms. I knock, and Donna lets us in. I introduce them and give them some privacy. This conversation must be between the two of them.

They talk for about thirty minutes, and Sasha returns to my office.

"Well?"

"She's terrified."

"I know, right?"

"Did she say you could *take care of business*?"

"Yes, but she doesn't want to know about it until it's done. She let me check her phone, and sure enough, there was a tracker on it. I removed it and told her to disengage with him. She shut her phone off, at least for the time being. Checking their phones should probably be a priority when they first arrive."

"Yes, I agree," I say. "Abusive men are an addiction. They make women rely on them for everything, and they don't know how to survive without them."

"She'll be okay. She's a strong lady. He just needs to go away permanently," Sasha says.

"Thanks, Sasha."

"I'm going to hang around for a while. Is that okay?"

"Of course." As Sasha walks out, Ethan walks in. I stand and rush into his arms.

"I've missed you so much," I say, pulling him close and kissing him hard.

"Are you okay?"

"Yeah, just a little unnerved by that jerk. But I need to be strong for Donna."

"You're the strongest woman I know. I love you." He holds me tight and kisses me on the top of my head.

"I love you. I want to stay here tonight. Is that all right with you?" I ask.

"Sure, as long as I get to stay with you." At night, the security room monitors the facility. It is staffed by former military women who are very capable of protecting the residents. Outside, we have two male guards who secure the perimeter.

"I just have a feeling this guy is going to come back when he thinks no one is here," I say.

"You're needed here. We're staying."

"Yeah, I'm staying too," Sasha chimes in, coming around the corner.

By nine o'clock, the moms have put the kids to bed, and the main floor is empty except for the security office, Ethan, Sasha, and me. The residents are aware they need to stay off the main floor at night for security reasons. Everything is calm until one in the morning, when we hear glass breaking. We both sit straight up in bed and look at each other.

"You stay here," Ethan says, jumping out of bed and pulling on his clothes and shoes. I know by now to do as I'm told, but I stand and pull on some clothes and shoes anyway. Ethan readies his weapon, gives me a chaste kiss on the lips, and leaves the room. I hear Sasha meet him in the hallway.

"It came from the construction office. It has to be him," she says.

"Let's go," Ethan says. I watch out my office door as they stop at the security office door and check the monitors. They confirm it is him and head to the bookcase/door.

I watch the bookcase click closed, and I head out into the hall. I run into the security office and close the door behind me. I watch the monitors with the team as Sasha and Ethan work their way down the hallway of the construction office.

"Call the perimeter guards and tell them to come in through the front," I say.

"Already on it," one guard says. "They're two minutes out." Just then, I see them sprinting across the grounds on the monitor.

They come to an intersecting hall. Ethan goes left, and Sasha goes right.

"We know you're here, Tommy. Just give up, and we'll take it easy on you," Ethan yells.

"Fuck you!" Tommy yells back. "Give me Donna!"

"She's not coming out, so you may as well leave."

"I'm not going anywhere without Donna. She's mine!"

"She doesn't belong to you, Tommy. She came here to get away from you."

"No! Goddammit! She's mine!" Ethan turns right at the next corner, pointing his gun out in front of him. He must catch sight of Tommy because he squeezes off a round and ducks around the corner. I lose track of Sasha on the cameras as Ethan yells again.

"Give it up, Tommy!"

"Fuck you!" Tommy runs into something, and it clangs to the floor. I see Ethan run around the corner, and he shoots his gun. Tommy shoots twice, and Sasha comes into the frame and shoots him in the head.

"He's down," she hollers out. But Ethan doesn't come into the frame.

"Ethan," I say under my breath. "Find Ethan, dammit! Where is he?" Security scans the cameras, but Ethan isn't in any frames. Running for the connecting door, I unlock it and shove it open.

"Ethan!" I yell as the lights come on, blinding me for a second. I run down the hall in the direction he did, and when I turn right into the storeroom, I see him...lying on the floor. He's unconscious, and there's blood, so much blood.

"Ethan!" I scream and fall to my knees by his side.

"Ethan, Ethan, baby, it's me. Wake up." I tap the sides of his face. "Call 911!"

Sasha falls to his other side, surveying the scene.

"I think the bullet went straight through." She applies pressure to the wound in his chest.

"Hurry, please!" I'm hysterical now. "Ethan. I'm here. You're going to be okay."

"Breathe," Sasha tells me, and I look straight through her, not comprehending what she's saying. This can't be happening. Tommy was an idiot. How was he able to shoot *Ethan*? This can't be happening.

"Is he breathing?" I whisper, begging he still has breath in his lungs. Sasha leans down to listen and look at his chest.

"Yes, it's shallow, but he's breathing." The two male guards burst into the building, out of breath from running.

Sasha barks, "You two, go outside and lead the ambulance to the front of the building and get them the fuck in here!" They turn tail and run.

Motioning to me, she says, "Here, put your hand on his chest and apply pressure. I'll be right back." She runs through the door and tells the security office to keep everyone out of there and to stay calm. She grabs her phone and runs back to me, taking her position at his side. She takes over, pressing on the wound. With her other hand, she dials Freddy.

"Ethan's been shot! Call Marissa to come to the shelter. And a cleanup team. Get Amelia and meet us at Johnsonville Memorial." She hangs up and pockets her phone.

I don't know how long it's been, but it feels like a lifetime when the paramedics finally come in the door.

"Please, you have to help him," I beg.

"Yes, ma'am, please step aside." I get up off my knees and step to the side. I'm covered in Ethan's blood. Sasha comes up behind me, pulls me farther away, and holds tight to my shoulders.

"He's gonna be okay. You have to let them work," she says in my ear. They start an IV and load him onto the gurney.

"Let's go. We need to get him to Johnsonville Memorial, stat!"

"I'm going with you," I yell, but Sasha holds me back.

"No, ma'am, there's no room. We have to work on him."

"I'll drive you," Sasha says. When he's loaded and the ambulance pulls out, we head for the garage. Sasha takes the keys from the board, and we jump inside the Escalade. She tears out of the underground garage as soon as the door opens.

We burst into the emergency room, looking for Ethan. I approach the first nurse I see.

"I'm looking for my husband, Ethan Martinelli. He was shot in the chest."

"Yes, ma'am, they brought him in a few minutes ago," she says.

"Where is he?"

"They took him straight to surgery. I'll take you to the waiting room."

"No!" I cry. "I need to see him."

"They got him, Lola. Let them help him," Sasha says. Amelia and Freddy enter the ER doors. I fall into her arms and burst into tears.

"What am I going to do, Amelia? I can't live without him." I cry, totally out of control.

"He's going to be okay, Lola. We have to think positively. Send him all our strength and prayers." I collapse to the floor and pull my arms tight around my knees.

Freddy doesn't hesitate. He picks me up and sets me on the couch between him and Amelia. Leaning my head on her shoulder, I cry.

Hours pass before the doctor comes to meet us.

"Mrs. Martinelli?"

"I'm Mrs. Martinelli. How is he?" I ask, jumping up from the couch.

"He's in critical condition, and we've moved him to the ICU."

"Is he going to be all right?"

"There was extensive damage to his chest, but the bullet missed his heart and lungs."

"Thank fuck," Freddy says, running his finger through his hair.

"He's resting now."

"When will he wake up?"

"He didn't wake up before surgery. We did an MRI of his brain, and there were no signs of a head injury. We'll have to wait until he wakes up on his own."

"When will that be?" Amelia asks.

"There's no way of telling. His body needs to heal. It will take time."

"I need to see him," I say. "Can you take me to him, please?"

"You'll have to get cleaned up first. It's a sterile environment up there."

"I'm not leaving!" I yell.

"It's okay," he says in a calm voice. "There's a shower in my office. I'll have a nurse bring you some scrubs, and you can clean up there. It's private. No one will bother you."

"Thank you so much," I say, letting out a breath.

"Let me know if there's anything else I can do for you, ma'am. Mr. Martinelli has done a lot for this hospital. We will do our best for him."

"Thank you."

"I'll go to the penthouse, pack you a bag, and pick up some food. I'll be back as soon as I can," Amelia says.

"I'll drive you in the Escalade," Sasha says.

Amelia places a quick kiss on Freddy's lips, and they're gone.

"Freddy, you know what to do, right?" I ask, placing my hand on his forearm.

"Yes, Lola. I'll make sure The Organization is on high alert. I'll have guards posted by the door in the hall. I'll take care of everything until Ethan feels well enough to return. We have plans in place for situations like this," Freddy says.

"Thank you."

The nurse comes, and I follow her in my bloody haze to the doctor's office. She shows me where everything is and gives me the scrubs, leaving me to myself. I turn on the shower, remove my bloody clothes, and step under the spray. I watch as the red water circles the drain. I use the wall to hold myself up as tears stream down my face. It feels like my heart is ripping in two. What if he doesn't wake up? What am I going to do if Ethan doesn't make it? I can't live without him. I fall to my knees as my cries rip from my chest.

"Ethan! I need you! Please come back to me!"

When the water begins to run cold, I drag myself from the shower floor. Taking the towel from the hook, I dry off and dress in the scrubs. When I open the door, Freddy stands in the hall waiting for me. He escorts me to the ICU, and a nurse ushers me into his room. I'm not prepared for what I see. He has tubes coming from his arms, his chest, his mouth, and his nose.

"Where can I touch him?" I ask quietly. The nurse gestures for me to sit in a chair on the side of the bed. She points at his hand.

"Do not put *any* pressure on his chest, and do not try to wake him. He's heavily sedated, and we want him to stay that way so he can heal," she says.

"I won't. Thank you." Pulling his hand to my lips, I kiss his knuckles, then open his hand and press it to my face like he does when he kisses me. Tears stream from my eyes. After some time, exhaustion takes over, and I fall asleep with my head on his bed by his side.

Amelia touches me on the shoulder, and I'm instantly awake. I look at Ethan and then at her.

"How ya holdin' up, sweetie?" Amelia asks quietly.

"Okay, I guess." I look Ethan over before I move away from him.

"I brought you some clothes and food. You need to try to eat and keep your strength up."

"Maybe. Is there a sweater in there? It's freezing in here."

"There sure is, and I brought some of Ethan's sweatshirts and sweatpants. I thought you might want to wear them."

"You're amazing. Thank you," I say, giving her a big hug.

"Anything new yet?"

"No, they're concentrating on keeping him comfortable so his body can heal." After putting the bag on the chair in the corner, I pull out one of his sweatshirts and pull it over my head. The scent of him envelops me. Amelia stays by his side while I use the restroom, eat a little of the salad she brought, and drink some water.

"Thank you so much," I say. "I don't know what I would do without you, Amelia."

"Can I do anything else for you tonight?" she asks while cleaning the area.

"No, I'm good."

"Freddy handled the cleanup at the shelter, and I spent some time with Donna. Sasha is with her now. She couldn't believe Tommy had come there with a gun. She feels so bad about Ethan. Marissa and the staff are taking care of things at the shelter, but I'll keep an eye on them. Don't you worry about anything. I have it all handled. Ethan is all that matters now."

"Thank you for handling everything." She gives me another big hug.

"Are you okay?" Her brows pinch as she looks at me.

"I'm not feeling so well. Maybe I shouldn't have eaten that salad. Can you stay with him a little longer?"

"Of course."

I take off for the bathroom and make it just in time to throw up. I stay inside until all the food leaves my body.

"Are you okay?" she asks when I walk back into the room.

"Yeah, my stomach just can't handle food right now, I guess. I'll be fine."

"If you're sure?"

"I'm good. You go on home. Thanks again, and tell Freddy thank you too."

"Call me if you need anything. I'll be back in the morning." She hugs me tight and leaves.

I spend the next few hours running back and forth to the bathroom. One nurse finally catches on.

"Are you okay? You know you cannot be in here if you're sick. You could endanger his life further."

"I'm fine. The salad my friend brought me must've been bad or something."

"I'll get you something to settle your stomach."

"Thank you so much. I would appreciate it."

Ethan made it through the night, but he hasn't moved a muscle. My neck is stiff from this god-awful chair. At eight the following morning, Dr. Ramirez comes in. He has me wait outside while he checks Ethan over. Not long after, another doctor goes in to join the consultation. When they finish, they both come out to fill me in.

"Mrs. Martinelli, this is Dr. Sloan. She's a neurologist."

"Nice to meet you. How's he doing? Can we wake him up now?"

"No, we aren't going to wake him up yet. His body will do that when it's ready. His heart rate is strong, and his blood pressure is good. There's no sign of infection, and he made it through the night without incident."

"How long will it take until he's strong enough to wake up?" I ask.

"It could be a few days, or it could be weeks. The body is a mysterious thing. It will take as long as it needs to recover," Dr. Sloan says. My hand flies to my mouth. Before I know what's happening, I run into the bathroom and throw up again.

"Mrs. Martinelli, are you okay? Were you hurt yesterday during the event?" Dr. Ramirez asks.

"No, I was in the other building. I...I... I'm fine."

"If you don't mind, I would like to take a look at you."

"Why?"

"Because the night nurse said you were throwing up, and she had to give you Zofran to settle your stomach. Please, it will take just a few moments of your time. He'll be fine."

"What if he wakes up, and no one is here?" Panic laces my voice.

"I'll have the nurse sit with him until we're done."

"Okay."

Chapter 56
Lola

Two Weeks Later

"He has been *resting* for two weeks now and hasn't even twitched. Isn't there something we can do?" I argue with Dr. Ramirez.

"His body has had a chance to heal, so we're going to lower his pain medication slowly. It may help him to wake up, but be aware he may be in a lot of pain at first. We can readjust his medication at that time."

Thank God, they are finally doing something to help him wake up. The waiting game continues. Freddy, Amelia, and all his sisters have come to visit and sit vigil by his side with me. Giving me breaks to shower, eat, and nap.

Four more days have passed, and still, Ethan hasn't moved. I'm becoming impatient waiting. The news from the doctor is the same every morning during rounds. They've removed some tubes, and he's breathing on his own, but he's still sleeping. He looks stiff as a board.

When the doctors gave me the same spiel this morning, I couldn't take it. It's been weeks. I thought I had cried every tear in my body, but they're back now with a vengeance. I place my forehead against Ethan's and plead with him to wake up.

"Please, Ethan. I need you to open your eyes, baby. Please come back to me. Come back to our family." I sit back in the chair that knows my ass all too well, and I lower my head to the bed by his side and sob.

My tears soak the sheet under my face, and then I feel it—his fingers move in my hair. Is this real? Am I sleeping? His fingers slide haphazardly through my curls. I lift my head a few inches off the bed and turn to look at him. His eyes are still closed.

"Ethan?" I whisper. I sit up and take his hand in mine. "Ethan, baby, can you open your eyes for me?" I run my thumb along his cheek. "Please, Ethan, try to open your eyes." His nose crinkles a little, and I can see his eyeballs moving back and forth under his lids like he's trying to find his way back to me. I turn off the overhead light with the remote, and his eyelids start to flutter.

"That's it. You can do it." His eyelids open into little slits. "Oh my God, Ethan." His eyes search the room and land on my face, and the tiniest curl comes to the corner of his mouth. But then his eyes shift around, and his brows crinkle in confusion.

"You're in the hospital," I say calmly. "I'll be right back."

I run to the door and throw it open.

"Help, somebody!" I yell and run back to his side. Two nurses and a doctor rush through the door.

"His eyes are open." I move out of the way, and they start taking vitals and checking him over.

"Mr. Martinelli, I'm Dr. Jacobson. Can you understand me?" Ethan stares at him, and then, with the smallest of movements, he moves his head. I let out a huge breath. "You've been shot. You're at Johnsonville Memorial. You have been asleep for two and a half weeks." Ethan's eyes grow wide. "Would you like to try to speak?" Ethan nods his head ever so slightly. He opens his mouth, but no sound comes out.

His eyes start to panic, but the doctor puts his hand on his arm. "It's all right. You had a tube down your throat to help with your breathing for a while. It may take a little longer until the swelling in your throat goes down before you can speak. Are you in any pain?" Ethan points his finger toward his chest. "I can give you some pain medicine to help with that." He turns to the nurse and gives her the order for some medication. When everyone moves away from him, I rush back to his side and kiss his lips.

"I love you so much. I've been so worried about you."

Wasting no time, the nurse comes back in with a shot in her hand. "This is going to make you sleepy."

Ethan puckers up for a kiss, and I laugh through the tears.

"I'll be here when you wake up. Until then." I kiss his lips, and his eyes slide closed.

"He'll be asleep for a few hours. Why don't you try to get some rest, Mrs. Martinelli," the nurse suggests. After the first night, they brought in a more comfortable chair that turned into a little bed. That's where I set up camp. I feel like I can relax a little bit since he woke up, so I snuggle down on the chair bed and finally get some sleep.

I'm awakened by a raspy voice.

"Lo… Lo…" I snap out of it and jump out of my little bed.

"I'm here, Ethan," I say, taking his hand in mine. His body still looks stiff as a board, but his face is soft, and I swear his eyes get brighter when he sees me.

"You can talk, thank God." I kiss him on his lips and push the button for the nurse.

"How are you feeling?" I ask.

"What… happened…" He works so hard to get out the words.

"Donna's husband broke into the shelter. You and Sasha went to find him, and he shot you, and then Sasha shot him."

"I… don't… remember…"

"That's okay. It's all over now. Freddy arranged for the cleanup and has been handling both sides of The Organization. Amelia has been running the shelter and keeping me stocked with clothes and food."

"I… love… you…" The words come out low and gravelly.

"Shh, I love you too." The nurse comes into the room, takes his vitals, and asks him on a scale of one to ten what his pain level is. He holds up eight fingers.

"Okay, that's still a little high." She turns to me. "I'll speak to the doctor and be right back."

"Can I get you anything?" I ask. He puckers his lips. "I'll give you all the kisses you want, my love."

The nurse comes back in.

"The doctor would like to hold off on the pain meds while we get you to radiology. Afterward, I'll give you something for the pain. Does that sound good to you?"

"Yes…" Ethan rasps out.

"Good, I'll be back with transport to help move you in just a few minutes," the nurse says.

"Thank you," I say.

About five minutes pass and the nurse and two big men come back into the room.

"Mrs. Martinelli, would you mind stepping outside, please? The first time a patient gets moved around can be a little upsetting," she says.

"I'll be right outside." I press another kiss to his lips and wait outside.

I'm standing in the hallway when I hear Ethan roar in pain. I try to rush into the door, but the nurse is right there to stop me.

"He's fine. They already have him moved to the gurney. He's okay," she says calmly. Running my hands across my face, I stand on the wall opposite his door.

The men bring him out on the gurney, and there are tears in his eyes.

"Are you okay?" I ask. He nods.

"He'll be back before you know it," the nurse says. While he's having a CT scan and MRI done, I shower and put on clean clothes. Changing my little bed back into a chair, I wait patiently for him to return.

The gurney stops outside the door, and I jump to my feet. As they wheel him inside the room, I see he's sound asleep.

"What happened?" I ask.

"We had to sedate him after the first test. He was in too much pain. He'll be out for a few hours. Why don't you go get something to eat?"

"No, I'm fine. I'm not hungry," I say.

"You really should try to eat something. You need to keep up your strength now," the nurse says. "I'll bring you something."

"Thank you."

I text his sisters in the group text and update them.

They just brought him back from radiology, and they had to sedate him because of the pain.

LIL

When do you think we can come to see him?

When he wakes up, I'll ask him what he wants to do.

MEME

How does he look?

He's still pale.

GILLY

Tell him we love him.

I will.

LIL

How are you holding up?

I'm tired, but okay.

MEME

Do you need anything?

No, I'm good. I'll text again when I know more.

Ethan sleeps through the night and wakes me with a tap on the leg. I leap up from my little bed.

"You're awake." I kiss him on the lips. "How do you feel?"

"Better, I think."

"Your voice sounds better." I press the button for the nurse.

"My throat doesn't hurt as much today." In walks Dr. Jacobson and a nurse.

"Well, good morning. How are you feeling today?" The doctor checks his pupils and looks under the bandage on his chest.

"Better, I think," Ethan croaks.

"Good, good. How's your pain level today?" Ethan scrunches his brow as if he's trying to decide on a number.

"Like a five?" he finally answers.

"That's better."

"Can he have visitors?" I ask. "His sisters are chomping at the bit to come and torment him."

"I think a few visitors for a short time would be okay today if *he* wants them," the doctor answers. Ethan nods. I text his sisters, telling them to come this afternoon.

"How are you feeling today, Mrs. Martinelli?" the doctor asks.

"What's wrong with you?" Concern grows in his eyes. "Were you hurt that night?"

"No, Ethan, I'm fine," I say, placing my hand on his arm to calm him.

"I'll leave you two alone, and I'll check in later."

"Thank you, Doctor," I say, following him to the door and closing it behind him.

"Lola. What's wrong?"

"I don't want you to get upset. I'm okay."

"Please. I won't be able to rest until you tell me the truth." I kiss him on the lips and take his hand.

"The night they brought you in, I was sick to my stomach."

"And..."

"Dr. Ramirez insisted I get checked out in case I had the flu or something, so I didn't make you sicker."

"And..."

"Ethan," I say quietly through a smile.

"There's something you're not telling me, Lola. What is it?" He winces when he tries to sit up in the bed.

"Okay, stop. I'll tell you. But you have to stay calm."

"You're scaring me, please." Worry etches across his face.

"I'm pregnant." Tears fill my eyes.

"You're... pregnant." He takes a minute to process it, and I'm not sure if he's happy or not.

"We're having a ...baby?"

"Yes, Ethan, you're going to be a dad."

"I don't... I can't... I... Come here, I need to hold you," he says with tears running down his face. I move in, careful not to touch his chest, and he holds me tight.

"Are you happy?" I ask.

Pushing me back so he can see my face, he says, "You have no idea how happy I am." He peppers my face with kisses and then moves a hand to my belly.

"Are they okay in there?"

"Yes, he or she is warm and cozy in there," I say, putting my hand on top of his.

"I'm gonna be a dad... Oh my God. *You're* gonna be a mom!"

"Yes." I say, nodding my head wildly.

"Does anyone else know?"

"Just you, the doctor, and the nurse who were just in here."

"Can we tell my sisters when they come?"

"Of course." I giggle.

"I love you, Mrs. Martinelli."

"I love you, Mr. Martinelli. Now try to get some rest. This baby and I need you." I have never seen his smile so wide.

Epilogue
Ethan

Eight Months Later

My recovery has been a long one, but the upcoming arrival of our baby has given me a goal to work toward. I was in bed for so long that my legs were weak. I spent some time in physical therapy, teaching my body how to move again.

Our beautiful baby boy, Dominick Martinelli, was born one week late, but he is healthy and happy. Momma and baby are doing just fine. We arrive at the penthouse to a crowd welcoming us home from the hospital.

"He's so adorable," Amelia coos.

"That's my nephew you're slobbering all over," Gilly snips.

"I'm not slobbering on him," Amelia barks back.

"It's okay. Everybody will get to see him," Lola announces. "Just don't be getting all up in his face. You know, germs and everything." She waves her hands around.

"Yeah, you're right." Amelia and Gilly back off.

Lil comes over to Lola and proceeds to mother her.

"Here, sit down in the recliner. You need to get off your feet."

"Thank you."

"Have you gotten any sleep?"

"Not yet."

"Well. We won't stay long… Will we, everybody?" she says loudly, eyeballing everyone.

"No, we just wanted to drop off some presents and meet the little guy," MeMe says.

Everyone takes turns meeting our little guy and dropping gifts at Lola's feet. There are teddy bears, soft blankets, a bassinet to put beside the bed, and a swing. My sisters provided a few refreshments and helped to clean up.

"Thank you, everyone, so much for everything," I say, and they gradually start to filter by to say good night.

"Rocky, can I talk to you for a minute, please?" Gilly asks and pulls me off to the side.

"What's up, sis?"

"Is this whole security guard thing really necessary? I cannot *stand* Nico. All he does is try to boss me around."

"Maybe you need someone who can keep you in line, sis," I say.

"Yeah, right? There's no man out there that can keep my baby sister in line," Lil chirps.

"Oh, you be quiet," Gilly snaps.

"I think it's important for you to have security. Lil and MeMe have husbands protecting them, but you're still my responsibility."

"I'm almost twenty-nine years old, *Rocky*. I think I can take care of myself."

"That might've been correct when you were traipsing all over the world on your adventures, where no one knew who you were. But you're home now. I need to be sure you're safe."

"Fine, but if I kill him, it'll be on your conscience," she says, releasing a deep breath.

Unable to contain my laugh, I say, "I'll understand."

"C'mon, Nico, I'm leaving." She snaps her fingers and heads for the door. Nico's eyes widen, and he shoots me a glare as he moves toward the door. He doesn't seem to like Gilly any more than she likes him.

Baby Dominick starts to fuss.

"What's the matter with my little man?" I gather him in my arms from Lil. Lola started to get up, but I motioned for her to stop. "I got this," I say, and she relaxes back into the recliner. I hear Lola and Lil talking from the bedroom while I change Dom's diaper.

"I'm so proud of the man Ethan has become," Lil says.

"I love him so much," Lola says.

"You need to make sure you get your rest when the baby sleeps, and make Rocky wait on you hand and foot for the first few days because it won't last long. Take it from someone who knows."

"I will," she says with a giggle.

"And if you need anything, any hour, you text or call me, okay?"

"I will, thank you." They're hugging when I come back in the room, patting Dom lightly on the bottom.

"Okay, it's time for bed," I announce.

"I'm heading out," Lil says as I walk her to the door. "You take good care of her, little brother."

"Don't worry so much. I'll take good care of both of them." I lock the door behind her. After walking over to Lola, I reach out for her to take my hand. She does, and I help her stand from the chair. She winces with discomfort, and we head to bed for the night.

Lola and I are sitting at the table enjoying a peaceful lunch the next day when both of our cell phones ring.

"Hello," I say. Nico is on my phone.

"Boss, you're going to have to take me off this assignment with your sister," Nico says.

"Why would I do that?"

"She doesn't listen to me, and she punched me. Can I hit her back?" Nico asks.

"Hell no, you can't hit her back!" I yell into the phone. Lola's eyes go wide, and she answers her phone.

"Hello?" We hold both phones up so we can share both conversations as they complain about each other.

"Lola, I'm sorry to bother you with the new baby and all, but you're the only one who can make Rocky listen. He has to give me a different bodyguard. Nico is a jerk," Gilly says.

"What did he do?" Lola asks.

"He's treating me like a child," Gilly says.

"How?" Lola asks.

"I just wanted to go shopping. I wanted to wander around, try on a few clothes, and enjoy myself. But he's ruining it."

"What did she do, Nico?" I ask.

"She's dragging me to all these stupid little shops, and when I try to give her my opinion, she gets all mad."

"Don't you know you never give a woman your unsolicited opinion, Nico?" I say.

"But she's not picking out anything that looks good on her."

Our mouths hang open in disbelief at what he just said.

"Is that the way you worded it to her?" I ask Nico.

"Yeah, basically," Nico responds.

"Why did you punch him?" Lola asks Gilly.

"How do you know I punched him?"

"He's on the phone with Ethan."

"Son of a bitch!"

"Calm down. Why did you punch him?"

"He said a dress made me look fat."

"What! Maybe he just doesn't know how to talk to women."

"He can talk to my fist." We both snicker at her words.

"How about you try to be nice or just watch from a distance and don't comment at all?" I ask Nico.

"That wouldn't be any fun."

"It's an assignment, Nico. It's not supposed to be fun."

"But I like to make her mad. She's so funny when her face scrunches up, and she yells at me."

We both gasp in a breath and look at each other.

Lola mouths, "He likes her."

"I'll talk to Ethan," Lola says to Gilly.

"I'll think about it. For now, take care of my sister," I say to Nico.

"Thanks, Lola," Gilly says.

"Will do, Boss," Nico answers.

We all hang up.

"This is going to be fun."

If you liked this book...

Please leave a review on Amazon or Goodreads.

Follow me on...

Tik Tok: @authormkmanson
Instagram: authormkmanson
Facebook: authormkmanson

Coming Soon in 2025...

Tell Me
Forced Vacation
Come Back

Promises To My Baby Boy

I promise to treat you with love, patience, kindness, and respect.

I promise to play ball, cars, blocks, and anything else that brings you joy.

I promise to help you with your math homework when it's beyond your mom's realm of understanding.

I promise to read you a story, tuck you in each night, and fight the monsters under your bed.

I promise to support you in all of your life choices.

I promise to guide you as you grow into the man you want to be.

I promise to be the best dad I can be.

Your Dad (Ethan)

Acknowledgments

D.C. You have been supporting me from the first spicy scene I asked you to read. You were the first one on board when I thought I might want to try this whole writing thing. You have read my most intimate thoughts from my past and accepted me without question. Your unwavering loyalty and friendship have meant the world to me, and I am thankful you came into my life. One day I will write something that will make your facial expressions change.

T.D. I am sorry I brought you over to the dark side of romance, but isn't it so much fun? Your input and honesty have helped me to continue to grow and improve as a writer. Thank you for your help with grammar and coming up with a book title, sorry you have to wait until book four to see it. I can always count on you to come up with the perfect word or a name I need. I am so honored to call you, my friend.

K.L. Thank you for taking a scene I'm struggling with and ripping it apart, so I can put it back together better than before. You challenge me to be a better writer, and I respect all your opinions and critiques. You have been a true friend and confidante.

Thank you to the Mexican dinner group. You know who you are. Daquiris for all when I make the best sellers list. You are all so special to me and I will never forget your support and encouragement.

To Frank. Thank you for being up for all the challenges I throw your way. From the logos to the covers, your creativity has been spot-on.

Thank you for always standing behind me, pushing me to follow my dreams when I get nervous. I love brainstorming with you at midnight and laughing ourselves to tears. You make me so proud every day.

To Austin. Thank you for all of your love and support, even though you don't know what the hell I have gotten myself into. Your stories, drawings, and painting abilities amaze me and I am so proud of you. We need to get your comic book out there next.

To Katie. Thank you for giving me ideas that kept me up until all hours of the night. Watching you make books as a kid, I always wondered how the ideas and stories came to you. Finally, at my advanced age, I have figured it out. I just needed to take the time to slow down and listen to those little voices in my head. Your strength and love mean everything to me. Keep following your dreams and I will always be there to support you. Who knows, maybe there is a cookbook in your future.

Christy Jones. You are such an inspiration to me. Your can-do confidence has shown me what a strong woman can achieve when she puts her mind to it. You built your business from scratch and made it a success. You are amazing to work with and I am so proud to call you, my friend.

Christy McPherson. You have been my best friend since ninth grade. I can tell you anything and you don't judge me. You are my ride or die, and I would cut a bitch for you. I love you and I can't wait to lie on the beach and drink margaritas when I retire.

Thank you to my first Beta readers, Shae and Beth. It was great experience to have fresh eyes read my work. I appreciate your suggestions and be patient, Sasha is coming soon.

Thank you to all the readers out there who took a chance on this new indie author. I hope you fell in love with the characters as much as I have loved putting them on the page for you. Come along on the ride with me and find out what happens to your favorite characters in the books to come.

About the Author

M.K. Manson began a journey of self-discovery on her 58th birthday. It started her on a path to become a dark romance author.

She has been a lover of smut for years. Whether listening to audiobooks or poring over paperbacks, she reads all genres and loves a dark and twisty story. Give her a spicy why-choose romance any day of the week, and she's a happy girl.

With four dark mafia romance books self-publishing in 2025, she is on her way to her life's goal of being a best-selling author.

For more information on M.K. and her books, follow her online on Tik Tok, Instagram, and Facebook at authormkmanson.